MAZE OF SOULS

ELLIE JORDAN, GHOST TRAPPER, BOOK SIX

by

J.L. Bryan

Published 2016
JLBryanbooks.com

Copyright 2016 J.L. Bryan
All rights reserved.

This book or any portion thereof may not be reproduced or used in any manner whatsoever without the express written permission of the publisher except for the use of brief quotations in a book review.

All characters appearing in this work are fictitious. Any resemblance to real persons, living or dead, is purely coincidental.

Acknowledgments

Thanks to my wife Christina, who always reads the ugly, ugly first draft of everything.

I appreciate everyone who has helped with this book. Thanks to beta readers Daniel Arenson and Robert Duperre, Annie Chanse, Rhiannon Frater and Connie Frater, and as Isalys Blackwell. Rhiannon Frater in particular went to a lot of trouble to help improve this book. Proofing was done by Thelia Kelly and Barb Ferrante. The cover is by PhatPuppy Art.

Thanks to my agent Sarah Hershman and to everyone at Tantor Media who have made the audio versions of these books. The audio books are read by Carla Mercer-Meyer, who does an amazing job.

Thanks also to the book bloggers who's supported the series, including Heather from Bewitched Bookworks; Mandy from I Read Indie; Michelle from Much Loved Books; Shirley from Creative Deeds; Katie and Krisha from Inkk Reviews; Lori from Contagious Reads; Heather from Buried in Books; Kristina from Ladybug Storytime; Chandra from Unabridged Bookshelf; Kelly from Reading the Paranormal; AimeeKay from Reviews from My First Reads Shelf and Melissa from Books and Things; Kristin from Blood, Sweat, and Books; Aeicha from Word Spelunking; Lauren from Lose Time Reading; Kat from Aussie Zombie; Andra from Unabridged Andralyn; Jennifer from A Tale of Many Reviews; Giselle from Xpresso Reads; Ashley from Bibliophile's Corner; Lili from Lili Lost in a Book; Line from Moonstar's Fantasy World; Holly from Geek Glitter; Louise from Nerdette Reviews; Isalys from Book Soulmates; Heidi from Rainy Day Ramblings; Kristilyn from Reading in Winter; Kelsey from Kelsey's Cluttered Bookshelf; Lizzy from Lizzy's Dark Fiction; Shanon from Escaping with Fiction; Savannah from Books with Bite; Tara from Basically Books; Toni from My Book Addiction; Abbi from Book Obsession; Lake from Lake's Reads; Jenny from Jenny on the Book; and anyone else I missed!

Most of all, thanks to the readers who've supported this series. There are more books to come!

Also by J.L. Bryan

The Ellie Jordan, Ghost Trapper series
Ellie Jordan, Ghost Trapper
Cold Shadows
The Crawling Darkness
Terminal
House of Whispers
Maze of Souls

The seventh Ellie Jordan book will be available in May/June of 2016

The Jenny Pox series (supernatural/horror)
Jenny Pox
Tommy Nightmare
Alexander Death
Jenny Plague-Bringer

Urban Fantasy/Horror
Inferno Park
The Unseen

Science Fiction
Nomad
Helix

For The Smiths
(Jeremy and Christina)
(not the band)

Chapter One

I should have known it wasn't real right away. My childhood home, an unremarkable split-level in the suburbs, had burned down more than a decade earlier. It was impossible for me to be standing in front of the house, or walking up the driveway, or ascending the steps to the front door.

The door opened as I approached.

Outside, the sky was blue and the grass was green, the front lawn manicured in putting-green style as my dad had always kept it. My mother's roses bloomed in the first-floor window box. The house looked serene, as it might have on any spring day of my childhood.

Inside, everything was blackened, reduced to ash and rubble by flames that still sputtered here and there.

I stepped inside, and the door closed behind me.

"Mom? Dad?" I called out.

They didn't answer, but I heard a thumping coming from upstairs.

I walked up the fire-damaged steps, which wobbled and cracked beneath my feet. Small flames rose and flickered on the steps. They spread up the already-charred wall in little drips.

My stomach dropped as I approached the fire-scarred door to my parents' room. It was ajar, but only slightly.

"No," I whispered. I knew something terrible had happened to them, and that I was much too late to stop it.

Shaking, I pushed open the door.

The master bedroom actually looked intact, not charred like the rest of the house. Framed family pictures sat on my mother's dresser. My father's slippers lay on the floor by the bed.

Two black body bags were tucked into the bed, the flowered coverlet drawn most of the way over them.

"Mom?" My voice was a hoarse squeak. I was a child again, small as I walked toward the bed where the body bags lay under the sheets. They were zipped tight, and they were definitely not empty. "Dad?"

I approached the body bag on my mother's side, lying motionless on her pillow. My hand, smaller than it had been in many years, reached out and touched the pull tab of the zipper. It was hot enough to scald my fingers, but I held on anyway, and I pulled. It wouldn't move.

"Eleanor." The voice was faint inside the thick black plastic. It was my mother, the only person who ever really called me by my full name. Well, almost the only person.

"I can't do it," I told her, still grappling with the hot metal in my small, useless fingers.

The curtains burst into flames, the fire spreading unnaturally fast across the wall, cracking picture frames and igniting furniture.

The body bag folded upright, as though the body inside—my mother—had just sat up inside.

"I can't do it!" I screamed, while the fire spread to the bed and swept across it, setting alight the pillows and sheets on which my dead parents were resting.

"*Eleanor,*" another voice sang out. The other person who liked to call me by my full name.

I looked toward the bedroom door, past the flames that had quickly engulfed the whole room. He stood just outside the door, a shadow at first, then his features glowing red with the reflected glare of the fire. Anton Clay, dressed in his dark frock coat and silk cravat, watched me with a smile on his lips. He looked haughty as ever, a man who'd died young, burned to death by his own hand. Of course, he'd taken a number of others with him, including a lover who'd spurned him. He'd murdered her whole family, too.

"Help me," I said, as if I didn't know better. I was desperate.

I looked back at the bed, but it was burned to cinders. No blankets, no body bags, just a heap of dark, with smoke-blackened box springs and bones poking out here and there.

"Ellie!" That wasn't a voice from my childhood. It was the screaming voice of Stacey Tolbert, who'd worked for me at Eckhart Investigations for several months now, helping me to find, trap, and dislodge unwanted ghosts from our clients' homes.

I ran toward the scream, out the doorway and down the hall, Anton watching me with his arms crossed, relaxed and smiling, reflected fire dancing in the depths of his eyes.

The hallway no longer seemed to be part of my parents' house. I was running through some kind of smokehouse, smelling of fire and meat, a building that might have been found on Anton's old plantation. It was long and dark, lit only by fire visible through tiny, barred slits in thick wooden doors. The air was acrid and thick, hard to breathe.

"Ellie!" Stacey stood behind one door, her face close to the bars. She screamed as the smoke closed around her, swallowing her up.

"Ellie..." Calvin's voice rasped weakly through another door. That was my mentor, retired police homicide detective Calvin Eckhart, who taught me what I know about ghost hunting, which is a pretty good amount by this point. I could barely see him through the barred hole, surrounded by smoke and fire, slumped down in his wheelchair like he was already dead, the metal spokes of the wheels sagging in the heat.

I tried both doors. They were locked and woudn't budge; they might as well have been made of stone. I opened my mouth to speak, to tell Stacey and Calvin I was trying to save them, but smoke filled my lungs. I coughed, then lost my balance and fell to my knees. I was useless.

I could hear their screams inside the doors, but only briefly, and then they fell into low whispers, like the ghostly voices of the dead.

The sound of heavy chains scraped across the floor toward me. Anton Clay appeared from the smoke, grinning wickedly. He dragged my boyfriend Michael on the chain behind him, heading for a door to another fire-and-smoke-filled cell.

"No," I managed to cough out. I willed myself to rise up, to stand up and confront him, but my body was much too weak. I couldn't pick myself up off the floor.

Anton paused, looking down at me. Michael waited obediently, wincing at the glowing hot chain around his neck.

"I will take them all, Ellie," Anton said, his voice smooth as silk. "Come to me, or I will take them all from you. I will make you come and beg to join them."

There was a shudder, and burning timbers fell from the smokehouse roof. The entire building was on fire around us.

Anton snapped his chain, and Michael dropped to all fours. I couldn't help Michael, and he couldn't help me. I was powerless to move.

"Remember you are mine," Anton whispered, leaning in close to me, our lips almost touching. "Always."

I awoke in a sweat. I lay in my bad, in my little brick studio apartment, my cat watching me indifferently from a chair. With the blackout curtains up, I couldn't tell whether it was day or night.

After some deep, blissfully smoke-free breaths, I took a moment to remember what was true and what wasn't. My parents really were dead. Anton Clay, a ghost from almost two centuries ago, had burned our house down around them, and I'd barely escaped. I had encountered the ghost on my way out, and he had looked at me, and he'd haunted me ever since.

That was years ago, though, when I was fifteen. This wasn't the past. Stacey and Calvin weren't dead, and neither was Michael.

I'd simply had yet another dream about Anton Clay and how he wanted me dead. I didn't know whether my dreams had any connection to the real ghost, or whether he even thought of me at all. In my dreams, though, he was obsessed with finding me and killing me.

It can be hard to separate the reality from nightmare, especially when my waking reality is filled with its own nightmares. I don't need old ghosts pursuing me out of my past. I have enough of them in my present and my future.

I tried to put aside all thoughts of Anton Clay as I got ready for work.

Chapter Two

"By my calculations, this place is halfway between Savannah and Augusta," Stacey said, glancing at the van's GPS display. "So that puts us about an hour away from civilization in either direction."

"It's not an hour from *all* civilization," I said. "There was a little white church back there. And a gas station a few miles before that."

The particular stretch of highway on which I drove was admittedly pretty remote. High pine trees lined either side of the blacktop. Here and there, we passed a mailbox, usually close to a driveway of sand and gravel twisting out of sight somewhere behind the pines.

We passed stands of thick old Lowcountry oaks, the Spanish moss hanging so thick and long from their curled limbs that it nearly touched the ground. Moss-caked cypresses grew around murky ponds just large enough to conceal an alligator or two.

"Are we there yet?" Stacey asked, fidgeting impatiently in her seat.

"Don't make me turn this van around, kids," I replied. "Aren't you supposed to be navigating?"

"The van navigates itself." She pointed to the GPS again. "I'm supposed to be looking for hand-painted signs hanging on trees. Like that one, maybe?"

A wooden sign mounted between two pines certainly matched the client's assurances that we "couldn't possibly miss it." The hand-painted plywood billboard advertised a place called Pine Hollow Farm, conveniently located just 1.2 miles ahead on the left past Old Neville Pond. Jack o' lanterns and a smiling, dancing scarecrow adorned the sign. Supposed attractions of the farm were advertised inside scattered cloudbursts: "CORN MAZE!" "PUMPKINS PICK-UR-OWN!" "FALL FUN!"

A smaller board with the words TEMPORARILY CLOSED hung on the front of the sign.

"Sounds like they've got a real tourist resort happening out here," Stacey said. "Or they did."

"There's another one." I didn't have to point to the next big slab of wood. Like the first, it was attached to roadside trees by ropes, not nailed in place, presumably so it could be removed when Halloween season ended.

"HAYRIDE in the HAUNTED WOODS!" the sign offered, along with cartoony ghosts and gravestones. A skeletal horse drew a black wagon. "PINE HOLLOW FARM, JUST .6 MILES AHEAD ON LEFT – PAST OLD NEVILLE POND." Another board that read CLOSED TODAY hung on the front of the sign.

"That looks seriously haunted," Stacey said. "It's going to take Pac-Man and a mouthful of power pellets to eat all those ghosts."

"Maybe we can just haul them away in that horse-drawn death wagon."

Another sign suggested we "STOP AT THE PINE HOLLOW GENERAL STORE TODAY!" for such treats as "ORGANIC VEGGIES" "HOMEMADE JELLY" and "BOILED PEANUTS." It assured us we were only .3 miles from the turn-off at the pond. No CLOSED sign had been added to this one.

"Any idea what we're facing out here?" Stacey asked.

"The lady said something's been tormenting her kids and

scaring visitors to the farm," I told her. "Not in the way they're *supposed* to be scared, I guess. They've seen figures in their house and around the grounds. That's about all she wanted to say on the phone."

"Sounds like some real trouble. Never fear, there's *another* sign..." Stacey pointed to a wooden billboard ahead, mounted on posts instead of temporarily tied to trees. This one had a couple of painted horse silhouettes and offered horse boarding and riding lessons. A big arrow on the sign pointed down a dirt lane that snaked away between the pines.

"That must be Old Neville Pond." Stacey pointed to a low body of black water with cypress trees at the edges. It didn't look much larger than a cheap plastic kiddie pool. "Not as major a landmark as advertised."

"Maybe it used to be bigger," I said. "You know, global warming and all."

I turned down the sandy dirt lane and soon passed rows of greens waiting to be gathered from the field. Beyond a small apple orchard and the pumpkin patch promised on the sign, we reached a cluster of small, fairly decrepit wooden buildings surrounded by gardens. A stable with a corral sat farther back on the property. Three horses wandered in the corral—one large and white with brown spots, including a big white star on its forehead; another, smaller horse looked paint-splattered with red; a third was even smaller with a golden coat.

"Aw," Stacey said. "This reminds me of my grandparents' house."

I thought of visiting my own grandmother in her apartment full of weird big-eyed children paintings and a standing cloud of cigarette smoke. Stacey's family farm sounded like a much happier environment, certainly a healthier one.

One cabin-sized building stood at the front, with a wide front porch and a sizable dirt parking area. The sign above proclaimed PINE HOLLOW GENERAL STORE in a jaunty Hee-Haw font next to an almost lifelike painting of a cornucopia.

An OPEN sign hung behind the screen door leading inside. We parked and climbed the three steps to the porch, passing rows of aromatic green herbs growing in little potted plants along the porch railing. Pumpkins carved into jack o' lanterns also decorated the porch, the candles inside them currently unlit since it was daytime. Rocking chairs flanked the front door.

"Hey, it looks like a Country Barn," I said, referring to the chain of kitschy, faux-folksy restaurants owned by Stacey's family.

"Hush your mouth." Stacey opened the screen door, jingling a bell at the top. The wooden door inside was propped wide open, inviting us into a place that was recently built but was intended to look old and rustic. Jars of the previously-advertised preserves and jellies sat on one wooden shelf. Other racks offered small baskets of seasonal produce—apples, pumpkins, squash—and tourist bric-a-brac like keychains and t-shirts advertising the corn maze and haunted forest of Pine Hollow Farm. The smell of hot apple cider permeated the room.

"Hey there." A woman in her thirties stood up behind the counter, nudging her glasses up her nose and giving us a broad smile. She wore overalls and a long-sleeve shirt polka-dotted with jack o' lanterns. "How can I help y'all?"

"Are you Amber Neville?" I asked.

"I sure am."

"I'm Ellie Jordan, with Eckhart Investigations." I produced a business card from my purse. "We spoke on the phone earlier."

"Oh, thank goodness." She slumped a bit, her customer-service mask of good cheer dissolving into a worried frown. "I'm glad you're here. I didn't know if y'all were for real or not."

"We definitely are," I said.

"I'm so sorry," Amber said. "I didn't mean to sound..."

"It's perfectly okay. I'm a skeptical person, too."

She laughed, but there wasn't any real joy in it. The laugh of the person who can't believe how bad things have grown around her. "I used to be skeptical. I wish I still could be."

I quickly introduced Stacey as my tech manager, then asked, "What kind of trouble have you experienced here?"

"I don't know where to begin." She shook her head. Her hair was long and dark, her scuffed and dirt-stained overalls manufactured by Calvin Klein.

"Are you the owner of the farm?" I asked. Simple questions to put the client at ease.

"Yes. Well, my husband and me. Mostly him. Jeremy inherited the farm from his family."

"So he grew up here?"

"No, in Augusta with his parents. That's where I'm from, too. Jeremy's great-uncle left him the place about a year ago. We decided to try to make the farm work, you know? Move the kids out here, away from all that crime in Augusta, the drugs...all of that." I got the sense she was talking about something specific but didn't want to say it.

"How many kids do you have?"

"Three. Corrine's sixteen, Castor is thirteen, Maya's six."

"They must keep you busy," I said. "Along with the rest of the farm, with the corn maze and everything."

"The maze, the haunted woods. Agri-tourism, they call it," Amber said. "We even changed the name to Pine Hollow Farm because of the local ghost legend. The farm used to be called....I don't think they called it anything in particular, really. You'd be surprised how far people would come for these little attractions, though. Then we had to shut down."

"Why was that?"

"Where are my manners? Would you two like a cup of hot cider? Fresh brewed from our orchard."

"No, thanks," I said, but Stacey accepted. Amber poured the hot liquid from the steaming urn and added cinnamon before handing it over. It smelled sweet and tasty.

"When did you start having trouble around the farm?" I asked. "When did the strange occurrences begin?"

"Oh, well, now that I can look back on it, I'd say just after we moved here," Amber said. "For me, anyway. Every once in a while, when I was out in the gardens or the woods alone, I'd hear horse hooves, moving at a gallop. There'd be nobody around. I'd go and check Pixie and Starburst, thinking Corrine might be out riding one of them, and they'd be just as calm as you please over in the corral. And every once in a while, usually late in the day when the shadows are growing dark, I'll think I see somebody out of the corner of my eye, watching me. Then I see one of the scarecrows and just tell myself it was my mind playing tricks. I never believed in ghost stories."

"What changed your mind?"

"Other people started seeing things just the past few weeks," she said. "The horses have been making noise at night like something's troubling them. Both my daughters have seen horrible things, Corrine when she was out riding, Maya right in our own house at night..."

"You live here on the property?"

"Yes, our house is just down the way. Other kids saw things, too. Corrine's in the drama club at school—which is great, and really helped her make some new friends after we moved here last year—anyway, she and some of her friends were in charge of haunting the woods. They'd haunt the corn maze at night, too. They'd put on costumes and try to scare people who pass through on the hayrides. They always had fun. Then they all quit a about a week and a half ago."

I jotted this down. Today was October twenty-seventh, just a few days until Halloween. "Why did they quit?"

"Strangers in the woods," Amber said. "Scary-looking people. Several kids saw them, said they approached them. They weren't normal, you understand, like real people in costumes. They were more like shadows. You could see through some of them. And they just disappeared in an eyeblink."

"And you believed their story?" I asked.

"Only because of the other things," she said. "What my daughters have seen. These things are coming into my house at night now. Terrorizing my kids."

"What exactly have they seen?"

"There's a girl who climbs up the stairs on her hands and knees," Amber said. "Wearing a bloody dress. My youngest daughter Maya is the one who sees her. She's crawled right into Maya's room before, too. Right up to where she was lying in bed.

"And Corrine saw something while out riding in the woods by herself. Heard it first—a man on a horse, all wrapped in shadows. He chased her for a minute while she rode hard back to the house, and then he just disappeared. This happened a week ago."

"Do you know of anything that might have triggered all this?" I asked. "Has anyone here attempted to have any kind of séance or invite any supernatural activity?"

"Nothing like that," she said. "Just all the Halloween decorations, and the kids pretending to be ghosts, and the haunted hayride past the old cemetery...but it was all in fun, nothing serious. Do you think that could have stirred up something supernatural?"

"Possibly. Where's this old cemetery?"

"Back in the woods. Just follow the same dirt road you drove in on, and you'll see it eventually."

"It's on your land?"

"Oh, yes. The centerpiece of the haunted woods. A real graveyard. Some of Jeremy's ancestors are buried there."

"He doesn't mind using his own family cemetery that way?"

"Jeremy says if you have to live near a graveyard, you may as well cash in on it," Amber said. "Especially with the ghost legend."

"What's the ghost legend?" I asked. By general unspoken consent, we'd settled into the rocking chairs by the fireplace, Stacey and Amber both sipping warm cider. There was no fire, but it made for a cozy setting, anyway.

"It's just an old story," Amber said. "There's probably no truth in it. They say after the Revolution, an ex-Hessian mercenary—you know, German soldiers who fought for the British? One of them used to ride up and down that old dirt road out there, preying on the horse and wagon traffic between Savannah and Augusta. A highwayman. One day he killed a young woman, shot her with a pistol while robbing her. There was a big manhunt and he was killed. And they say his ghost still rides around here. You think it was him that chased my daughter out there?"

"I don't know much just yet," I said. "Did your daughter describe what he was wearing?"

"You'd have to ask her," Amber said. "She doesn't speak much to me these days. I think she's upset about all her friends getting scared here. She says they're avoiding her at school. She never wanted to move here from Augusta, and the friends she did make at her new school meant so much to her..."

"That sounds tough," I said.

"And I won't let her ride out there anymore," Amber said. "Not in the woods, not after she saw someone chasing her."

"She still wants to ride in the woods after that?" I asked.

"Don't ask me to explain her to you. I've been trying to figure that girl out for years."

"I don't suppose the old legend offers a name for the highwayman?" I asked. "Or the young woman he murdered?"

"Sorry." Amber shrugged.

"We'll dig into the local history and see what we can find. Honestly, it sounds a bit like *Legend of Sleepy Hollow*, with the Hessian horseman and everything. Someone might have just adapted that story into a local tall tale."

"That's why we cooked up the name Pine Hollow Farm, to put people in mind of the Headless Horseman," Amber said. "Corrine plays the horseman in the Haunted Woods. She wears a black hood, black cape, and charges out on Pixie to scare the hayride passengers. Well, not since we shut down, of course..."

"Your older daughter plays the horseman?" I asked, scribbling notes. "The same daughter who was chased by a figure on horseback?"

"Maybe he didn't care for her portrayal of him," Amber said, with another of her not-very-happy smiles.

"When your daughter's friends witnessed the shadow people in the woods, did the description match any of the other entities you've mentioned? The figure on horseback or the girl who creeps inside your house?"

"Not as far as I could tell," she said. "They didn't talk about a horseman or a pale girl. They didn't tell me much at all, though. Maybe they gave Corrine more details."

"Would you mind if I spoke to her?"

"You'll have to wait until she's home from school," Amber said. "I thought it might be easier if we had this meeting during the day when nobody else was around."

"Is your husband away, too?"

"He's at work. Jeremy teaches high school English in Waynesboro. It's a long drive."

"Can you show us where the incidents have occurred?" I asked.

"All right," she said. "But I won't go near the graveyard or the woods around it. I'm sorry. I'm sure professionals like you can handle that area, but it's too much for me."

"I understand. Stacey, let's go grab a video camera."

Outside, while Stacey took a handheld camera from the van, I looked ahead along the dirt road. It passed a two-story farmhouse with a giant wraparound porch. The house looked old but recently restored and painted. Farther along, I could see the corn maze itself, sprawling for several acres on one side of the dirt road. A scarecrow stood by the maze entrance.

The dirt road continued away into pine woods, where it disappeared into the shadows. Though the day was warm, I shivered, apprehensive about going in there. After you spend enough time chasing ghosts, you start to develop a little bit of a sixth sense about them, even if you're not particularly psychic.

I could sense dark things in that forest, things I knew we would have to face before it was all over. The only question was how dangerous they were to the living.

I had a feeling we'd be getting the answer to that one before too long.

Chapter Three

"You think there's any truth to the old ghost story?" Stacey asked as she fired up her video camera. I grabbed a Mel-Meter and a couple of other basic items from the van, loading them into my utility belt.

"We can probably find out whether this road actually existed in the eighteenth century," I said. "If it was used for traffic between the cities, it should be mentioned somewhere. It does run parallel to the Savannah River, so it's in the right place for an old road between the cities of Savannah and Augusta."

"And maybe we can find out whether the headless horseman was real, too," Stacey said.

"Nobody said he was headless."

"Oh, right. I mean, um, the Hessian horseman."

"Everybody ready?" Amber descended the steps from the little store. The wooden door remained open behind her, with only an unlatched screen door to keep people out.

"You didn't lock up?" I asked.

"A few people from town come out here to buy produce, and

they just leave the money on the counter if we're gone."

"Wow," Stacey said. "You'd get robbed blind if you tried that in the city."

"That's why we don't live in the city anymore." Amber led the way as we walked up the dirt road.

"You said the horses were acting strange?" I asked. Animals tend to be the most sensitive to the supernatural. They're usually the first family members to detect a haunting, followed by the kids, the wife, and the husband, in that order.

"They seem loud and troubled some nights, and they've been skittish. Especially Pixie, after she and Corrine were chased by that dark shadow."

"Which one's Pixie?" Stacey asked, pointing her camera at the horses.

"The little gold champagne mare," Amber said.

"Aw, she's so cute. I love that red Appaloosa, too. My grandma had a black-spotted Appaloosa. Dolly."

"That's Hector. He's our boarder. We're hoping to get a few more."

"You have a number of buildings here," I said, nodding at an old barn that still looked abandoned.

"We've tried to restore what we can," Amber said. "There are a couple of overgrown buildings in the woods, too, but there's not much we can do with them, except use them as haunted houses for the hayride."

"Sounds like you had a fun little business going here," Stacey said.

"We did. We opened up at the beginning of September. School and church groups came out, and we had a Girl Scout camp-out, but now I don't feel comfortable inviting anybody here at night. I'd hate for someone to get hurt, or worse..." The worry was clear on Amber's face. "I don't want my kids to get hurt, either. Do you think you can help?"

"We'll have to try to figure out the identities of the ghosts causing your problems," I said. "It's a process. We'll set up cameras and other gear and stay here overnight to observe."

"Okay. I haven't really discussed it with Jeremy. I mean, we talked about it, but I didn't tell him I'd, um, found your agency online and invited you over..."

"Unfortunately, there's no quick fix. We'll have to hang around for a while. He'll notice we're here."

"It's going to be an awkward dinner conversation." Amber sighed.

"Has your husband experienced anything?" I asked.

"He says he's seen shadows in the woods that looked like people. Then they disappeared. He's not convinced it's...ghosts, or whatever you'd call them...but he was rattled when he told me about it. The next day he declared we should try to forget about it and move on."

"But he was open to the idea of calling in paranormal investigators?" I asked.

"He's having some trouble admitting that the problems are real."

"Denial is normal when you encounter something that doesn't fit your belief system," I said.

"Well, I hope he's ready to move on to the bargaining phase soon." Amber led us down the sandy dirt road, past a large dirt parking area and right to the main house, which had a saltbox shape, two stories at the front sloping down to a single story at the back. A brick chimney rose at one side, big enough to fit Santa Claus and multiple reindeer. The broad wraparound porch looked welcoming. The farmhouse had been painted a cheerful yellow and white.

"How old is that house?" I asked.

"It was built in the early nineteenth century, but the foundation goes back even earlier, to colonial times," she said. "We've invested a lot in this place over the last year. The idea that it's not safe for our family is just so troubling..."

"We'll do all we can do to make them safe," I said. "I promise you that."

We crossed the front porch, past a swing and a couple of jack o' lanterns, and Amber led us through the door.

The interior of the house looked warm and cheerful, with plenty of sunlight, a silky blue color on the walls, and family photographs displayed on the wall above an antique side table.

Open doorways led to a dining room on one side of us and a book-lined sitting room on the other. The rough-hewn planks of the staircase rose directly ahead. The foyer narrowed to a small hallway past the stairs, visible through a propped-open door.

"Are those the stairs where your younger daughter saw the ghost?" I asked.

"Maya has seen it here a few times. Trying to climb up on its hands and knees. It looks like a woman in a bloody dress."

"And that same apparition has entered her room?" The wooden steps and banister were thick, scuffed, and ancient, but polished to a gleam. My Mel-Meter ticked up by a milligau, indicating anything from a weak residual haunting to a few electrical wires in the walls nearby.

"Oh, yes," Amber said. "This was only two nights ago. That's when I got serious about calling you, whether Jeremy agreed or not. It's one thing to see something strange in the woods, or to feel like the scarecrows are watching you, but it's another when things start coming inside your house and threatening your kids."

"Can we see her room?" I asked.

Amber led us upstairs. The kids' bedrooms were fairly small, but they each had their own. Maya's room wasn't surprising for the nest of a six-year-old girl: Disney character figurines, a pink plastic dollhouse, a half-constructed farm puzzle, coloring books, and stuffed animals heaped in a basket by the small bed.

I took some readings, but there was nothing to indicate a supernatural presence in the girl's room. The scary bloody woman must have hid elsewhere during the day.

We checked the other rooms, too, taking some baseline readings with my Mel-Meter so we could identify any strange electromagnetic activity later, if the ghosts returned to the house during the night. Castor, the boy, had a drum set in his room and laundry scattered all over his floor. Corrine, the older girl, had decorated her room along a psychedelic theme, with glow-in-the-dark stars on the ceiling and twinkling Christmas lights on the headboard. I also looked into the sunny master bedroom, decorated with a few old antique end tables and a wardrobe.

We took a quick look around the downstairs. At the back of the house was a comfortable, spacious living room, with a laundry room connecting it to the garage. The garage had a work area with a blowtorch and a welding mask, and I was a little surprised to learn these things belonged to Amber instead of her husband.

The front sitting room was furnished with oversized chairs. Board games and books, mostly cracked old paperbacks, stocked the room's built-in shelves. Overall, it seemed like it should have been a happy place for a family to live, but there was a heavy, oppressive feeling in the air, even with the early afternoon light pouring inside.

Returning outdoors was a relief.

"Where have you seen the troubling things you mentioned?" I asked Amber. We walked past a garden protected by a scarecrow in an old flannel shirt. A cheap straw hat stapled to his head shaded his blank, cloth-bag face.

"I've felt people watching me in the gardens and the orchard, but it gets worse closer to the woods. More than once I've felt like someone was following me in the corn maze while I was cleaning it up—visitors leave trash in there every night we're open. Once I turned and thought I saw something like a shadow of a person slipping away through a row of corn, but when I stepped closer there was nothing there. It gave me some pretty bad chills."

We drew closer to the maze. The scarecrow by the entrance held a sign with corn maze rules, displayed in a dialogue balloon spoken by a cartoony ear of corn with eyes and a mouth: no picking the corn, no cutting between rows or damaging the plastic netting that ran between them, no drinking or smoking, no littering, no kids under twelve without an adult. Sounded reasonable to me.

"You'd better let me show you around the maze," Amber said. "It can take more than an hour if you don't know your way."

"That's one impressive arch," Stacey said. She actually whistled at the huge archway over the entrance, made of old shovels, pitchforks, and other farm implements twisted and braided together. "Did you make that in your metal shop in the garage, Amber?"

"I actually did, yeah," Amber said, blushing. "I'd never sculpted with a blowtorch before. It was fun. I have ideas for more things I want to make."

We followed her under the arch and into the corn. The high

golden stalks immediately walled off the world outside, closing off everything but a narrow path leading away to the left and the right. An earthy vegetable smell hung in the air.

"How many people come out here on a typical day?" I asked Amber.

"Sometimes we get a few hundred on Saturdays."

"Wow, sounds busy." I wondered if the influx of visitors had stirred up spirits unhappy about the invasion of their territory. A farm this old could have quite a collection of restless ghosts.

I took more readings as we walked. The electromagnetic activity seemed to kick up when we walked north, towards the dense pine woods beyond the maze, and slacked off whenever we moved south, away from them.

Amber led us through one turn of the maze after another. We passed a gazebo with a bench where people could rest. Artificial spiderwebs and black plastic spiders hung underneath the slanted roof.

At a big clearing near the center, where several paths came together, a row of three scarecrows stood mounted on wooden frames, elevated off the ground a few feet so they seemed to tower above us.

"The butcher, the baker, and the candlestick maker," Amber said, as if introducing us to them. The scarecrows definitely followed the theme. The butcher's hands, made from old gardening gloves, grasped a plastic butcher knife and a fake meat cleaver, and he wore an apron stained with fake blood. His face was a simple cloth bag that would have been less creepy with some eyes. The baker wore a tall, jaunty chef's hat and had oven mitts for hands. The candlestick-maker grasped a pair of electric candles, and another fire-safe battery candle burned inside his grinning plastic jack-o'-lantern face. Tiny birthday-sized electric candles glowed on the brim of his straw hat.

We continued through the twists and turns of the maze. As we approached the back again, near the woods beyond, I knew something was happening because my Mel-Meter ticked up by several milligaus.

"What is that?" Amber whispered as we turned a corner. We

stopped, looking at the scene ahead of us.

"Is this one of your staged hauntings?" I asked Amber. "Something you set up?"

She shook her head, her eyes wide. "No, no. Not at all."

A few feet away, there were hoof prints in the dirt path ahead of us. They ran from the back wall of the maze, where the corn stalks had been trampled. The orange plastic netting barrier, which marked the paths of the maze and kept people from wandering outside of it, had ruptured open to reveal the pine woods beyond. It looked as though someone had ridden a large, strong horse right out of the woods, breaking through the mesh-plastic barrier and into the corn maze, and then the horse and rider had inexplicably vanished a couple of yards along the path. Broken corn cobs were strewn all over.

"Any chance your daughter crashed through here on her horse?" I asked, approaching the ripped netting. "Or a neighbor?"

"If somebody did, they didn't mention it to me," Amber said. "It's a long way to the nearest neighbor's house. About a mile. Anyway, I think a horse would have tangled in that plastic netting, not broken through."

"The hoof prints just end right here," Stacey said. She checked the rows of corn on either side of the path. "Either that horse disappeared into thin air, or somebody lifted it away with a choppa."

"With a what?" I asked.

"A choppa," Stacey said. "You know, a helicopter? I was doing Schwarzenegger from *Predator*. 'Get to da choppa!'"

Sometimes I wish Stacey would stay quiet when we're meeting new clients.

"I'm sure Amber would have noticed a helicopter airlifting a horse from her yard." I looked closely at the torn edge of the orange netting. It was ragged, with a lot of stretching and ripping of the plastic. "It doesn't look like anybody cut it with a blade, either. Something bashed right through here. Amber, any idea when this might have happened? When was the last time you saw this portion of the maze intact?"

"I suppose it could have been anytime in the last two days," she said.

I stepped through the ruptured fence and over low weeds toward the woods beyond. Poison ivy curled up the trunks of the trees, and brambles and thorny vines blocked access between the trees. There was a lot of wild blackberry, which is an awfully pleasant name for a fast-growing invasive vine with thorns like fangs.

Some of the undergrowth had been ripped and trampled, right in line with the break in the outer wall of the corn maze. I motioned for Stacey to take pictures.

"That's weird," Stacey said. "The undergrowth damage stops a few feet back. Like the horse just popped in here out of nowhere."

"Then popped right back into nowhere after it crashed into the maze," I said. My Mel-Meter indicated the woods were several degrees cooler than the maze—not surprising, with all the shade from the tree canopy above—and the electromagnetic reading ticked up as I approached the weed-choked pines.

"Watch out," Amber cautioned as I inspected the edge of the woods. "Those are some pretty hostile plants right there."

"Where can we go deeper into the woods?" I asked.

"There are a few paths. You'll see some as you walk down the road." Amber wrapped her arms around herself, as though just the idea of following that road into the woods made her cold.

We finished the corn maze, which didn't take very long with the owner leading the way, and then Stacey and I returned to the dirt road. Amber accompanied us until we reached the place where the shadow of the woods fell across the road, as though to divide the dark land of the dead from the sunny land of the living.

"I'm sorry, I just can't go any farther," Amber said, remaining in the sunlight as we stepped into the shade. "And my kids'll be home from school soon, and I should get back to the store..."

"That's fine, Mrs. Neville," I said. "We'll just have a look around. How far away is that old cemetery?"

"It's a little hike, but you won't miss it."

"Okay. Thank you."

"Be careful in there," Amber said. She backed away a few paces, looking between me and the shaded dirt road that curved away into the woods, as if reluctant to leave us.

"We'll be fine," I told her. "We've faced some challenging ghosts in our time." *Challenging* seemed like a more polite word than other options like *murderous* and *insane*. "What about traffic? Will there be cars and trucks on the road?"

"Oh, no. It just runs out and gets swallowed by the marshes alongside the river. You don't need to worry about anybody running into you back there." Amber tried to smile, but she still looked worried as Stacey and I walked along the dirt road into the shadowy woods. We lost sight of Amber and the farm buildings as we followed the road.

The woods were quiet. The pines soared above us, walling in the dirt road as surely as the rows of corn and plastic netting walled in the dirt paths of the corn maze, as if the woods were just a larger, wilder labyrinth. Leafy oaks stood scattered among the pines, their foliage the colors of sunset.

Weeds and pine needles filled the ditches on either side of the road. The road itself seemed narrower now. If two vehicles came along from opposite directions, it would take quite a bit of awkward maneuvering for them to pass each other.

"Don't you love fall?" Stacey asked. "All the little festivals, the changing leaves, kids in Halloween costumes, the dead spewing up out of their graves to haunt the living..."

"It's a nice time of year," I agreed. "So you and Jacob are definitely attending the Lathrop Grand Halloween ball, right? Madeline Colt insists we come, and it was nice of her to invite us. Don't strand me there with no one to talk to."

"Oh we're definitely going. I still can't believe Madeline would ever want to see us again after we trashed the place. And then all those news stories about the bones we found."

"Apparently the publicity's been good for the hotel, and Madeline already has a crew working double-time to renovate the fourth floor, now that the ghosts aren't making it impossible."

"Good. I hope we billed like crazy."

"We did. Is it getting colder?" I checked my Mel-Meter and confirmed a small temperature drop of five degrees since we'd started down the shady portion of the road into the woods.

"Feels like it. There's our first haunted house." Stacey pointed at a decrepit shack overgrown with ivy, its remaining boards gray, warped, and weather-beaten. Thorny vines snaked in and out of the dark gaps in the walls. An empty doorway invited us inside. Well, it wasn't exactly *inviting*—it slanted to one side on the crumbling wooden foundation, a weird cavelike mouth leading into a pitch-black interior. Colorful Halloween decorations, including a cardboard jack o' lantern and a string of miniature green skeletons like evil Christmas lights, had been tacked to the front of the old building, along with a hand-painted sign that warned *BEWARE THE HAUNTED WOODS!*

"How old do you think this shed is?" I asked Stacey, while drawing my flashlight and pointing it into the dark doorway.

"I don't know. Probably long enough for thousands of generations of spiders to come and go, leaving only their webs behind. If you listen closely, you can almost hear the whisper of their little feet and fangs..."

"Very funny. You've got a point about the cobwebs." My flashlight beam found thick curtains of webs and gray dust, but not much else beyond some crumbling remnants of furniture at the back. The place looked like a deadly sneeze attack waiting to happen. "I guess nobody's gone inside in a while. Not even those drama-club kids who pretend to be ghosts and monsters."

"They probably just jump out from behind the shed," Stacey said. "Why go in there and get your nice ghost costume all filthy? Or, let's say, the clothes you and I are wearing right now. Those would be pretty filthy if we went poking around in there..."

I checked the doorway with my Mel-Meter, but there was nothing suspicious, no weird energy that didn't belong. I smelled animal droppings—maybe raccoons, squirrels, or rats nested somewhere inside.

"I'm with you, Stacey. Let's keep our boots free of rat poop if we can."

"That's all I ask."

The cemetery lay farther along the dirt road, its outer wall so shrouded in wild ivy that I could barely discern the bricks and rusty iron beneath the green growth. Portions of the wall tilted forward over the drainage ditch alongside the dirt road, as though waiting for a good hard shake to send them crashing down. Good thing we aren't prone to earthquakes in this part of the country. Orange and black crepe-paper ribbons decorated the old walls, along with cardboard cutouts of jack-o'-lanterns and witches, though this added Party City décor actually made the cemetery a bit less scary.

The old cemetery gate stood open at the side of the road. The area of the drainage ditch just below it was partially filled with weedy gravel, as if there had once been a kind of mini-causeway across the ditch, from the dirt road to the front gate. The footing looked unstable there now.

I stepped over the ditch and touched the rusty wrought-iron gate. It was rooted in place, left open so long that the gate's lower edge had submerged into the reddish earth below it.

"Looks like it's been stuck open for years," I said. "That's not good."

"A leaky cemetery?" Stacey asked.

"The worst kind. Ghosts will respect the cemetery walls even if they've deteriorated over time. But leaving a gate permanently open?" I shook my head. "Most people would know better than that, even just subconsciously."

"So we could be looking at a lot of comers and goers," Stacey said. "Spirits wandering freely every night. Does that mean all we need to do is close up the gate? Or is that like closing the barn door after the horse gets out? I mean, the haunted barn, and the ghost horse, obviously." Her voice was fast and chatty, a sign that the eerie woods and old cemetery were getting to her.

"We'll try it, but I doubt it will be that simple," I said. "Always observe carefully before acting. Let's have a look inside."

I walked through the open gate. The air was much colder inside the cemetery walls, and my meter confirmed a ten-degree decline as I entered. I didn't need any instruments to tell me about the little bumps that formed on the back of my neck and spread along my back, or the shiver that passed through my body. Stacey shivered, too.

"Chilly," she whispered, then panned her video camera around.

The cemetery possessed a wider variety of trees than the pine woods around it, with ornamental trees planted to beautify the burial ground sometime in the distant past. Curtains of Spanish moss hung from thick, curling oak limbs overhead. Crepe myrtles sprawled nearby, their leaves gone the color of dried blood for the autumn and slowly dripping to the thick pine-needle carpet below. Dark cypress trees loomed farther back, also shrouded in moss, and I could hear gurgling water somewhere in that direction.

"It's really quiet," Stacey said, breaking the silence by commenting on it. The surround-sound chirping of cicadas, so common that I'd barely noticed them as we walked through the woods, was now distant, as if none wanted to come sing to the dead buried here.

"I'm getting three to four milligaus on the Mel-Meter," I said. "I'm guessing we're not standing near any electrical lines, so that's pretty high."

"You'd think a haunted cemetery would have more graves," Stacey said.

"They're all around us. You're standing on one." I pointed to a chunk of stone behind her, mostly swallowed by ivy, the faint traces of eroded inscription still visible near the bottom.

Stacey gave a sort of *yeep!* sound and hopped away from the old headstone, swinging her video camera around in front of her like a talisman for warding off the dead.

"There are more back here. Everything's overgrown." I drew my flashlight to help us find some more badly worn headstones.

The cemetery was in deep disrepair, but had never been fancy. I discovered more stones, many of the names lost to erosion. The most prominent grave marker, a granite obelisk, stood about waist-high and belonged to a Hiram Neville, buried in 1823. Most of the markers were smaller, many of them sunken almost entirely out of sight. Cracked granite slabs weighed down grave sites, with weeds growing up through them like fingers reaching up from below the earth.

The cicadas and birds might have avoided the cemetery, but flies seemed perfectly happy there, growing thicker and more noticeable as we trudged deeper in among the moss-draped trees and sunken headstones. I batted some of the peskier insects away from my face.

If there had ever been footpaths, or any regular rows or organization to the cemetery, those had long since vanished. It had the air of a swamp graveyard, and it looked as though the dead had been tossed here and there over the generations without much planning, like thoughtlessly scattered seeds.

After stepping around a massive fallen cypress, we finally reached the back fence, made of a low brick wall topped with rusty-spike fencing that would not have looked out of place enclosing the entrance to some medieval dungeon. Chunks of the fence had buckled inward or outward over the years, as if the spongy soil beneath them had been unable to support the weight of the bricks and iron.

The fence overlooked a drop-off to a wide, shallow creek that ran behind the cemetery. Across the creek, heavy old pines cast their shadows onto thick weeds that covered the ground.

"It's like a chain of islands back there," Stacey said, taking video as she nudged her way into place between me and a nearby half-sunken headstone. "This creek connects to another one back there. See?"

"It looks as complicated as that corn maze," I said. A few small creeks split apart and rejoined here and there in the areas of the woods we could see, slicing the land into a swampy patchwork. The soil of the tree-filled islands would be soft and spongy like that in the cemetery. It was probably just wet, slippery mud all year round, with the canopy above keeping the sun away.

Tearing ivy from the fence, I discovered the iron gate, which barely looked wide enough for a human being to pass. This one, at least, was solidly closed and latched. Beyond the gate lay an old wooden footbridge over the creek, most of its floorboards missing, connecting the back of the cemetery to the marshy island behind it.

"I dare you to walk across that bridge out there," Stacey said.

"Maybe not today," I said. I stepped closer to the gate, toward the fallen carcass of the old cypress tree, checking the area around it for electromagnetic activity. The readings clicked upward.

"Looks like this gate was a handy shortcut for the creepy swamp people of olden days," Stacey said. "They could slither in here, bury their dead by moonlight, hold their dark moon-worshipping funeral rites—"

I spun back toward Stacey to snap at her for her disrespect of the dead around us—okay, maybe I just wanted her to stop trying to scare me—and something caught me around the ankle and dragged me down into the muddy earth.

I heard my voice cry out as my hip splatted into the wet soil, and that wasn't the end of it. I kept dropping, the wet cemetery seeming to open up just enough to swallow me whole, red mud slurping me down like a giant's mouth lined with quicksand. Sharp points jabbed into my arms and legs.

Something long and stiff broke my slide into the darkness below the cemetery. I screamed, slapping at what looked like a bony arm seizing me across the chest. A thick tree root, I finally realized, not a hungry corpse trying to pull me underground and eat my brain.

"Ellie?" Stacey stood over me, looking worried.

Now that I'd stopped sliding, I could catch my bearings. I was facing the underside of the fallen cypress near the back gate. Some of the huge old roots jutted out above the ground, while others, like the one that had caught me, remained submerged beneath the soil.

I wasn't lying flat on my back, but slantwise in the mud, my boots well ahead of my shoulders. It looked like I'd tangled in a clump of ground ivy that had concealed a deep pit left by the roots of the toppled tree. Now my feet were at the watery bottom, and there was mud all over me.

"Are you hurt?" Stacey asked.

"Mostly embarrassed," I said.

Stacey helped me up, and we looked down into the muddy pit, half-expecting to see bones and skulls revealed by my little slide. I'd just taken an unlucky step into a big hole. Nothing undead had attempted to draw me down into the depths.

Still, it was a little unsettling, walking into an open, watery pit in a cemetery. It certainly made the place feel hostile.

"Okay, I think we've seen enough back here," I said. "We could spend all day exploring those trails and creeks, and I don't want to. Let's get cleaned up. We still have a lot of area to cover before nightfall."

"I don't need to get cleaned up," Stacey said. "I'm fine. I didn't fall in the mud and get filthy like some of us."

"Yeah, okay," I said, annoyed. "That's more time you can spend setting up cameras and microphones. Let's get moving."

On our way back, we tried to close the front gate of the cemetery, working it back and forth in the mud in an attempt to free it, but it didn't budge. We'd have to return later with some tools and try again. For now, the spirits were still free to come and go. After all these years, I wasn't sure the rusty old gate would hold them in again, even if we could close it. The ghosts had long since grown accustomed to ignoring the boundaries of the cemetery.

Hopefully, we'd get a clearer picture of the haunting after night fell, as we watched and listened in the darkness.

Chapter Four

Getting mud off oneself is typically a simple operation, but here there were a couple of problems. I didn't want to ask a brand-new client I'd just met about borrowing her shower so I could stain it red with mud, but it wasn't exactly convenient to zip back home, which would take at least an hour each way. We could have found a motel in the nearest town, but that would have wasted time. I'd been planning on sleeping on the drop-down cots in the van if necessary. They were narrow and uncomfortable, but they were free.

Anyway, I'm embarrassed to relate that I ended up hosing myself off behind the stable, out of sight of everyone except the red-speckled Appaloosa named Hector, who watched me curiously, snorting occasionally. The snorts sounded a little derisive to me.

Stacey stood guard at one corner of the stable while I quick-changed into fresh clothes from my overnight bag. The horse kept looking at me, blinking, but other than that it was a successful covert mission.

By the time we returned to the house, things were much louder because the kids were home from school. The thirteen-year-old boy

Castor, wiry and dressed in a Deadpool t-shirt, was attempting to ride away on his bicycle, heading for the highway and not the woods. The girl, six-year-old Maya, was running after him, screaming, disheveled ribbons trailing at the tips of her disheveled red hair. It was easy to imagine her mother carefully arranging the hair into orderly braids in the morning, only to have the girl destroy it all in the course of the day at school.

"You can't go!" Maya shouted at her brother as she chased him up the dirt road away from the house.

"*You* can't come!" he shouted back over his shoulder, his long bangs fluttering in his face. "Go inside and play with Corrine."

"She never plays with me." Maya threw a pine cone, hitting her brother square in the lower back. Castor scowled in response but didn't slow down.

"Maya, get out of the road!" Amber emerged onto the front porch with a slam of the screen door, covering her cell phone with one hand as she screamed at her daughter. "You're not allowed in the road."

"But Castor's in the road—"

"He's allowed."

"But I don't want to be by myself! And Corrine locked her door!" Maya screamed. I remembered Maya was the one who'd seen the bloody-girl apparition inside the house. I could see why she might not want to be alone at home.

"I'm right here, Maya. You won't be by yourself. Now get out of that road this second!" Amber gave Stacey and me a frazzled shake of her head as we approached the porch. She quickly ended her phone call.

"Who are they?" Maya asked her mother, pointing at me.

"They're detectives," Amber said. "They're here to help."

"Help with what?" Maya stopped at the foot of the porch steps and gave us a suspicious look, narrowing her green eyes.

"The problems we've had around here," Amber said.

"You mean the ghost?" Maya looked at me. "She comes inside at night. Sometimes you can't hear her or see her, but she's there."

"What do you think she wants?" I asked. "Any ideas?"

"I don't know. She's all covered in blood and she shows her

teeth."

"Like she's smiling?" I asked.

"No," Maya said. "Like she's biting."

"You don't have to talk about this if it scares you, Maya," Amber said.

"Talking doesn't scare me." Maya clambered up the steps toward us. "It felt cold." She shuddered, drawing her arms in close. She wore a sleeveless black dress printed with scores of tiny white bird shapes. Goose bumps were rising on her bare arms. Amber stepped over and hugged the girl's shoulders. Maya asked, "Why is it bothering me? Can it hurt me?"

"Kids are usually better at seeing ghosts than adults are," I said. "It's normal that you're the first person to see the ghost. We don't know what it wants or why it's here yet, but we're going to figure that out. And then we're going to get rid of it for you. That's what we do."

"That's right, Maya. That's what they're supposed to do." Amber gave me a look that was difficult to read—a little angry, a little suspicious, and very tired. I could see how stressed she was, and now she had to worry about whether we were legitimately going to help or just some kind of scammers. It's good to be cautious, since there are definitely some shady types around the fringes of the ghost business. One such company, fairly shady if you asked me, but definitely not small, was in the process of buying the little hometown detective agency where Stacey and I worked.

"And then everything will be okay?" Maya asked.

"We can usually improve things," I told her. "Right now we need to get set up." I quickly explained the drill to Amber, while Maya listened intently. We would need cameras and microphones inside her house as well as around the property. "I'll need to spend the night in your front room to watch for the apparition that's getting into your house."

Amber nodded. "You may as well get started. And I'd better get supper ready so I can feed Jeremy while explaining I already hired y'all. The news will go down easier with mashed potatoes and blueberry pie. He'll be too stuffed to complain. Maybe you two should join us. There's plenty. "

I was about to turn her down—better to retreat to the nearest Waffle House for food rather than sit in the middle of family drama and a potential big argument—but Stacey was faster and graciously accepted the invitation. I would have poked her in the ribs as punishment if I could have done it out of the client's sight.

Then we got to work. Our first priority was to wire the front stairs and upstairs hall with the works—thermal, night vision, motion detectors, microphones. In Maya's room, we set up a high-sensitivity microphone and remote sensors for electromagnetism and temperature. Maya had reported the bloody-girl apparition crawling right up to her bed, so we wanted to monitor her room as she slept.

While testing and checking our gear upstairs, we finally met the other daughter, Corrine, when she emerged from her room and stared at us. Her hair was dark like her mother's, but cut short, and she had the same glaring green eyes as her younger sister.

"Hi," I said, after she'd stared at us for a few seconds. "I'm Ellie."

"Mom!" Corrine shouted, rather than replying to me. "Why is there a camera crew up here? Mom! Tell me this isn't a stupid intervention!"

"It's not an intervention, Corrine," Amber said, appearing at the bottom of the steps. Maya stayed close by her mother's hip, close enough to create a serious tripping hazard. "It's an example of why you shouldn't huff off to your room without speaking to me when you get home."

"Would you just tell me what's going on?" Corrine snapped.

"We're paranormal investigators," I said, hoping to defuse the situation. "We're here about the problems you've been having. In fact, I'd really like to hear about your experience with the horseman—"

"Oh...*no.*" Corrine covered her mouth with one hand and backed away like she was a vampire and Stacey and I were huge bales of garlic. "You don't have a show on TV, do you?"

"No—" I began.

"Oh, you just have an internet show? That's even worse."

"We don't have a show at all," I said, trying not to sound as annoyed as I felt. "We're just here to identify and remove the ghosts."

"This is so weird." Corrine took a backward step toward her room.

"It gets a lot weirder than this," Stacey said. "This is the calm part. Wait until things are creeping out of the walls and attacking everybody."

"You want to see a ghost, just go out riding in the woods at night," Corrine said. "Don't take Pixie. She scares easy. In fact, don't take any of our horses. I don't want them getting hurt."

"We don't want to risk any harm to your animals," I said. "Have you seen strange things anywhere besides the woods?"

"I've been seeing strange things since we moved here," Corrine said, crossing her arms. "Like boys who wear hunting clothes to school. I mean, do they think we can't see them because they're dressed in camouflage? And what's the point of wearing camouflage and a bright orange jacket together? This town is so stupid. Not that there's actually much of a *town*..."

"I'm guessing you didn't want to move here from Augusta," I said.

"No, I wanted to lose all my friends and spend my weekends cleaning up pig poop," she said. "That's exactly what I wanted my life to be. Totally. Now I can't even ride my horse very far because..." She cut herself off and shook her head. "You know why."

"I'd really like to hear more about—" I began, but she backed into her room and closed the door. "—that ghost you saw," I said, finishing my sentence for the benefit of no one in particular.

Back downstairs, the house smelled of Amber's cooking. The strongest scent was the baking of homemade bread, a simple yet somehow rare luxury, at least for me. My own cooking usually involves opening a box or can, dumping it out, and heating the contents. Hey, it takes skill to microwave macaroni just right. Amateurs have to boil it on the stove.

As we grabbed armloads of our most weather-resistant gear from the van, a beige Toyota Corolla, about ten years old and with a deep dent in one side, rolled down the road and pulled into the

Neville's driveway. It parked next to the big Suburban, which was much newer and apparently Amber's vehicle. Farther along the drive, near the barn, sat an old pick-up with rust all over its shell, and it wasn't clear whether it was still operational or just a decorative heap of junk.

Amber's husband Jeremy drove the Corolla. I recognized him from the family pictures in the house—unkempt red hair, thick glasses, tie slightly askew, coffee stain on his white shirt. It wasn't hard to see him as a frazzled and overworked high school teacher.

Jeremy climbed out of the car, dragging with him a cracked vintage attaché case that could have been used for handing off Cold War secrets in some 1960's espionage film. It was decorated with a score of travel stickers, indicating that the briefcase had visited London, Alaska, Mars, the desert planet Arrakis, and Gotham City. I strongly doubted it had actually gone to some of those destinations.

He looked over at us, two strange women standing next to a big blue cargo van with armfuls of assorted electronic gear. There was an awkward, quiet moment, during which his wife failed to materialize from the house to assure him we were supposed to be there.

"Are you...here about the cable?" he asked, looking at the van.

"No—" I began.

"That's too bad. Because we don't have any out here. I mean there are literally no cables in the ground. And the dish cuts out all the time."

"How's your cell reception?" Stacey asked.

"About what you'd guess."

"Your wife contacted us." I said, stowing my gear back into the van so I could introduce myself and hand him a business card.

"Private detectives?" he asked, looking at the card.

"We specialize in the paranormal."

"Okay. I'm just going to head inside, then." He gave us a look like he was trying to back away from a couple of escaped homicidal maniacs. "Has she already paid you any money?"

"Nope." I didn't like the sound of that question or the general direction in which it pointed. "We were about to head over to the maze and the woods to set up for an observation tonight. If you like, though, I can come in with you and explain more about—"

"Oh, no, go sit out in that old graveyard all you want. Don't say we didn't warn you." He walked up the steps and away into the house without a backward glance.

"That went surprisingly well," Stacey said. "I thought it was going to take a bad turn."

"It still might. Come on, it'll be dark soon."

We set up our observation gear at some of the more obvious places, like the outer edge of the corn maze that had been shattered by the Amazing Disappearing Horse. By the time we reached the cemetery, the sun was so low that it was completely blocked by the thick woods around us. I kept both of my tactical flashlights set to "flood" mode while Stacey set up the gear that would enable us to watch and listen for the dead.

I wanted to urge her to hurry, but I didn't want to distract her. I was sure she wanted to get out of those dark woods as much as I did. It grew colder and colder as the minutes crawled past. I heard the crunching of dried leaves and old pine straw, indistinct noises that could have been human footfalls or small animals emerging from their burrows for the night.

There was a strong feeling of being watched by invisible eyes, a sensation I never enjoy, as you could probably guess. We hadn't collected a blip of hard data yet, but my gut was telling me the place was severely haunted and quite dangerous, and the most reasonable course of action was to run away screaming until I reached a well-lit patch of civilization.

I didn't do that, since I was supposed to be the professional ghost hunter here, but I definitely imagined in great detail how nice it would be to get away from that place.

In time, we were finally ready, with multiple microphones prepared to catch any voices of the dead that might choose to speak. I was glad to have Stacey around to analyze the hours of ambient noises our recorders would collect. It would be her job to separate the specters from squirrels, to find anything resembling a human voice.

We made our way back to the rusty gate, which was still mired in the layers of dirt that had probably held it open for decades. I stopped and looked back at the cemetery, which now looked like a dark jungle. The feeling of being watched was more intense than ever, and I could feel a kind of cold seething in the air, as if shapes or monsters were ready to spill out from behind the crooked tree trunk and old headstones.

"We're listening," I said out loud, addressing the unseen and restless spirits that I could easily imagine gathering to watch us. "If you have anything to say, any message for the living, go ahead. We'll be listening even after we're gone."

We stood there, quiet and tense, the darkness growing colder. Then we moved on, back up the shadowy dirt road, shining our flashlights into the gloom.

Chapter Five

"So do you catch a lot of these ghosts?" Jeremy asked us from the head of the old picnic-style table on their back porch. This was the setting of the dinner into which I'd been roped. It was a pleasant enough environment, with herb and flower gardens in smelling distance and swarms of fireflies blinking in the nearby woods.

The food was appealing—fried chicken, potatoes, cole slaw, and the afore-smelled homemade bread, which was soft and heavenly. Sweat tea. The family situation was awkward, though. Family dinners are not great environments for me, anyway, putting me in mind of my own lost family. Even with Michael and his sister Melissa, just sitting around a table with a prepared meal puts me in an uncomfortable place.

Tonight, at the Neville family table, Amber was extra-upbeat, or pretending to be so, while Corrine played the sullen teenager, Maya stared at us and barely ate, and Castor focused on his phone, as if having a couple of paranormal investigators at dinner was totally normal.

Jeremy kept asking questions, and it was a little hard to tell by his tone whether he was genuinely curious or mildly hostile to our presence.

"We're able to improve things for most of our clients," I said, answering Jeremy's question. "Sometimes a ghost can be pressured into moving on. Sometimes we trap them and take them away."

"How do you trap a ghost?" Jeremy asked. "Prop up a cardboard box with a stick? Put a bowl of Boo Berries underneath?"

"You must have discovered our operations manual," I said. "We also have a variety of complicated gadgets from the Acme corporation. They were originally designed to catch roadrunners, but I'm sure they'll work fine."

"They didn't work that well for the coyote," Jeremy said.

"Wile E.," Castor said without looking up from his phone. "His name is Wile E."

"The key is to bait the trap properly, and for that, we need to determine who's haunting this house and why," I said. "Maybe you can help with that, Mr. Neville. Your family has owned this farm for generations. Do you have any idea who the ghosts might be? Their names, specifically, would be a huge help."

"I heard the legend of the horseman ghost growing up," he said. "But I only visited this place a couple of times, when they had family reunions here. That's it. It belonged to my great-uncle, and I happened to be his closest living relative when he died. When they told me I'd inherited the farm, all I planned to do was sell it off."

"Why did you change your mind?" I asked.

Jeremy seemed hesitant to answer. For a moment, all I could hear was the swarms of crickets in the night, and then Amber spoke up.

"We came out to look at the place," Amber said. "It was really run-down then...not that it's in great shape now, but we have put a lot of work into it. At the time, it was like the old place spoke to us. I'd been working as a claims adjuster, you know, car insurance, and that job had literally given me an ulcer. Too much stress, and too many hours, and I never saw my kids...I needed a change. We all did."

"And Corrine got arrested for selling drugs," Castor added, still not bothering to look up from his phone. "So we had to blow town."

"Shut up!" Corrine snapped. She stood abruptly and stomped out of the room, muttering, "This is so stupid."

Amber flushed red, and her husband shook his head, not looking at anybody.

"It's true," Amber said. "Kids, if you're finished eating, you can go."

"I'm still eating!" Maya said. "I want to hear about the ghosts and how Corrine got in trouble."

"I already know all about it," Castor said, sounding bored.

"Castor, why don't you take Maya and go play?" Amber said.

"I don't want to go play," the boy replied, still staring at his phone.

"Castor!" Amber snapped, and the boy finally rolled his eyes and took his little sister out of the room.

"Corrine was fourteen," Jeremy said, giving a shrug when Amber glared at him. "She was supposed to be at her friend's slumber party. The police called us at three in the morning. She'd been caught—pulled over in a car driven by a couple of boys. Seventeen-year-old boys. In Corrine's purse, they found twenty ecstasy pills and a lot of cash. We're lucky she only got community service and probation."

"You didn't have to tell them all that," Amber said.

Jeremy shrugged. "Augusta has too much crime these days. This place seemed safer."

"Corrine grew up in a daycare center while we were both away at work," Amber said. "I felt like I'd missed her childhood and I wasn't there for her. I wanted a chance to do better with the younger kids. The farm seemed like a more wholesome place."

"Do you really believe you can help?" Jeremy asked. "How many of these have you done? How many ghosts?" He winced a little as he said the word, as if he couldn't believe this was really happening. That's totally normal.

"I've worked scores of cases," I told him. "Most of them resolved to the clients' satisfaction."

"And what about the others?"

"Sometimes a situation is intractable," I said. "Sometimes the living have to surrender to the dead. Move out and move on. I can't say much about your particular situation because I don't know much yet."

"I'll tell you one thing," Jeremy said. "These mashed potatoes are the best thing that have happened to me all day." He ate another spoonful of them, chased it with tea, and sat back. "I didn't want to believe any of this was happening. I mean, I like horror. I've got a dedicated shelf out in the front room. It's the one with the raven perched on top. I've got H.P. Lovecraft, Edgar Allen Poe, Stephen King, Anne Rice, Peter Straub, Bentley Little, Clive Barker...but I never believed any of it. On the other hand, I've read enough to know there's no safety in skepticism, am I right? The guy who refuses to believe in the monster always gets killed by it. I don't want to be that guy. I don't want Amber or the kids to be that guy, either."

"I think we need to see what these ladies can do," Amber said to him. "Everything's getting worse around here. I dread turning out the lights at night. I'm scared to take my eyes off the kids for half a second. This was supposed to be safer than life in the city."

Jeremy nodded. "I think we should go ahead. I'm not crazy about being backed into a corner like this, but as long as they're here, let's see what happens."

After supper, Jeremy started asking questions about the cameras and other gear set up inside the house. I let Stacey explain all of it to him while I checked around the house again.

I took more electromagnetic and temperature readings in the upstairs hall, focusing on the area from the top of the stairs to Maya's door. Castor drifted back to his room, ignoring me and appearing to be absorbed in his phone, but he left his door open and sat on his messy bed at an angle that just happened to let him watch me as I worked.

Back downstairs, I found Amber and Maya finishing a quick clean of the kitchen.

"I'm putting Maya to bed," Amber said. "Jeremy's outside with your partner."

"He seems okay with us being here," I said.

"Very okay." Amber glanced at the kitchen window, as if trying to see what her husband was doing with perky blond Stacey out in the yard. The van's interior light was on, but Jeremy and Stacey were somewhere in the back, probably looking at the bank of monitors and other equipment. "He's asking her a million questions about your ghost work. Sorry."

"I'll go check on them," I said. "Good night, Maya."

"Are you going to stop the bloody lady tonight?" Maya asked, her face solemn as she looked up at me.

"I will personally stand in her way," I said. "But if you see anything in your room that scares you, just say something out loud. We'll hear you over the microphone and come help right away."

I headed outside and approached the van. The rear doors were open, and Jeremy stood there, leaning on one of them while he watched Stacey and the array of monitors inside.

"But how do the more powerful ghosts get that way?" Jeremy was asking her as I approached. "What's the difference between a weak haunting and a strong one?"

"It's all about energy," Stacey said. "The bad ghosts can learn to feed on the living. They can also learn to understand and control some of their, you know, ghostly abilities. Calvin says that the worst thing is a ghost that's old *and* powerful, one that probably doesn't even remember its time as a human..."

"What about good ghosts?" Jeremy asked.

"They're usually trapped here by their relationships with not-so-good spirits," Stacey said. "Like murder victims who get tangled up with their murderer's ghost."

"Ghosts obsess over certain moments of their lives," I said, by way of announcing my presence. Jeremy and Stacey both jumped, having been too busy to notice my approach. "They all do. Whether they're 'good' or 'bad' is just a question of what effect they have on the living, really."

"You scared me," Jeremy said.

"Ellie spends a lot of time around ghosts, so now she acts like one," Stacey said. "Moving silently, creeping up on people, dragging chains around in attics—"

"She's joking," I said. "Mostly. So here's the plan, Mr. Neville.

You and your family should go about your typical night as if we weren't even here. We'll stay out here in the van and keep watch on all the cameras we've set up. When your family goes to bed, I'll come inside, sit on the stairs, and watch for the ghost that your daughter's been seeing. We'll work outward from the ghosts invading your house to the ones wandering your land."

"Hey, you know," Jeremy said, "when I watch that *Ghost Investigators* show, they usually have the residents of the house leave during the investigation."

"I don't do that," I said. "I want the family to follow their usual routine, because I want the ghosts to follow *their* usual routine. Sending the family away could change the ghosts' behavior. Maybe the ghosts would just lay low until we left. We wouldn't want that."

"No, we like them to come right up and grab us in the dark," Stacey said. "It saves time."

A shriek sounded over one of the audio monitors in the van. A little girl's voice.

"What was that?" I asked, drawing my flashlight as Stacey turned toward the monitors.

"It came from Maya's room," Stacey said.

"Help!" Maya's voice whispered over the speaker. "A ghost! There's a ghost in my room!"

Jeremy bolted away from the van toward his house. Up on the second floor, the window to Maya's bedroom was pitch black.

I told Stacey to stay in the van and watch over the monitors, and then I ran along just behind Jeremy.

Maya's voice cried out a third time over the speaker in the van, begging for help.

Chapter Six

Jeremy and I burst through the front door, startling Amber, who joined us, bewildered, as we ran up the stairs, our shoes and boots thundering on the wood-plank steps. The noise was enough to make the two other kids open their doors and look out.

The door to Maya's room remained closed, the lights turned off inside.

Jeremy had been in the lead since we left the van—he was a husky, tired-looking guy, but he'd moved with lightning speed at the sound of his daughter in distress. Now he shoved open the door, calling her name as he flipped on the lights.

Maya was sitting up in bed, watching everyone crowd into her room. She smiled and looked generally non-terrified despite her recently screamed claims of seeing a ghost.

"It worked!" she said.

"Are you all right, Maya?" Amber asked.

"Just trying it," Maya said. "They told me I could yell if the bloody lady came back."

"So you didn't really see anything?" Jeremy asked.

"Not yet," Maya said. Her smile slipped a little. "Maybe later."

"Okay, good, uh, systems check, everyone," I said. "I'm glad you're safe, Maya."

"Can I get up and watch the Muppets?" Maya asked.

I eased out of the room, letting her parents deal with that one. Corrine and Castor gave me questioning looks, and I told them everything was okay, but they still looked puzzled.

I was actually a little upset but I kept it to myself. Maya was just a kid. She had no way of knowing that I'd seen a ghost murder my family when I was a child, that I was here to keep her from suffering the same fate, if the ghosts on the farm turned out to be truly dangerous. Her scream instantly stirred deep emotions and visions of Anton Clay—always smiling, always impeccably dressed, except when I saw him as a charred skeletal corpse coming to burn my soul from my body. Even then, he seemed to grin.

I returned outside and climbed into the van, where Stacey was on her drop-down cot. I lowered the cot on my side and sat down. It was extremely uncomfortable, as always, but very slightly better than sitting on the van's rubbery floor.

When Maya was squared away and back in bed after her false alarm, the house began to fall quiet. From what I heard over the microphones, Jeremy and Amber spent their last hour before bed in the reading room at the front of the house while a scratchy Stone Roses album mumbled quietly on their old record player—acting like everyone was normal, just as I'd requested. They seemed like a nice family, I thought, the parents making some career and financial sacrifices to try to provide a warm, close-knit life with their kids.

On the little black and white monitors, small shapes moved in the cemetery. We had two night vision cameras out there, plus a microphone that picked up intermittent dry leaf-crunching sounds. Nocturnal scavengers nosed past the tombstones, first a pointy, white-faced possum, then several minutes later a raccoon, one of nature's cutest and most hostile critters. The microphone began to pick up a low buzzing sound, as if flies were getting active, too.

"Okay, looks like the family's all gone to their rooms," Stacey said, while I hooked on the radio earpiece that would keep me in touch with her. "You shouldn't just sit on those old stairs all night.

You'll get sore glutes."

"I'm bringing my air mattress."

"Don't forget to stretch and walk around, though. You want to stay loose and limber in case Bloody Betty comes crawling inside."

"Is that what we're calling her?" I asked.

"I like the sound of it," Stacey said. "So what do we call the headless horseman?"

"He's not headless. He's *Hessian*," I reminded her. After strapping on my utility belt, I hopped out of the van and onto the gravel.

"Okay, so something German. Hans? Headless Hans?"

"He's not headless—"

"Hansy the Horseman? Horsey Hans? Work with me, Ellie."

"Maybe Lars." I closed one of the rear doors to the van.

"Lars Horseman?" Stacey frowned. "No way. That's not alliterative and it doesn't rhyme—"

"Keep working on it." I closed the other door and headed back to the house.

I eased the house's front door open and shut as quietly as I could and tiptoed across the aged hardwood floor. I inflated my air mattress at the foot of the steps, wincing at the loud whine of the little electronic pump. No family members came down to complain, though.

With that loud chore done, I climbed a few steps and sat down on the staircase. I'd brought my tablet, which enabled me to check our video feeds from around the farm, but I left it off for the moment.

I turned off all the lights and sat in the quiet house, listening to the occasional low creaks and moans of the old wood, the scrape of fallen leaves pushed across the front porch by the wind. Someone walked around upstairs, ran the water for a moment, returned to bed.

The house shifted into a different character by night. The handmade rustic feel, with lots of exposed planks, bricks, and timber beams, was charming by day. At night, in the heavy shadows broken only by moonlight, it took on the feeling of a place with odd angles and warped boards, where things did not quite fit together and something darker could reach out from between the walls or through the floorboards.

I rubbed my hands together as if cold, trying to ward off the growing sense of foreboding. This house had presence, history, layers of emotional energy accumulated over the generations. In the stillness and silence of the night, the soul of the house could emerge, along with any spirits that had been dormant during the day, waiting their turn to creep out under cover of darkness.

"Ellie, I caught a shadow figure in the maze," Stacey whispered. "I'm watching it at quarter-time now. It was on the camera near the maze entrance."

"Was the figure going into the maze or coming out?" I whispered back.

"It was inside the maze. Just passing by the entrance, but not coming out."

"I don't feel like getting lost in that maze by myself tonight," I said. "Let me know if you see anything else, but I want to wait right here for Bloody Betty."

"Okay. It's getting spooky, Ellie. I forget how silent it gets out in the country."

"Would you feel better if I told you a ghost story?" I asked. "I know one about a girl alone in a van on an old farm. It was all quiet until the wind started to blow, and then she heard the barn door creak—"

"Hush your face," Stacey said.

"You missed the part where it turned out to be a friendly unicorn with a pizza. Your loss." Joking was a way to avoid acknowledging my growing sense of foreboding, tinged with a glimmer of fear that could grow into full-blown panic. Nothing had actually happened so far, aside from a possibly-natural cold spot and shadows in the maze, but my nerves were firing off like I was under attack by a pack of rabid monkeys.

I took some deep breaths, then distracted myself by making another orbit of the first floor, checking for unusual temperatures or other activity. I passed through the dining room into the brick kitchen, where it looked like most of an interior wall had been knocked out to open the kitchen up to the living room. A large old brick chimney and fireplace sat next to a shining chrome-and-black modern stove that looked brand new.

The walls had been pretty recently painted, a buttery yellow in the kitchen area giving way to a silky blue over in the living room space. Their furniture was an eclectic mix, a jumble of modern sleek-lined black chairs and handcrafted antique pieces of heavy dark wood, probably a combination of the house's original furniture and whatever the family had brought from their old suburban spread back in Augusta.

I swept my Mel-Meter around the old chimney, but I picked up nothing except the ghostly smell of old smoke, which was perfectly normal for a fireplace that looked like it had hosted centuries of flames and ash.

The living room didn't offer any exceptional readings. I opened the door at the far end, down four thick lumber-slab steps into the laundry room. The walls were all brick, with remnants of old plaster clinging to them here and there.

Spirits typically like the dark, lesser-used places in a house, little spots where they can nest without much interference: the basement, the attic, the crawlspace, the small area at the very back of a sloped closet. The dusty, little-seen space under the bed.

The laundry room was a few degrees colder, and I did detect higher electricity here, but nothing wildly out of step with my earlier readings. The laundry room was at an outside edge of the house, lower than the rest of it, and of course had large electrical cables to power the laundry machines. Along with the garage, it was a later addition to the early nineteenth-century farmhouse, made of visibly newer and more modern brick.

I passed through another door and into the dark garage, where Amber's metal-working bench occupied one corner. Another area, used for storage, was a jumble of old and new, like a broken antique bedframe parked next to a stack of sealed plastic Container Store tubs labeled with magic marker. CLOTHES. SCHOOL. TOYS. MEMORIES.

Stacey's voice crackled over my headset, but the reception was poor in the garage. I couldn't make out what she said, but her tone was urgent.

"Repeat," I said, hurrying back through the laundry room and up the steps to the living room, in search of better reception. "Stacey, repeat whatever you just said."

"—moving in," Stacey said, her voice a little clearer now. "Severe temperature drop outside the front door from our sensors out there. Motion detector is pinging. Now it's moving in."

"Moving in?" I dashed through folding doors into the front room stocked with old paperbacks and board games.

"The thermal in the foyer is picking up a cold shape. Be careful, Ellie. I'm ready to jump in anytime."

"Hold your position."

Usually Stacey would snark out some kind of cop or military movie cliché at this point. The fact that she didn't told me that she was seriously spooked by whatever she was seeing on the monitors.

I slowed and drew my tactical flashlight as I stepped into the foyer, narrowing the iris so it would give me a focused, slicing light-saber sort of beam, in the event that I chose to click it on. I kept it dark for now—this was meant to be an observation, not a fight. I didn't want to run off the ghost I'd been waiting to see.

There was no denying how cold the foyer had become. On my Mel-Meter, the temperature dropped from a perfectly pleasant sixty-eight degrees to a frigid thirty-nine as I crossed the threshold. The air was bitterly cold. My earlier feelings of foreboding returned in full bloom now, and I fought to stay calm.

Something was definitely in the room with me.

A thin white mist hung about an inch above the floor, thickest near the front door. It was spreading slowly from the door toward the stairs, as if carried on a trickle of air current.

This kind of frosty mist or cold fog is commonly associated with high-energy hauntings. It's essentially the reverse of seeing heat ripples in the air, radiating from a hot surface in the summertime. The mist results from the sudden cooling and freezing of the humidity in the air as a ghost passes through, hungrily slurping up what energy it can from the ambient heat of the room.

"Ellie?" Stacey asked.

I tapped my microphone with my finger to indicate that I wouldn't be speaking for the moment. I didn't want to run off the ghost.

I eased around the slowly flowing mist and scooped up my thermal goggles from the little heap of gear next to my air mattress. Then I moved up a few steps and turned to face the mist, claiming the staircase for myself. I didn't want to scare the ghost away, not at the moment, but I also had no intention of letting it slip past me to harass Maya in her room, or any other member of the family.

The mist inched forward, slowly making its way from the front door to the staircase. As the first frosty tendrils reached the bottom step, I spoke up. I kept my voice low but firm and filled with intention.

"Stop," I said.

The mist may have slowed, or possibly not—it had been moving at a snail's trot already. Gradually, it filled in more of the space in front of the bottom stair, and seemed to ease a little ways up and over the lip of the stair. The slow pace of the thing was almost maddening. I could feel the individual seconds dragging on and on.

I took the opportunity to strap on my thermal goggles and try for a more in-depth look at the entity. Sometimes this gives me the rough shape of the ghost and tells me whether it presents itself as large or small, maybe even whether it's male or female.

In this case, though, what I saw was a deep blue, almost black mass of no clear shape, chilling the space around it. It was like a black cloud rolling its way over the floorboards toward my boots.

"Stop there," I said. At this point, I had my flashlight in one hand and a microphone drawn from my utility belt in the other. "Can you tell me your name?"

If there was a response, it wasn't audible to me. Maybe I'd recorded something out of the range of my hearing, though.

"Can you tell me why you're here?" I asked, still pointing the microphone at the cold front gathering on the first stair.

No words came back, but there was a sighing sound in the air, barely audible, coming and going like a soft breeze.

"Are you lost?" I asked. "Are you scared? I can help you move on—"

The darkness surged forward, like a flood of black water

pouring upward and swallowing one stair after another, climbing up to my feet in an eyeblink. I stumbled back, startled at the sudden change in the entity's speed. The plodding slowness of the mist had given me a false sense of security.

I glimpsed her shape for only an instant through my thermal goggles, a blurry black-ice outline suggesting a woman from the waist up, the freezing shapeless darkness spreading out behind her like a impossibly large shadowy skirt big enough to enclose half the foyer and the front door.

The thermals revealed no details, only the shape of a slender, slightly curvy abdomen, and long arms ending in claw-tip fingers.

One purple-black hand seized my ankle. Pain scorched my skin. Her fingers were freezing, cold enough to kill the skin and possibly the bone beneath.

I lanced her with my flashlight, but this entity wouldn't be deterred. She gripped harder, and I'm pretty sure I heard the bones inside my ankle squeak in protest, and then I toppled backwards onto the stairs.

My head banged against wood, and I smelled horses.

I bounced, jarring my head again, but the real pain was in my lower body.

Male voices muttered around me, and red light oozed from the ends of burning sticks, the crude pine torches of the old days. Visibility was poor.

I realized I was moving, lying in the knobby bed of some kind of wagon. The scrape of wooden wheels filled my ears as I jostled over an uneven road.

Looking down at myself, toward the pain in my lower half, I glimpsed my legs by the red torch light. I wore a red dress—no. A simple white cotton dress, perhaps no more than a slip or a petticoat, most of it red with fresh blood.

I was dying. Stars rolled past overhead. Men walked alongside the slow wagon and spoke to each other in low voices, too quiet for me to make out the words, but they were seething with emotion. I could smell the acrid sizzling pitch of their torches. Their faces were in shadow, but I could see they wore white wigs and triangular black hats.

The wagon must have hit a stone, because the whole thing bucked, and my head slammed against the wooden floor of the wagon again—

—and I was lying sprawled in front of the staircase in the Neville house, disoriented, my head throbbing. It looked as though I'd fallen down the few steps that had been below me, conking my skull along the way.

The front door swung open. Stacey entered and ran toward where I lay at the foot of the stairs. My hips were on the inflatable mattress, but the upper half of my body had landed past it and crashed straight into the wooden floor.

"Ellie! What happened?" She swung her light around the room as she dropped to her knees beside me.

That was a good question. A fine question. It took a moment to gather my wits around the pounding in my head and remember just what had happened. As soon as I did, I sat up—while Stacey cautioned me to lie still—and drew my backup flashlight from my belt, since I wasn't sure where the first one had landed as I fell.

I switched it on and looked up the stairs. I didn't see anything, but that doesn't mean much in ghost-land.

"See if the ghost is still here," I said. I found my thermal goggles on my forehead, knocked askew but fortunately not broken. Those things are expensive. I drew them back down over my eyes and looked up the stairs from where I still sprawled on the floor.

I couldn't see any cold spots or other remnants of the freezing mist. I saw Stacey's warm red form move closer to the stairs, taking readings with her Mel-Meter.

"Nothing weird here," she said.

"Help me up." I pushed my thermals up onto my forehead, then Stacey loaned me an arm so I could regain my feet. I felt slow and dizzy, but I was starting to panic. "We need to get upstairs."

"Wait, let me check you for head injuries and stuff—"

"Bloody..uh...what's her name—"

"Bloody Betty?"

"She could be up in that little girl's room right now. I sure didn't stop her."

"I'll go check. Wait here." Stacey raced up the stairs. I shambled after her, leaning on the wide wooden banister for support. My head hurt and I urged my boots to move faster instead of clomping along as though stuck in the mud. I lost sight of Stacey as she reached the top of the stairs and continued on toward Maya's room.

As I climbed the stairs, I noticed a disturbing numbness in my ankle and foot where the ghost had grabbed me. The numbness flared into a burning sensation that reminded me of the time when I was eight years old, having a great time at the beach with my parents until I happened to swim into the long tendrils of a jellyfish. The pain had seemed to last forever.

There was no time to stop and de-boot and de-sock myself to check myself for damage, though. I reached the second floor and found Stacey outside Maya's room, taking readings. The upstairs hallway was dim, lit only by a little moonlight and the glow of Stacey's Mel-Meter.

"Nothing here," she whispered, shaking her head.

"I'm going to check anyway," I whispered back. With my flashlight off, I took hold of the doorknob and turned it as quietly as I could, not wanting to disturb the little girl if she was resting peacefully.

Her room seemed cool but not unnaturally so. Moonlight trickled in through the curtains, but for the most part the room was all shadow. I took a step inside for a closer look, to make sure the girl was sleeping soundly in her bed. A floorboard creaked, and I tensed, hoping I hadn't woken her.

Nothing moved in the dark room.

Leaving Stacey in the hall, I tiptoed deeper into the room, taking readings with my Mel-Meter. It registered a spike as I approached the sleeping girl. Her long red hair reached out in all directions across her pillow, tangling and knotting even in her sleep, making me think of Medusa and her coif of live snakes. My hair's pretty difficult to manage, too, but at least it's not venomous.

I waved the meter past the girl's alarm clock, which looked like a small aquarium with a couple of plastic goldfish suspended in blue gel. A lamp shaped like a giant seashell sat beside it. So did a LeapFrog digital tablet. This little cluster of electronics and wires could account for some of the energy I was detecting, but I still thought the reading should have been less pronounced.

The reading ticked upward as I lowered the meter toward the floor. Here was a wheeled car that resembled a shark, its angry yellow eyes and open jaws pointed at a pink plastic palace full of little doors and slides. There might have been batteries in these toys, but they were turned off at the moment. Why the high electrical readings? If it was a ghost, though, it was fairly good at hiding itself, because I wasn't getting any other signs, like temperature fluctuations or goosebumps on my neck.

In the doorway, Stacey gave me a big shrug, silently asking just when the heck I planned on wrapping this up and moving on. I gave her a big shrug in return. I didn't know.

I followed the ever-increasing electrical readings right to the floor, feeling myself relax as I did so. It had to be some kind of cable or wire running beneath the floorboard.

Then I heard something giggle under the bed.

Tensing, I pointed my flashlight at the ruffled bed skirt and reached for it with my other hand. The bed skirt was long enough to touch the floor, concealing the entire space below the bed. A full-grown man could have hidden under there.

I held my breath as I raised the bed skirt. I saw a pale little shape that I first thought to be the plastic hand of a toy doll.

The giggle sounded again, and two white eyes glowed in the darkness under Maya's bed. My first impression was right—it was a plastic baby doll toy, larger than life size, with eyes that lit up as it giggled. Its rosy plastic cheeks and lips were frozen in an immutable smile, its white teeth bared at me.

The giggle stopped, the eyes turned black, and the doll vanished again as darkness reclaimed the space under the bed. I'd probably jarred the doll to life with my poking and prodding, maybe causing the bed skirt to brush against it.

Tricked by an oversized baby doll—judging by its size, the thing probably ran on six or eight fat D cell batteries, or maybe something with an even bigger kick. This mistake wasn't going to win me any of the major ghost-hunter awards, but I don't suppose those actually exist, anyway.

I nudged the massive doll the rest of the way under the bed, hoping it wouldn't giggle again and wake Maya when I dropped the bed skirt back into place.

The pale woman surged up from the darkness behind the doll. Her face was a white death mask, but her hand was a gleaming blood red, droplets of gore hanging from her long fingernails. I had a good look at those as they swiped at my face, as though she intended to skewer my eyes. The air was instantly ice-cold all around me.

I screamed and leaped back from the bed, at the same time clicking on my tactical flashlight to blast the attacking ghost with thousands of lumens of white light.

Above me, Maya seemed to bounce on the bed, and she let out a scream of her own. Stacey, over in the doorway, screamed along with her about a second later.

Once again, I would not be winning any awards in the category of Most Professional Ghost Hunter for my performance this evening.

My flashlight flooded the room with white light. Stacey added her own and lifted the bed skirt on the other side of the bed to soak the bloody dead woman in light from another angle.

The woman was already gone, though. Our lights revealed, in searing white, the giant giggly baby doll and an assortment of stuffed animals, balled-up socks, and dust bunnies. Or maybe they were lint bunnies. Definitely some sort of harmless under-the-furniture floor fluff.

"Is she here?" Maya asked. "Do you see her?"

"I saw her," I said. "It looks like we scared her away for now."

"You know how to scare her?" Maya asked.

"Light," I said. "If you keep a flashlight by your bed, that's like a weapon you can use against her."

Maya nodded, her eyes wide and frightened, her red tangles bouncing everywhere. "Is she really gone?"

I checked my Mel-Meter. The unusual high electricity readings had vanished. "She's not in the room," I said. "We're going to figure out how to kick her out forever. Are you okay, Maya? Did she hurt you?"

Maya shook her head.

"What about you, Ellie?" Stacey asked.

"I'm fine." With the immediate shock averted, I had time to notice the stinging pain around my ankle again, but then the family members arrived, clamoring up the hall from their respective rooms in response to our screams.

Maya's room grew crowded fast, and everyone looked at me, ready for an explanation of what had just happened.

I cleared my throat.

"Okay," I said. "My associate Stacey and I have made our initial assessment, and in our professional opinion, this house is definitely haunted. You have at least one semi-conscious apparition, she has a lot of energy, and she is not happy."

"Can you get rid of it?" Jeremy asked.

"As soon as we know who she is and why she's here, we can figure out how to remove her." I felt drained, as if Bloody Betty had sucked out most out of my energy when she'd grabbed me. I was doing my best to sound confident and together despite being badly shaken by what I'd just witnessed. I've gotten pretty good at faking it.

The ghost had inadvertently given me something, too—a glimpse into her own memories. I needed to write down every detail I could remember as soon as possible, before it began to fade like a dream. If it contained any clues to her identity and how to deal with her, then it was worth a conk on the head and a jellyfish sting from beyond the grave.

Chapter Seven

We explained the situation as well as we could. Though the family members had their share of conflicts with each other, they certainly drew together in a moment of crisis, revealing a bond that lasted until it became apparent that the supernatural flare-up was, hopefully, concluded for the night. Bloody Betty had made her visit and moved on.

The family broke down into bickering before returning to their rooms. Maya went with her parents. Stacey and I moved cameras into her room to keep a close watch for the rest of the night, recording everything in case the ghost returned to make a repeat performance.

"Why are you limping?" Stacey asked as I returned to the van with her. It was well past midnight.

"Our cold friend grabbed me," I said, and quickly recounted the attack and my glimpse of being someone else, somewhere else. "It feels like she did some damage."

I climbed into the back of the van, sat on my bunk, and winced as I slid off my boot. The movement didn't feel great against my injured ankle. Then I pulled off my sock.

"Yowtch," Stacey said, then let out a little sympathetic hiss of pain.

Reddish-purple fingermarks were visible on my ankles, showing exactly where she'd seized me.

"Looks like frostbite," Stacey said.

"I'm sure it's pretty mild." I winced as I wiggled my foot back and forth. "Because the feeling is coming back fast. A little too fast, really."

"Jinkies, that was one frosty phantom," Stacey said.

"Jinkies?"

"You know, like Velma on *Scooby-Doo*—"

"Obviously. But you see yourself as the Velma of our group?"

"Of course. I handle the high-tech gadgetry, right? That's Velma."

"So who does that make me?" I asked, narrowing my eyes. "Daphne?"

"What's wrong with being Daphne?"

"Just watch the monitors, Stacey," I said. "We can't have any more incidents tonight."

"Like sneaking into a little girl's room and waking her up by screaming at the top of your lungs?" Stacey asked. "I don't remember Calvin teaching us that technique on training days—"

"It was pure customer service, that scream," I said, trying to salvage my dignity. "Making the client aware of a hostile apparition."

"Are we sure she's hostile?" Stacey asked.

"She could have broken my neck," I said. "Whether that was intentional or not, she's dangerous."

I got to work at my laptop, writing down the rapidly-melting details of my vision. Ghosts are energy with consciousness, and sometimes contact with them can transfer emotions, visions, or memories. Some ghosts even know how to manipulate this, making the living feel depressed or violent, or inducing frightening hallucinations. In this case, I didn't think it was intentional. A snippet of the ghost's memory had simply leaked into me.

"I saw a couple of the men," I told Stacey, by way of jogging my own memories. "They had pitch torches. Their clothing was definitely eighteenth century. One guy had a tricorner hat. I'm not sure if I was still dying or already dead at this point. There didn't seem to be a rush to take me anywhere."

"You?" Stacey asked.

"The girl in the wagon. I saw the vision from her viewpoint."

"Bloody Betty."

"Her name wasn't Betty, it was..." It was on the tip of my tongue, but it wouldn't quite drop off. I was sure I could remember it if I tried.

"Did she give you any ideas about what's going on around here? Or how to get rid of her?" Stacey asked.

"No, just that tiny look at her life. I assume she's soaked in her own blood, but I don't know if she was injured, or if it was a death during childbirth situation, or what exactly happened to her."

"Maybe it wasn't her own blood," Stacey said. "Maybe she killed somebody."

"Considering what an unfriendly ghost she is, I wouldn't be surprised."

The rest of the night was fairly quiet. The most unusual readings came from the cemetery—cold spots, shadows, occasional weird creaking sounds. I was glad to be looking at it on video rather than sitting out there in person, watching for disturbing shapes in the fog. As the hours passed, I stretched my legs a few times, taking walks around the dark yard while picking up some extra readings.

The family was up and moving before dawn. Corrine tended the horses while her mother and younger siblings took care of other chores. Jeremy was off to work in the early darkness, with a long commute to the high school where he taught. Soon all three kids had left for school, too.

We sat down with Amber in the little general store and showed her the thermal video clip from the previous night. Her eyes grew saucer-sized as she watched the low flood of freezing purple-black spread across the foyer floor toward my red and orange shape on the stairs. She jumped as the dark mass suddenly swelled toward me and swept me off my feet in a not-so-romantic fashion.

I winced at the sight of my form tumbling down the stairs and landing on the floor, the air mattress protecting my hips but not my head as I sprawled across the boards. It was embarrassing.

"If you look closer, you can see the ghost's shape..." Stacey backed up the video, zoomed in and played it very slowly, so Amber could see what I'd glimpsed through my goggles. The front edge of the dark mass formed into the shape of a woman from the waist up, her arms reaching out to grab me at floor level, while the back end of her remained a shapeless mist that spread out across the foyer.

Stacey paused the video when the woman-shape was clearest.

"Oh, my..." Amber covered her mouth. "You can really see it there."

"You're sure you don't have any idea who she could be?" I asked.

Amber shook her head.

"Could Jeremy know? Or does he have an older relative who knows the history of this place? And have you checked the house for any old family records?"

"We've already been there, done that," Amber said. "We tried to figure things out before we called you, but we don't have any more ideas."

"I've emailed a friend of mine at the Savannah Historical Association, but I doubt he'll have anything for us," I said. "They focus on the history of Savannah and its immediate surroundings. Stacey and I will probably need to hit the local library, the county courthouse, anywhere there might be records. Stacey loves that kind of research."

"I hope we'll get to dig through lots of dusty yellow land deeds!" Stacey said, faking a smile.

"Don't forget tax records," I said.

"My favorite."

"In the meantime, Stacey and I should probably get some rest. I saw a place called Old Walnut Inn at the last town we passed. Is that a good place?"

"I wouldn't know," Amber said.

"It definitely *looked* cheap," Stacey said. "Like Bates Motel cheap."

"I could probably find a place for you to stay here in the

house," Amber said. "We could make up the couch..."

"Thanks, Mrs. Neville, but I'm sure that would be inconvenient." I rushed to answer before Stacey could accept the invitation. Amber seemed to be offering reluctantly, being polite but probably not wanting a couple of weirdo ghost investigators camping out in her living room, snoring the day away like unwanted, unemployed relatives. "Is it all right if we leave our gear set up for tonight? That would save hours."

"Of course," she said, trying to smile but not quite making it. "How long do they usually take, these ghost bustings of yours?"

"Every case is different. I promise we'll move as quickly as possible."

Soon after that, we climbed into the van and backtracked a few miles. The Old Walnut Inn, despite its genteel-sounding name, was more of a roadside motel with a peach and pink trim that probably hadn't been updated since sometime around 1961. It was an L-shaped building arranged around a fenced swimming pool area. The pool had long since been filled with cement, yet the outdoor lounge chairs and umbrella tables remained, as if faithfully waiting for the return of the lost water and whatever good times may have happened in decades past.

The interior was pretty much what the outside implied—outdated, worn, threadbare, the lights reluctant to switch on. The room was clean, though, with a pair of double beds that seemed reasonably comfortable and not gross. Plus it didn't cost much more than we would have spent on gasoline to drive the heavy cargo van home to Savannah and back again.

Stacey secured the window curtain to keep all the light out, while I removed my sock to have another look at my injury. The reddish fingermarks remained, but the stinging feeling meant that the damage couldn't have gone too deep. Serious frostbite would have left my foot numb, probably blistering by this point.

Stacey laughed, and I looked over at her. She was reading something on her phone.

"What's that?" I asked.

"Just Jacob." She shook her head as she put her phone away.

I texted Michael to see what he was doing. His schedule at the fire station shifted unpredictably but usually involved getting up well before daylight, and of course I mostly work the graveyard shift. I'm often going to sleep when he's getting ready to start the day.

There was nothing from him, though, not even a reply to my quick message from earlier letting him know I'd be away from the city for the night. Then I noticed my new message hadn't gone through but had instead gained me an error message with an exclamation point. There wasn't much of a phone signal available out at the farm. It was possible he'd replied long ago and I still hadn't received it.

We slept for the rest of the morning. I tossed and turned. Anton Clay lived in my dreams, and he had a way of showing up and ruining them, Freddy Krueger-style. An idyllic beach setting with Michael and Stacey suddenly became an inferno, the sky blood-red, the ocean water boiling, the bodies of dead fish and strange tentacled things rising up to cover the ocean all the way to the horizon, their pale corpses washing up on the smoldering sand.

It was a relief to finally awaken for the day, but I couldn't say I felt particularly rested.

The only spot for breakfast, especially around noon, was the Huddle House, a diner-style chain restaurant that flourishes wherever Waffle House isn't. They seem to specialize in finding new things to stuff inside hash browns. I ordered the garden omelet since I didn't want to spend all day in bed sluggishly digesting fried potatoes. Stacey seemed to thumb her nose at my choices by ordering the French toast with the strawberry mess on top.

"Grant just got back to me," I told her, skimming Grant's email while waiting for my eggs full of peppers and tomatoes to get cooked and find their way to our table. "He doesn't have any information on the address—the farm is too far from Savannah. So it looks like a real poking-around sort of day. You can sift audio and video footage from last night, see what we missed. I'll be looking into old paperwork in old buildings."

"Okay, I like that arrangement," she said. "I hope you find something worthwhile. Nobody seems to know anything so far."

"It's a long shot," I said. "Even if there is something to the legend of the Hessian horseman, it won't be easy to find records from the eighteenth century, especially in a place this far from any large city. There may not be anything to discover."

"I'll work extra hard to find any ghostly faces or voices in our data, then."

"Are you saying you're usually lazy about it?"

"Ha ha." Stacey chewed her lip, looking worried, and not even the arrival of French toast seemed to cheer her up. "What if we can't find any history on this one, Ellie? What do we do then?"

"Then we observe the ghosts and try to figure out what they want. Bring in Jacob for a psychic reading. Let him know we might need him soon—like, as soon as he can make it up here. He might be our only hope at getting a clear picture of what's going on down at the farm."

The nearest courthouse and library were both located in the city of Sylvania, the county seat, population three thousand. Stacey rode in the back of the van, already at work on the previous night's data, while I let the GPS guide me into a cute little village of colorful, old-fashioned masonry buildings, centered on a town square with a fountain and trees. It was a little reminiscent of the squares of Savannah. I was surprised to see how cheerful and alive the town seemed. Many of these little old towns that I see are desolate, with lots of empty shop windows.

My first stop was the courthouse, where I could research the history of land deeds in the county. Records were spotty, as I expected, especially since a fire had destroyed the courthouse in 1897, but some of the paperwork had been saved.

I collected any names of female residents of the land that I could find, paying extra attention to those who'd died young, since that can point to tragic or violent deaths that might lead to a haunting. There was a Henrietta Neville who died at age fifteen in 1891. A Ruth Neville died in 1853, just seventeen years old. The yellowed death certificate, handwritten in a barely legible scrawl, offered no details, only mentioned a vague "head injury."

Some of them cross-checked with the handful of names I'd been able to collect at Jeremy's family cemetery. There was Hiram Neville, born in 1746 and buried in 1823—I'd seen his big headstone, mostly eroded and sunken, but his name and year of death had been a bit legible. Judging by his advanced age and the size of his grave marker, I was guessing he'd been something of the family patriarch during his era. Hiram was the first to own the land, receiving it in a decree from the royal governor of Georgia in 1770, probably in exchange for some sort of cash payment. He was also interesting to me because he would have been alive during the American Revolution, during the time when Hessians were riding around Georgia killing rebellious colonists for the British Empire.

I also found a death record of a Rebekah Neville Hudstrom, buried in 1859. Edina Drayton Neville, age 11, died in 1903 of polio. In 1943, Minnie Neville, aged twenty, died in a horseback riding accident.

I had to wonder how many layers of hauntings we faced. Was the horse-mounted ghost really a Hessian soldier or somebody from later years? Was the horseman connected to the bloody girl ghost at all, or were they separated by generations? Once a place is haunted, it tends to accumulate more ghosts over the years, the energy growing denser and darker like a spiritual black hole. Nothing attracts a ghost like a haunted house, Calvin says.

I jotted notes, took snapshots of old documents, and put together what sparse history of the Neville farm I could. I desperately needed more information about the eighteenth century in particular.

The courthouse offered only some bare-bones information, but it was better than nothing. I traced the history of land ownership all the way from Hiram Neville to Jeremy's deceased great-uncle and then to Jeremy himself.

Outside, Stacey lounged in the back of the van with her headphones on, staring at the array of screens. With the windows open and the van's rear door ajar, the interior was pleasantly cooled by the autumn air.

"Find anything?" she asked, waving at her monitors. "I didn't."

"Not much on my end."

"No dead girls, huh?"

"Some dead girls, but not much information about them. Maybe the library has more."

"Sounds like an exciting adventure."

I did have some better luck at the library, as it turned out.

The library was, naturally, smaller than those where I usually did my research back in Savannah, pleasant and sunny despite the spiderwebs and bats hanging from the ceiling. Cutesy foam tombstones and plastic coffins decorated a large table that offered "Spooky Reads" ranging from classic Shirley Jackson to more modern and kid-friendly R.L. Stein offerings. I would have found the little faux-graveyard a little more adorable if it hadn't reminded me of the need to deal with restless things in the real one over at the clients' farm. Even in the daylight, just the memory of that swampy, isolated family cemetery was disquieting.

The librarian on duty was a middle-aged woman dressed in a bee costume, with a black and yellow striped top and a headband with shiny antennae that bounced as she moved. It wasn't quite Halloween yet, but I supposed she was really into the season. A long felt stinger wagged at the back of her black stretch pants as she turned to face me.

"Can I help you?" she asked, studying my face as if struggling to recognize me. "New patron?"

"I'm from out of town." I introduced myself and passed her a business card.

"Oh, a private investigator!" The librarian's voice dropped into a conspiratorial whisper, though we were alone in the room as far as I could tell. "Are you solving a murder? I just love those Kinsey Millhone mysteries." She pointed to a "Staff Pick" shelf where Sue Grafton novels were prominently featured.

"Nothing that exciting, I'm afraid, unless I run across an unsolved historical murder."

"That *would* be exciting!" The librarian's eyes lit up. "How can I help?"

"I'm researching a local farm. The new owners are trying to learn about their ancestors who lived there." I gave her the address of the farm, but avoided mentioning any ghosts.

"Oh, the Nevilles, of course! Amber is such a pleasant young woman. Her daughter always makes a wreck of the children's room. She's a little red-haired devil. Oh, she's not malicious about it, like some of the little...well, little *patrons*...that come in here. She's just so enthusiastic to read it all, you see. And then there's her son. So you must be interested in the horseman ghost."

"Have you heard about it?" I asked.

"Well, I didn't grow up here," she said. "I'm from Moultrie originally. After Amber and her family moved in and opened up that place for a tourist trap, I mean tourist attraction, you just about couldn't avoid hearing something about it. Most people don't think anything of it, of course."

"What have you heard?"

"Just that there's a ghost on horseback riding up and down the old roads out there," she said. "They say he'll clobber you if you get in his way."

"Anything about his identity?"

"Something to do with the Revolution. I want to say he was a Hessian—whoever came up with that tale didn't do anything but knock off the *Legend of Sleepy Hollow*, if you ask me. I don't believe a word of it, but I suppose it's fun to have such a local story. And of course there was that big battle not far from here. Big in Revolution-era terms, I mean, not so much in modern times. The Battle of Brier Creek, they call it, and serious history buffs from all over the country come here to see it. So we librarians are expected to know about it, you see, by those visiting buffs."

I wanted to cringe at her multiple uses of the word *buff*, as in history buff, movie buff, whatever—that word always rubs me the wrong way. I'd say it was one of my "pet peeves" but that term is another one of my, um...things that annoy me. That wasn't the librarian's fault, of course, so I kept a smile on my face and my mild irritation under my hat. Metaphorically. I wasn't wearing a hat.

I intended to ask her more about the local Revolution battle, but she saved me the trouble by launching right into it.

"...big defeat for the American side!" she was saying. "The patriots were trapped between Brier Creek and the Savannah River, you see. The British moved in, and hundreds of Americans died. Nobody even knows for sure how many. It was an awful sight, I'm sure. The victory encouraged the British to stay quite a bit longer. The British might have retreated and given up on the South if not for their big victory at Brier Creek. That's why the occasional history buffs come. It was a turning point in the war..."

I nodded along while she recited a short, well-practiced summary of the battle, but didn't hear anything that sounded too relevant to my case. I asked whether there was a connection to the Neville farm.

"Oh, none that I know of," she said. "I suppose some of them could have served in the Georgia militia there. We have a local genealogy database for the county. You can try that if you like. It's on the computer."

"That would be great, thanks."

"We also have archives of the *Telephone* going back years and years, if you'd like to look through those."

"I'm sorry?" I asked. "You mean the local phone book?"

The librarian chuckled, her shiny antennae bouncing on her head. "The *Sylvania Telephone*, dear. That's the local newspaper."

"That would be great. Though I'm guessing it wasn't established in the eighteenth century, by any chance..."

"1876," she said quickly. "When the telephone was very high-tech, you see."

She guided me toward the library's resources, and while I skimmed through records, she continued to tell me about significant events in local history, with an emphasis on the construction of "America's oldest welcome center" out on highway 301, which had once been the main route for Northern snowbirds bound for Florida before the interstate was built. This gave me some idea of why our motel hadn't really been updated in decades. It sat just off that highway and had probably lost most of its business long ago when the interstate was built many miles away.

This made me think of the old dirt road that ran through the clients' farm, and how Amber and Jeremy's version of the legend depicted the ghost as a highwayman, a former German soldier preying on travelers.

I asked the librarian if there were any old maps of the area. She found a photocopy of one from the early nineteenth century, but the hand-drawn lines and letters were blurry, not really giving me much insight. I took a photocopy of the photocopy to inspect later, maybe with a magnifying glass.

Researching the history of the land meant researching a branch of Jeremy's family. During the span covered by the local paper, I found a number of references, including the usual assortment of birth, wedding, and death announcements.

A pattern emerged over time. Over the previous century and a half, several of the men in Jeremy's family had apparently been accused of violent crimes, some of them convicted, at least one executed in the late nineteenth century. That was Oren Jubilee Neville, hanged in 1891 in connection with a local man found beaten to death on the Neville farm, his body in the high weeds not far from the road. Oren and the man had recently had a business dispute over the sale of a small piece of land.

This happened at least three more times over the next hundred years. Someone would go missing—once a local, twice just travelers passing through—and be discovered beaten to death near the road, on the family's property, and some member of the family would be charged. The most recent was in 1983, when a younger brother of the great uncle who'd left Jeremy the farm had pled guilty to aggravated manslaughter. That man's name was Lawrence Neville, arrested for apparently beating to death two college students from Augusta who'd been traveling the back roads of the state, camping and taking pictures of old farms and colonial-era ruins. He had died in prison.

The idea of restless ghosts wandering out from the family cemetery grew darker and darker as I read up on the family's history of violence. I wondered whether our bloody ghost-girl was a member of the family or a victim of its violence. Both things were possible. Unfortunately, the more I considered the glimpse I'd received when the ghost touched me, the more I became convinced that she'd lived in the late eighteenth century, and records from that time were spotty.

Eventually, the librarian sighed, shaking her head at my requests for information that the little library just didn't have.

"I wasn't going to say this," she told me, "But if you really want to drink from a fire hose of information about the Revolution around here, I suppose I could put you in touch with Virgil Rathmew. He's a local history buff. He actually wrote a book about the Brier Creek battle, but he couldn't find anybody to publish it. I suppose the big publishers want authors with advanced history degrees and such. Virgil has a certificate in air conditioner repair from Ogeechee Technical College, but that's about it."

"I'd be very happy to speak with him," I said.

"He's kind of an odd bird, though. I feel a little hesitant to introduce you, because I don't want you to go thinking everybody in town is like Virgil. Virgil's one of a kind. And that's not always a good thing..."

"Believe me, I'm not afraid of eccentric people. If he has information, I want it."

"I'll just look up his patron account and give him a call. Excuse me."

While the librarian returned to her desk, I gathered up the paper copies I'd printed of assorted newspaper articles and other details. It was late afternoon and the library would close soon. Between the courthouse and library, I'd skimmed hundreds of pages of documents, maybe more. My eyes felt worn down, and so did my forebrain, but I'd taken in a lot of raw data. I had a number of vaguely possible suspects for the identity of Bloody Betty, but nothing to point strongly to any specific one of them. As for the horseman, I had no real clues at all.

"Virgil's voice mail answered," the librarian said as I stood to go. "I gave him your name and the number from your business card."

I thanked the lady for her help, which had been considerable, and hurried out the door. The shadows were already long and deep outside. It was late October, and darkness came a little earlier every day.

As I approached the van, I checked my phone. Grant hadn't gotten in touch, though I wasn't counting on him to come up with much, anyway. Michael hadn't texted me back, either. I'd let him know I'd probably be out of town on a case for a few days. Usually he asked questions, wanted some assurances I'd be safe and not, for example, getting thrown out of high windows by angry poltergeists (it's happened). Maybe he'd worked an extra long shift at the fire station. Maybe he was still wrapped up in his latest restoration project, a massive grandfather-sized clock carved to look like a black castle, with spring-driven automata chess pieces that rolled out at different hours. The clock was bizarre and unsettling to me, but he was sure he could repair it and sell it for a sizable profit. He'd promised to take us on a little vacation together with the money, but that didn't make me like the clock one tick more.

    I thought about calling him, but the excited look on Stacey's face as I climbed into the van distracted me.

    "Want to hear the ghosts?" Stacey asked, grinning as she nudged her way up the narrow pass between the two front seats. She handed me her headset.

Chapter Eight

The headset filled my ears with static, the buzzing of flies, and the distant chirping of crickets. I closed my eyes and listened carefully. Something crunched in the leaves, maybe an animal that had nosed its way past the microphone in the cemetery the night before.

Then something breathed in my ear. It was heavy, masculine, just one slow breath in and back out, and it sounded very human.

I opened my eyes, and Stacey just nodded at my expression.

"Now listen to this," she said, grabbing another sound clip on her laptop screen. "It's also from the cemetery, from a little after two in the morning."

I closed my eyes and listened again to the ambient sounds of a quiet cemetery at night.

"Someone is watching," a voice whispered, making me jump. Voice apparitions are rarely so clear—breathing is creepy enough. To hear the flat, cold voices of the dead, even for just a few words, is always disturbing. It came again, closer, as if approaching the microphone.

"Someone is watching us."

"Do you have any video with this?" I asked Stacey.

"Sure do. The night vision camera picked up a little orb, smaller than a penny, passing near the microphone."

"We're getting somewhere with this case." I removed the headset and started up the van. "I'm just not sure where, exactly."

"Well, wherever we're going, they have talking dead people there," Stacey said. "That should be a comforting thought. Oh, Jacob said he can come up tomorrow night."

"That actually is a comforting thought," I said. "The Jacob part. Not the part with the talking dead people." I could still hear the flat, almost mechanical voice, devoid of any inflection. *Someone is watching.* I hate how ghosts sound when they talk.

We stopped at a restaurant in town long enough to order a couple of take-out salads, then returned to the farm as the sun sank away below the trees.

Taking our advice, the family members each slept with a flashlight in or near their beds, in case spirits bothered them at night. Stacey and I rigged up a pair of powerful floodlights on the house's stairway, where the bloody girl had attacked me the night before. These could be triggered by motion detectors or remote control from Stacey's workstation in the van. If Bloody Betty reached the stairs again, she'd be drenched in light. There was also a speaker that would blast Gospel music if Stacey activated it. These were our best attempts at securing those stairs so I could explore freely during the long night.

I didn't wait inside. This time, I set up shop on the front porch, with a thermal and night vision camera recording a wide sweep of the front yard. I remained out there while the hours grew late and the night grew quiet.

I watched and listened, creaking back and forth on a rocking chair.

One bit of information I'd picked up at the library seemed to confirm the possibility of a Hessian horseman ghost. A large number of the German mercenary soldiers had taken part in the British seizure and occupation of Savannah during the war. Many had stayed afterward, some of them having deserted during the war

—Hessian deserters were punished with death if caught by the Germans or the British, and several of those involved in the Savannah occupation had been executed. At the same time, the Continental Congress offered a reward of two hundred acres for any Hessian who deserted, so there were incentives to quit.

I found myself reading up on the centuries-ago occupation of Georgia as best as the Nevilles' spotty satellite internet service would allow. Jeremy had complained about the lack of cellular and cable or fiber-optic service out here, and I was ready to complain about it, too. Anyway, it was hard to stay online, and I got frustrated with the endlessly rotating circle that meant things were allegedly loading.

Several times, whenever I thought I heard something moving through the dry grass, I grabbed my thermal goggles. This enabled me to spot a possum scampering past the house, and then a stray cat about an hour after that.

Later, I texted Michael again, but he didn't reply. It was almost midnight, and not unthinkable for him to be asleep, but it was still odd not to hear from him at all. I considered texting his younger sister instead, just to make sure he was okay, but decided against starting down the road to Psycho Stalker Girlfriend Land. Surely Melissa would have called me if there was some kind of major emergency, anyway.

"There's something moving inside the house," Stacey said. I hopped to my feet, reached for a tactical flashlight, and headed for the front door. I was expecting the worst, that the ghost had decided to enter another way and was harassing Maya or somebody else upstairs.

I swung open the outer screen door, then shoved open the solid inner door and leaped into the foyer like a boss, ready to kick some supernatural tailbones.

The motion detectors on the stairs caused the floodlights to fire up, and the room filled with the sound of the Sensational Nightingales, an all-male quartet that was sort of the Menudo of Gospel music, enduring for decades by repeatedly replacing their membership, although the members are generally much older than the boys of Menudo. So maybe it's more like Jefferson

Airplane/Jefferson Starship/Starship, whatever that was all about.

The point is, lights and music flooded the place, which caused the girl on the stairs to jump and scream. She wasn't bloody and moaning or crawling around on the floor. It was just Corrine, startled by the gadgets that had sprung to life around her as she descended the stairs.

"Hey, never mind," Stacey was saying over my headset, just a bit late. "It's just one of the family members."

"What is going on?" Corrine shouted, covering her ears as if the music was deafening. Her eyes were squinted shut, too, against the searing white light that had suddenly appeared in the dark house.

"Sorry!" I said, killing the music and lights. The damage was done, though. We'd scared the older girl this time, and once again the family was springing out of their rooms, flipping on the upstairs lights as they came to see what had happened. Within a few seconds, the family had assembled on the top stairs, wearing their pajamas, all of them looking down at me.

I cleared my throat.

"Ah, sorry," I said. "It looks like Corrine might have triggered the little ghost burglar alarm we set up around these stairs, here."

"This is so stupid. I was just going for a glass of water." Corrine stalked down the staircase and tossed a glare at me as she passed by. "How are a bunch of lights going to get rid of ghosts?"

"They won't get rid of them, but a flood of protons can scramble a ghost's electromagnetic..." I gave up as she left through the doorway to the kitchen, clearly ignoring me.

"Will the screaming be an every night thing while you're here?" Jeremy asked. He stood with his arms crossed, his red hair messy and his eyes bleary, as though he'd had a series of long days with minimal sleep. "And if so, can we agree to schedule it sometime before midnight? Eight-thirty would be ideal."

"I told the kids to use the back steps if they had to go downstairs," Amber said. "Sometimes Corrine decides not to hear anything I say to her. She's trying to punish for moving us out here. Even if she does get to have a horse."

"A horse I'm not allowed to ride anywhere," Corrine said, returning from the kitchen with the glass of water. She rattled the ice cubes inside it, for no apparent reason other than to be loud. "Except in little circles around the corral."

"You came home terrified that someone had chased you in the woods," Amber said. "That's part of the reason these detectives are here!"

"Yeah, just *part* of it. Because you waited until Maya saw something, too. You didn't believe me or my friends. You thought we were..." Corrine's eyes shifted toward me for a second. "...making it all up. But we weren't. And now everybody thinks I'm a freak and we're all freaks with the undead wandering around our house at night." She stalked up the stairs and past her parents, then slammed the door to her room.

Amber took a deep breath. "So, I think we know how she feels about that."

"This is my fault," I said. "I'm sorry for causing loud problems. Late at night. Again."

"Are we clear to return to bed?" Jeremy asked. "Because that is where I'd rather be if at all possible."

"Yeah, everything's fine. False alarm."

"Come on, Castor." Jeremy put a hand on his son's shoulder and began steering him back towards his room. "Maybe tomorrow night you'll get your chance to scream everyone awake."

"I bet I can scream louder than Corrine," the boy said.

I mumbled some more embarrassed apologies as Amber gave me another long look, then led Maya away. The youngest girl was wide awake, asking whether the ghost had come back.

"We are really on top of this case," Stacey said over my headset, when I was finally alone again.

I stepped out onto the front porch before replying.

"Maybe you should have dealt with the family instead," I told her. "You've got that wholesome, innocent charm thing going. I never had that."

"Aw, you think I'm charming and innocent?"

"Or that you can act that way for short periods of time, at least," I said. "You're somewhat less likely to terrify children in the night than I am."

"I'm taking that as a compliment. You want to sit in the van for a while? I mean, the 'mobile nerve center'? I can get out and pace around, trying to look busy like you've been doing all night."

"I'll let you know. How long until Bloody Betty shows up?"

"Assuming she's on the same schedule as last night, we've got about twenty minutes," Stacey said. "Do you think she's that predictable?"

"We'll find out." I drew the thermal goggles over my eyes again and watched the yard. Tiny red and orange blobs of night creatures moved through the gardens, the corn maze, and the pine woods beyond. Small warm blurs indicated bats and owls among the trees. It wasn't the hot little shapes of living animals that worried me, though, not unless a coyote or puma came stalking out.

The thing that worried me happened about twenty minutes later. A deep purple-black mass of cold formed in the middle of the dirt road and began rolling toward me across the lawn. It was exactly reminiscent of the cold layer that had covered the foyer floor on the previous night. If I'd removed my thermals, I would have seen a thin layer of fog slithering its way through the grass and fallen leaves in the yard. Stacey confirmed this over my headset.

Tonight, I wanted to keep Bloody Betty out of the house altogether. The trick was figuring out how to stop her. The problem was that I still didn't know much about her. A name would have been extremely useful. Unfortunately, names and dates were exactly the sort of specific details that Stacey's psychic boyfriend Jacob had the greatest trouble fishing out.

All I had was a list of possible names, so I started testing them.

"Ruth Neville," I said. "Died in 1853. Age seventeen. Is that you?" My question didn't stop the fog at all, though that didn't really mean anything as far as whether she was actually Ruth or not. Many spirits will stop and pay attention if you say their names, but there are plenty who just don't care what you say to them.

I went on down the list, pausing after each name to judge whether the formless cold fog halted in its advance toward the porch steps or reacted in any way.

"Rebekah Neville Hudstrom. Dead in 1859, age twenty-five. Riding accident. That's all your obituary says. Want to tell me more about it?" I asked. "Were you murdered? Are you still haunting your childhood home?"

The ice-cold fog continued creeping forward. I stayed behind the railing, away from the steps this time in case she tried to yank me down again.

"Henrietta Neville," I said. "Died in 1891, age fifteen. Is that you?" I paused.

"Ellie, I don't think it's slowing down," Stacey said over the headset.

"I agree," I told her. To the approaching ghost, I said, "I know you aren't Edina Neville, dead in 1903, age eleven. Because I saw a little bit of your life, toward the end. You're from earlier than any of the girls I named, aren't you? You're something older. You've been here a long time. Who are you?"

I lifted the goggles from my eyes and squatted on the porch, as if the low patch of approaching fog were a small, easily frightened dog that I didn't want to intimidate. It was true that I didn't want to run her off just yet, but mostly I wanted to keep my center of gravity low in case she attacked. Even a weak ghost can use gravity to its advantage—nudging a heavy paint bucket off a shelf in your garage, for example, so it cracks your skull but looks like a simple household accident. Or giving you a push at the top of the stairs, that's an old favorite. Whatever can be done with just a faint shove.

All my nerves felt uneasy, and my stomach and jaw were both tight with tension. My palms sweated as I drew my tactical flashlight but kept it dark. Something unholy and restless was moving toward me, after all, and my body was sending the usual signals to fight or flee, to panic and scream, all of which must be held carefully inside if you're to have any hope of controlling the situation.

"Stop," I said, my voice colder and flatter now, with less pretense of trying to be friendly. It was almost like the voice of the ghost we'd recorded in the cemetery. "Stop there."

She didn't stop, and she was only inches from the porch now, her misty tendrils curling up onto the lowest of the three steps.

So I let her have it.

I activated both my flashlights, their beams narrowed and concentrated, each one hitting the little splash of fog with three thousand lumens of full-spectrum white light. The light doesn't actually hurt ghosts—though I often wish it did—but it's usually enough to scramble the unwanted presence and send it into retreat.

My beams came together to illuminate the puddle of icy fog from two different angles. Its tendrils curled back from the bottom step, and the entire fog patch shrunk away into the grass, breaking up into smaller rivulets I could barely see.

It retreated from the steps. I jumped down to the dirt, pressing the advantage I seemed to have gained. My lights shone like sunbeams onto the area where the fog had been, but now the fog had all melted away.

I drew the thermals down over my eyes again, turning the world back into a surreal, color-coded temperature map. This revealed the cold entity retreating to the road where it had originated. I chased her, spreading my flashlights to either side, as if I could herd the ghost away from the house.

The entity's temperature climbed, changing the thermal signature from a formless dark purple to lighter and lighter shades of blue. As the colors lightened, the ghost's form sharpened at the edges, suggesting a woman crawling across the lawn on her hands and knees. She was almost to the road.

"I can help you," I said. "You don't have to be trapped here. You can move on."

She grew pale and insubstantial as she reached the road, making it hard to distinguish her from the chilly night around us.

I eased my thermals off my eyes and up onto my forehead with the back of one hand.

She stood in the middle of the road, partially formed, and what I could see of her was frosty white and transparent. It was a meager apparition, no more substantial than a mist of breath on a cold black window, already fading.

A ruffled white cap surrounded her face. She regarded me with dark eyes, and I could just see the frown on her wispy, barely-visible lips. I got the impression of a young woman in her teens or early twenties. She wore old-fashioned stays, which is a vest ribbed with whalebone to give a woman the kind of posture and figure that were considered desirable about two hundred years ago.

She also wore petticoats, but these were harder to discern

because the lower half of her was dark, as though she'd been dipped in some black liquid. As her whole appearance was in shades of white and black, the blackened areas might have represented bloodstains. That certainly fit the glimpse I'd had of her, sprawled in the back of a wagon and soaked in blood.

The figure was moving away, but she looked back at me just before melting from sight. I continued after her down the road, even after she had vanished.

"She's a shy one," I whispered. "Looks like she was moving into the woods."

"And you're going to wait and see if our cameras out there happen to pick up something, right?" Stacey guessed.

"I'm following her. Maybe I'll learn something." I turned off my flashlights as I walked down the dirt road toward the pitch-black woods ahead. Above me were thousands of stars and a waning moon, so I could easily discern the road beneath my feet. The house and van grew more distant behind me as I walked, and the corn maze came up beside me as I approached the woods.

"Want me to come with you?" Stacey asked.

"Sure," I said. "I'd rather not die alone in the woods. It'll be more fun if you're with me."

"Thanks so much." Stacey's tone did not convey deep gratitude. The back door of the van opened, but she was well behind me and I didn't want to wait. The ghost of Bloody Betty was already out of sight, and I didn't want the trail to grow too cold. Or warm, I suppose, since we're talking about a cold ghost. This job can involve night after night of waiting around for something to happen. When it finally does, I want to grab on tight and see what I can learn.

My quick, confident strides began to falter as I approached the woods. At night, the darkness where the dirt road disappeared into the shadows of the trees might as well have been the looming mouth of a cave leading down into the underworld.

"Are you here?" I asked. "Is anyone here?"

"I'm coming as fast as I can," Stacey growled over my headset. "Don't go into the dark, scary woods after midnight by yourself, okay?"

"I wasn't talking to you," I whispered back.

I slowed to a snail's pace as I approached what looked like a veil of pure blackness across the dirt road. Not even a glimmer of light passed through the canopy of old trees overhead, their branches knitted together to form a dense ceiling not unlike the canopy that shades just about every street in downtown Savannah. In Savannah, though, there would be lights, crowds, and glowing shop windows. Out here, there was nothing but shadows, wild animals, and the empty dirt road that ran northward toward the river.

Something moved on the dark road ahead, a shadow within the shadows. It was near eye level, which meant it wasn't another raccoon or stray cat. I'd heard no beating wings to indicate a bat or nocturnal bird, and the shape had seemed larger than that, anyway. It was a person, or maybe a big animal, like a horse or a gorilla. A gorilla seemed doubtful.

I heard a sound like a flat sigh from the trees beside the road. That's the best way I know how to describe it, a human voice exhaling, long and slow, as if expressing ages of accumulated weariness.

Another voice, this one more of a low hiss, sounded from the opposite side of the road. Again, I saw movement in the darkness. Either this entity was moving fast, or there was more than one of them around me.

With my flashlights still off and pointed at the ground, I stepped across the threshold from the moonlit portion of the road into the darkness. It was like moving into another world.

The air was instantly colder and heavier, and it seemed to push against me, like invisible icy hands crawling over my skin.

Leaf-rattling sounds stirred around me, like animals closing in from different directions. Dragging footsteps sounded ahead, as if more than one person approached, their shoes scraping in the dirt, but I couldn't see anyone there. I couldn't see much of anything at all.

My heart began to hammer, and I couldn't take the strange sounds in the darkness anymore. I clicked on both my flashlights, sweeping them back and forth across the road, from one overgrown weedy ditch to the other.

A few gray shapes hobbled toward me, coming from the

direction of the cemetery down the road. They dissolved as soon as my lights hit them, but that didn't mean they were gone. They were Jeremy's dead relatives, I supposed, some of them with the violent histories I'd read about in the old newspapers.

Something grabbed my arm, and I turned, jabbing my light at the figure who suddenly stood beside me.

His face was full of holes. That was my immediate first impression, a face the color of dust with holes eaten into it by moths or mice. I could see bone through the dry, rotten face, all along the jawline, as well as several teeth, and the sharp point of one cheek bone. The eyes were hollow. It was a visage like that of an old corpse that had come shuffling out of its grave.

The apparition wore a wig that screamed eighteenth century, gray and thick, covered with dust and cobwebs and tied with a tattered black ribbon. His breeches and waistcoat, though threadbare, also indicated a ghost from that era.

I managed to take all of this in while also screaming my head off. He had, after all, grabbed my arm and didn't let go and back away when I illuminated his crumbling face. I pulled, but he held on tight, his eye sockets fixed on my face.

"*Go,*" he rasped in a voice that could almost have been mistaken for a handful of dry leaves rubbing together in the wind.

I don't think he meant *go ahead, make yourself at home in these woods. Come visit our bones and headstones! We love company.* That wasn't the tone I was picking up on here.

His fingers dug into my arm, and his skull face with its thin coating of ruined flesh moved closer to mine.

More shapes lurched down the shadowy road, shuffling my way.

This might have been a great moment to learn more about this particular ghost and his restless friends, but I was a little bit terrified that he was going to kill me right there, just as I'd joked about with Stacey. It didn't seem as funny this time.

I slapped the iPod on my belt.

A storm of sound filled the road, a religious cantata by Georg Böhm, one of Johann Sebastian Bach's teachers. I played a fast-paced section of the song, loaded with timpani and trumpets as well as violins and voices (the title was "Warum toben die Heiden," if you were curious). I had to holy up the place fast if I wanted to run off a whole gang of vicious ghosts right on their home turf.

Stacey arrived just as the ghost with the powdered wig vanished. She dashed right into the spot where he'd been standing, as though she hadn't seen him there at all, and swept her flashlight around, her jaw set, ready for battle.

"What happened, Screamy?" she asked. "Why'd do you break out the Beethoven?"

"It's Böhm," I said.

"Like I'm going to know right off the top of my head."

"I think you might have stepped right into a nasty-looking ghost," I said.

"What? Where?" Stacey jumped and backed up, swinging her flashlight around crazily, like someone who's just walked into a spiderweb.

"They were all over the place." I turned down the music and told her what had happened, keeping my voice low. "They seem to have backed off. Maybe they'll leave us alone for now."

"Let's not say things that could foreshadow getting attacked, okay?" Stacey said. "Like 'I think we're safe for now' or 'It looks like the evil ghost is gone.' Or 'I'll be right back, you wait here.'"

"Very funny," I said, but I didn't feel like laughing. The atmosphere in the woods was still thick and clammy. The spirits might have pulled back a little, but I doubted they'd gone far, and I was sure they were still watching us. We were intruders in their territory, after all, the land where they'd lived and worked and died, where their flesh and bones had long since mingled with the soil and groundwater, and their spirits still lingered long after their lives had ended.

"Any sign of Bloody Betty?" Stacey asked.

"She seemed to disappear," I said. "Maybe into the cemetery. I don't know, but I lost track of her."

Stacey and I backed away from the woods, walking so close to each other that our arms brushed together. Once we were several paces out into the moonlit area, we turned and ran, fleeing the ghost-crowded wilderness as quickly as we could.

Chapter Nine

On the bright side, we weren't having any trouble finding evidence to confirm that the Neville farm was haunted. This was definitely not a case of groaning floorboards, moaning pipes, or bats in the attic. These people had a major situation on their hands, and that meant a paying job for us.

On the dark side, we weren't dealing with simple nuisance ghosts. Bloody Betty, whatever her real name might be, had enough power to knock me over. The ghosts in the road and the woods were strong enough for a bit of auditory as well as visual manifestation, and at least one of them could touch me with his rotten hand. I had a feeling there was a lot of power in that old ghost who'd confronted me, just from the clarity of his appearance and the strength of his grip.

Stacey nicknamed the old colonial-era ghost Wigglesworth, after his dirty old wig.

We returned to the van, where I remained inside with Stacey for a couple of hours, watching and listening. After my close encounter with the dead but not departed members of the Neville clan, I didn't want to be alone again, not until the sunrise drew a little closer.

By now, we weren't surprised that our sensors were finding heavy activity in the cemetery. It was all stuff that would make hard-nosed skeptics turn up their hard little noses, like indistinct shadows and the soft walking sounds that came and went, but there was a lot of it.

We seemed to have successfully turned Bloody Betty away from the house for one night, letting Maya and the rest of her family have some peace, but I was worried about the scale of the haunting we faced and how to deal with it.

I had a little bit of a cheer-up moment when my phone buzzed and I saw it was Michael. It was about five a.m., time for him to get ready for his shift at the fire station. I hopped out of the van to pace the yard and enjoy a little privacy while we talked.

"Ghost-nappers," I said. "You kill 'em, we grill 'em."

"That...doesn't even make sense," Michael said, laughing.

"It's been a long night. I think I deserve a C for effort."

"It's a cold night," he said. "I'm thinking of starting a fire."

"It's like sixty degrees and almost sunrise, but okay. You know I think fires are horrible and pretty much the opposite of romantic, right?"

"I still think I can change your mind about that."

"Not likely." I didn't like the sharp tone that I heard in my voice. He was just trying to be jokey and playful, and probably didn't consider just what a sore spot he was poking there. My relationship with fire is a little more than sore spot. It's more like a deep hatred infused with fear, infused with more hatred. Still, my first instinct was to rip his head off, and I needed to dial that right down before I said something I regretted. "Where have you been the last couple of days? Avoiding me?" I asked. So much for dialing it down.

"Sick," he said. "I had the worst fever."

"You should have told me! I could have come over and taken care of you."

"Sure. Until you got sick. Then I would have to take care of you. It's the circle of illness."

"I wouldn't have minded," I said.

"You haven't heard me describe the symptoms yet," Michael said. "But I have to warn you, they may be disturbing to hear about, and impossible to unhear."

"I'll trust you on that. I don't need all the gory details."

"They weren't gory, so much as gooey, and I would say the color was—"

"Okay, got it," I said. "Are you feeling better now?"

"Mostly."

"Do you think you can make it to the Halloween thing at the Lathrop Grand on Saturday? Because I wouldn't mind an excuse to avoid it—"

"I'll be fine. I look forward to it."

"Really? You didn't say that last time we talked."

"It's a Halloween ball. We can make it fun if we have to."

I heard the creaking of a door opening. While talking on the phone, I'd wandered several paces across the front lawn. Now I turned and pointed my flashlight—right at Jeremy. He gave me an annoyed squint before raising his worn, travel-stickered briefcase to block the glare.

"I have to go," I whispered into the phone. "I just annoyed my client. He looks grumpy."

"I'm dying to see you again," Michael said.

"Keep taking that fever medicine." I hung up, then shouted "Sorry!" at Jeremy. He shuffled toward me, on the way to his car for his pre-dawn commute, portable glow-in-the-dark Cthulhu coffee mug in one hand.

"Did you catch any Deadites?" Jeremy shouted, though I was only a few yards away. He seemed pretty drowsy, a big red clump of hair sticking up in the back.

Jeremy tossed his briefcase in the car, then stepped closer to me instead of getting in the car and driving away. I gave him the best smile I could manage.

"You know, Deadites?" Jeremy asked. "I'm sure someone in your profession is familiar with the *Evil Dead* movies."

"They're a core part of the ghost-hunter curriculum," I said. "It's a mail-order course."

"Are you kidding?"

"Yes," I said. "But, seriously, we encountered several out on the road to the cemetery."

"They do like to hang around the woods, menacing people," he said, sounding almost apologetic for his dead relatives and their behavior. "If only we could control them, we'd have the best haunted-farm attraction in the state. Maybe the tri-state area."

"We did chase the bloody girl away for the night," I said. "We have a little footage of it."

Jeremy nodded. I tried not to breathe a visible sigh of relief when he finally turned back and climbed into his car. I didn't have any real accomplishments to report, but fortunately he had to get to work. It was a Friday. Jacob would be coming out this evening, thankfully, and that ought to shed some light on the ghosts and what they wanted.

I sincerely hoped it would, anyway, because I still felt very much in the dark.

Once again, the rest of the family rose early to tend the animals. Stacey and I slipped away as quickly as we could, back to the faded peach-and-pink comforts of the Old Walnut Inn overlooking what had once been one of the nation's busiest highways. We didn't see any traffic at all.

I slept for a couple of hours before my phone woke me up. I didn't recognize the number.

"Is this Detective Jordan?" a man's voice asked over the phone. He spoke with a low, hushed tone, as if calling to plan a murder.

"Well, I'm a detective," I said. "Private detectives don't usually go by—"

"It sounds like Detective Gordon," he snickered. "You know, from Batman."

"Okay. Who is this?"

"Apologies, m'lady," he said, and my skin crawled just a little. "I am Virgil Rathmew. A certain librarian informed me that you wanted to get in touch with me."

"Oh, yeah, good." I sat up, rubbing my eyes. Stacey scowled at me briefly from her bed, clearly annoyed I'd left the ringer at full volume on my phone while we slept, then she crammed pillows onto either side of her head.

"Might I ask the cause of your interest in our humble yet all-important role in the Revolution?" he asked. "Are you, perchance, investigating a crime that requires an expertise in that era?"

"Not exactly," I said. "We're just doing general research on a local family's history, that's all."

"I wonder why an out-of-town investigator would be called for that," Virgil said. "Rather than a prominent local historian and author."

"Uh, okay." I rubbed my eyes. "Sorry, I just woke up, and I'm not clear where this conversation is going right now—"

"I would say it's going *poorly*," Virgil said. "I am otherwise engaged until this afternoon, when I will be making the rounds at the Brier Creek battlefield. If you wish to join my lecture tour, it begins at one p.m. sharp at the Brannen's Bridge historical marker."

"Lecture tour?" I asked.

"Lecture tour, yes," he confirmed.

"I'm interested in learning whether there's any history related to Hessians in this area. Maybe associated with that battle."

The other end of the line was silent for a moment. "You want to know about the horseman on the Neville farm?"

"Well...yeah," I said. "Do you know anything about it?"

"I know they're attempting to exploit the old story for commercial gain," Virgil said. "I know the family who live there now are out-of-towners, virtually carpetbaggers from the city with no apparent respect for their own heritage."

"Why do you say that?"

"If they had any respect, they would not turn their family's tragedies into tourist fodder."

"So you've been to their attractions?" I asked.

"Attractions? You mean the corn maze and the 'haunted' cemetery? I've seen the signs and the *Telephone* article about it. That's all I needed to know. Some people disgust me. I doubt they even bothered to learn the real story."

"What is the real story?" I asked, daring to hope that he actually knew something.

"I must hang up now," he said. "My oven's beeping."

"Okay, then," I said, feeling a little concerned he might decide not to help me since he disliked my clients so much. "One p.m. at the battlefield?"

"Metal detector optional," he added, just before hanging up.

"Can't wait," I told him, though the guy didn't sound particularly friendly and I wasn't exactly looking forward to seeing him.

"Is it over?" Stacey croaked as I hung up the phone. She cautiously eased one pillow away from her ear, as if testing the air for noise.

"I know it was difficult for you, lying there and doing nothing at all with your eyes closed," I said. "On the upside, we now have an appointment with Virgil Rathmew, expert air conditioner repairman and part-time Revolutionary War expert."

"You were talking to that history buff guy?" Stacey asked, making me wince. "Can we go back to sleep now?"

I tried. With the motel room's curtains blocking the light from outside, Stacey was snoring softly within five minutes, but of course she hadn't seen all that I'd seen. Closing my eyes conjured fresh memories of the pale gray shades of the dead shuffling toward me, the man with the dirty wig and rotten face grabbing me, his sparse teeth and black gums visible through his tattered lips in a permanent death-grin, his nose decayed like a leper's—

Enough. I opened my eyes and took deep breaths, willing each part of my body to relax. I turned over on my side. As soon as the disturbing visions of Jeremy's dead relatives began to recede, they were replaced by Anton Clay, smiling at me while he burned all those I cared about. I dreamed of waking up in Michael's apartment, the whole place charred black, Michael and his sister both turned to ash and bone in their beds. Anton Clay's face smiled at me from a mirror, until I smashed it with a burned chunk of Michael's bedpost.

This job brings far too many nightmares. My next job is going to be something happy, like working at Disney World. Bright lights, toddler music all day, and thousands of screaming kids couldn't cause as many bad dreams as being attacked by the undead, am I right?

Hm. Maybe I'll stay where I am.

I slept fitfully, with unpleasant dreams, until my alarm awoke me at noon. I had to meet up with the renowned local history buff in one hour. The alarm had zero effect on Stacey, so I jostled her awake.

"Come on, Blondie," I said. "It's time for our educational battlefield tour."

"Huh?" Stacey half-opened one eye. "Thought you were doing that by yourself. I have to...watch hours of..." She yawned.

"After talking to that guy on the phone, I'm not going by myself."

"How bad can he be?"

"He calls me 'Detective Jordan.'"

"So?" Stacey waved me off and closed her eyes.

"He also called me 'm'lady.'"

Stacey opened her eyes again. "You're kidding."

"Not one bit."

"Ugh." Stacey sighed and shoved herself up to a sitting position, then stretched her arms. "And there's nobody else we can talk to?"

"The librarian said he's the guy who knows the most. Now get your boots on and accompany me to the park, m'lady," I said.

"Okay, I'm coming. Just don't call me that again."

"Call you what, m'lady?"

Stacey threw a pillow at my head. At least she was up and moving now.

About an hour later, we arrived at the bridge over Brier Creek, a muddy, swampy waterway wide enough for canoes and rafts, though probably not any boats larger than that. Cypresses grew thick along the banks, the trees and branches leaning inward to capture the sunlight over the creek.

The historical site consisted of a couple of markers and a picnic-table pavilion shaded by a rusty tin roof, which had accumulated layers of graffiti over the years. There were no other amenities. We pulled off the paved road and parked on a sandy dirt road alongside the little park area.

We looked at the two historical markers, both which were just signs mounted on posts, nothing fancy. The larger sign featured an engraved map of the battlefield site and a wall of text describing in long detail the battle that had occurred here in March of 1779. Essentially, it had been a case of Americans getting cornered and slaughtered by the British.

"Hey, listen to the story of this war hero." Stacey pointed at the second, smaller sign, topped with one of those Masonic compass and square symbols and the name GENERAL SAMUEL ELBERT. "After most of his men were killed, this General Elbert guy avoided death by making the sign of a Mason to a British officer, who was also a Mason and spared his life."

"Okay," I said. "What else?"

"That's it," Stacey snickered. "That's the whole story. And now this sign commemorates that amazing act of valor."

"We never stop to appreciate the sacrifices of those who use their social connections to save themselves," I said. "It really makes you think."

"General Elbert was a hero of the Revolution," a voice said. "However you may choose to decry him."

Uh-oh. It sounded like we'd stepped on some history-buff toes—not the most diplomatic way to begin our lecture tour.

I turned to see a man in a khaki shirt, red neckerchief, wraparound sunglasses and an Indiana Jones sort of fedora. He grasped a metal detector in gloved hands. He was shorter than me, a squat, wide man who must have weighed at least three hundred soft pounds. I guessed this to be our new friend Virgil, because his voice matched what I'd heard on the phone, but I couldn't confirm it right away because he didn't stop talking.

"Elbert served on the Georgia Council of Safety and led the Patriot cause in our state," the man lectured me. "He led more than one invasion of Florida, and later fought alongside George Washington at Yorktown. Subsequently he became governor of Georgia. So sneer as you please, madam, but you're sneering at a great American who fought for our freedom to stand here by this creek today as free Americans."

"Virgil Rathmew?" I asked. By this point, I'd heard enough of his voice that I was sure he was the same guy I'd spoken with on the phone earlier.

"I am." He kept his grip firm on his metal detector, not offering to shake hands. "You must be Detective Jordan."

"That's me. And this is Assistant Stacey. Thanks for meeting us here. Are we too late for the lecture tour?"

"Technically, yes, but as nobody else has arrived, we can begin on a delayed schedule," Virgil said.

"I guess it's our lucky day," I said. "Did you have anything to tell us about the Hessians, or maybe the Neville farm—"

"Enough." Virgil held up a hand as though I'd been yapping on and on for hours. "Please hold all questions until after the tour."

"What exactly are we touring?" Stacey looked around at the swampy stream, the two historical markers, and the concrete bridge above us where a car passed occasionally. She brought out a microphone. "Mind if I record you?"

Virgil activated his metal detector and began to walk.

"Imagine, if you will, that it is the month of March, 1779," Virgil said. "The colonies are at war for their independence. The British and their Loyalist suck-ups just lost a major battle at Kettle Creek, outside Augusta, and have begun a slow retreat to Savannah. Brigadier General John Ashe leads a force of Patriots, thirteen hundred strong, in pursuit of the retreating British. They camp here against the water, near the intersection of Brier Creek with the Savannah River—swampy, wet ground. The Patriots are working to rebuild a destroyed bridge here. They don't expect the British to sneak across the river farther north, at Paris' Mill, in order to turn around and attack them."

I thought the story was getting interesting, but then Virgil just had to back up, telling us the names and random biographical facts of all the British and American officers involved, and also the general disposition of both sides of the war up and down the whole continent. He walked back and forth at the creek bank, gesturing wildly as if there were anything to see. I listened for anything that could possibly relate to our case, while Stacey's eyes started to glaze over.

It was kind of impressive, though, just how much Virgil could rattle off from memory. He knew precisely how many muskets, horses, and cannons had been available on each side.

"The British surprise attack arrived on the morning of March third," Virgil said. "The Patriot force barely had time to assemble before the British drove them back into the swamps. Most of the Americans were ill-prepared and simply ran—including their supposed leader, General Ashe. Only about two hundred of them stayed to fight, and most died. Do you know who stood and fought that day? Do you? It was those men under the command of Samuel Elbert, whose memory you were so roundly dismissing when first I sauntered over here."

"I solemnly apologize to the memory of Mr. Elbert," I said, trying to sound solemn. "It sounds like a terrible event."

"Blood and the screams of the dying filled the swamps," Virgil said. "They say Americans were tied to trees and tortured to death by the British. Yet the Battle of Brier Creek is today nearly forgotten, while the *Kettle* Creek Battlefield has enormous fancy monuments, a forty-acre park, and plans for a full-use recreation area. Meanwhile this spot, just as sacred, just as infused with the blood of patriotic early Americans, is nothing more than a place for passing motorists to toss their Burger King bags out the window as they cross the bridge. Nobody wants to remember the defeats, only the victories. But those who died here deserve our respect, particularly those who stood and fought despite overwhelming odds."

"Is there any connection to the Neville farm?" I asked. It was possible that ghosts left by such a battle could have wandered through the swampy woods to the farm, which wasn't terribly far away. As the crow flies, they would have arrived at the swampy cemetery first, before reaching the corn maze and then the house. It was possible the gray shadowy things in the woods, including dusty skull-faced Mr. Wigglesworth from the eighteenth century, were actually related to the battle and not to Jeremy's family.

"If you're working for the family, surely you know all about their ancestry," Virgil said.

"I know about some of them," I said. "There was a guy named Hiram Neville, right?"

"And what do you know of him?"

"Not much. He would've been in his early forties during the

Revolution, though."

"I cannot say I'm surprised that people who would turn their own heritage into a cheap tourist mill would have so little knowledge of the very heritage they are exploiting," Virgil said.

"So, what are you saying, exactly?" Stacey asked, easing the microphone closer to his face. "There was a connection?"

"Hiram's son Albert fought in the state militia," Virgil said. "He died at age nineteen, fighting on the Patriot side at the siege of Augusta in 1780. You can look it up. But you're more interested in his daughter, of course."

"I am?" I asked.

"Mildred Neville," he said. "Died sometime during the Revolution. Murdered by a highwayman, said to be a former Hessian mercenary who'd fought for the English before deserting. He moved on to a career of petty robbery, preying on merchants and farmers as they traveled the isolated country roads."

"You're right," I said. "I'm *very* interested. How did she die?"

"It would have been a flintlock pistol or a sword. Possibly a dagger. It was unlikely to be fast and painless, in other words."

I nodded, thinking of my brief vision of the bloody girl in the wagon.

"Was she killed in a robbery?" I asked.

"That is the usual circumstance for death by highwayman," Virgil said.

"How do you know this story? I couldn't find anything at the library or courthouse."

"An oral history, which I took myself from one Dorcas Harding Baker, aged eighty-three at the time. She passed on, oh, many years ago now. She'd heard the details herself from her own grandmother. The Hessian highwayman who terrorized the roads between Savannah and Augusta in the old days, until he was finally captured and executed. Not arrested or tried, from what I understand, but very much executed."

"Do you have this in writing?"

"In my own hand," Virgil said. "My penmanship is exquisite, too. Mother always said so."

"Would you mind making a copy of it for me?"

"I could provide that, as well as copies of my annotated county histories," Virgil said. "Volume I spans the 1700-1800 era. Will a three-ring binder format suffice for you?"

"Sure, thanks," I said. "So do you know anything else about the horseman?"

"Captured and killed, as I previously mentioned. Stabbed and shot multiple times, then quite possibly dabbed with pitch and set on fire."

"Ugh," Stacey said. "What a story to hear from Grandma."

"Do you have his name? Any idea where he came from? Do you know his regiment or anything?"

"I don't recall any additional details about the man," Virgil said. "It was the girl's death that proved the flashpoint. Word was sent out, and they finally hunted him down. Hiram got his chance to avenge his daughter's death, hands-on. They say the ghost rides up and down the old, forgotten roads late at night, and that was the alleged point of the story. Mrs. Baker claimed to have seen it herself one night as she walked home through the woods from a church revival. She said it was a dark shadow of a man on a horse—just a shadow, black, no features. That's how she described it to me. Said it chased her all the way back to church, and she hid there until morning. She mostly talked about that ghost, to tell you the truth. The rest was primarily the set-up for the ghost story."

"I would definitely like a copy of that transcript," I said again, just to be clear. "And any other information you have about the Neville family from that era."

"I may have more. My basement is a treasure trove of local history. I may open it to the public one day—*after* my county history book is published. I don't want anyone stealing my ideas."

"We don't plan to write any competing county histories," I said. "I promise."

He stood quietly for a moment, as if appraising us through his midnight-blue sunglasses, then shook his head.

"I'll fish around in there and see what else I can find," he said. "Letting outsiders in is just too big of a risk."

"I understand," I said, as though I did. "If you could provide us with copies of anything you might find, we'd truly appreciate it."

"We'll see what we can do, Detective Jordan," he said. "Now, if you'll just follow me to my truck, we'll begin the second phase of our tour."

Stacey cast me a worried, questioning look as we followed him up the dirt road to a pick-up truck parked in the shade of an oak. It looked as if he'd deliberately parked out of sight so he could spy on us or sneak up on us, since that was what he'd done. I suppose it was possible he just wanted the shade of the old tree to keep his truck cab cooled off. Virgil drove a shiny brand new Ford F-450, which is not a cheap truck. I supposed he did well in the heating and air conditioning game.

"You'll have to help me unload the canoe," Virgil said, gesturing toward a dingy plastic watercraft roped into the back of the truck. "I've got a herniated disc."

"Why would we need a canoe?" I asked, although I was afraid I already knew the answer. I was about ready to wrap up our interview with Virgil, since he didn't seem to have any more specific information about our case. He seemed to have other plans, unfortunately.

"The British crossed at Paris' Mill, upcreek from here, to sneak back down the far side of the creek and surprise the American forces," Virgil said. "No tour of the Brier Creek battle site would be complete without a visit to the old mill site where that critical crossing occurred. A modern bridge spans the site now, but the ruins of the dam can be found just upcreek from there."

"How far away is that?" Stacey said.

"Just fourteen miles northwest of here," he said. "We'll be paddling against the current, but it's not a strong one."

Stacey cast me a panicked look. "Fourteen miles? That would take all day, and into the night..."

"Thanks anyway, Virgil, but we don't want to put you to that much trouble," I said.

"No trouble for me. You two will paddle while I narrate the battle. I can't paddle, between my herniated disc and my bad knees." He was unhooking the bungees that held the canoe in place.

"We don't have time, unfortunately," I said. "Can't we just drive to the other spot?"

"The entire length of the creek between Millhaven and Brannen's Bridge is of historical significance," he said. "One cannot truly grasp the scope of the battle by taking shortcuts."

"We'll have to miss some of that scope, then," I said. "The Cliff's Notes version is fine for us."

Virgil stared at me, possibly—I couldn't see much through those wraparound shades.

"I mean to impress upon you the importance of all that occurred so you can pass it on to your clients," he said. "That family ought to have more respect for the history they're using to scare up tourism dollars."

"We will be sure to relay all of that," I said, though I didn't really intend to harass my clients with this man's cantankerous opinions.

Virgil pointed northward along the creek. There wasn't too much to see, since the old forest enclosed the little waterway on both sides, reaching in from either bank to swallow most of our view of the dark water below.

"Thataway lies the old dam, about fourteen miles north of here," he said. "Had we taken the canoe, I could show you the remnants of the old mill. While a smaller decoy force downstream kept the American patrols distracted, British Lieutenant Colonel Mark Prevost led the bulk of the redcoats and Loyalist militia up this way. The bridge had been previously destroyed, so the British had to rebuild it quickly before crossing. One can imagine the Americans in their camp, feeling secure, unaware of the force secretly making its way southward..."

Virgil went on and on, using his hands to demonstrate battle lines and troop movements while occasional cars and trucks whipped by on the small bridge above us. Stacey recorded him with her microphone. After twenty or thirty minutes, she looked beaten down by the detailed minutiae of Virgil's recount. I was starting to feel that way, too—Virgil didn't stop long to breathe, and certainly not long enough for anyone else to speak or ask a question. Still, I listened closely, never knowing when some scrap or crumb of data might turn out to be important later on.

I heard every detail and repercussion of the battle, too, right down to the court martial of the American general in charge.

My head swam with Virgil's relentless lists of names, dates, facts, and figures. This guy was one extreme history buff. He seemed to have the entire war memorized, but we only needed to know about a tiny sliver of it, if that. I remembered the librarian's comment about how talking to Virgil was like drinking from a fire hose.

"I suppose you'll want to visit Kettle Creek Battlefield next," he said with a sigh, while Stacey and I were edging toward our van.

"No!" I said, much too quickly to be polite. "I mean, um, I don't think that's going to be relevant to our research here. But thank you for everything—"

"Good," he said. "Kettle Creek always gets more attention than Brier Creek. I wouldn't want those twerps at the Kettle Creek Battlefield Association getting big heads."

"Oh, you guys have a rivalry?" Stacey asked. "The Brier Creek fans versus the Kettle Creek fans? Battle of the Creeks?"

"There *aren't* enough Brier Creek fans to constitute a fan base, sadly," Virgil said. "I've considered creating an association myself."

"You should go for it," I said.

"Do you think there would be sufficient interest?"

"You won't know until you try."

"The fallen soldiers of Brier Creek deserve it," Virgil said. He seemed to be musing to himself rather than speaking to me as he looked up along the creek.

"Yep," I said, kind of lamely. "We'd better get going, it's pretty late in the day. Thanks again for all your help."

"Perhaps I will create an association of my own," he said, still looking along the creek. "In which case, I'll send membership packets for both of you. Membership fees will be substantial, but well worth it."

"Okay, we'll look over...all of that," I said. "Please let me know if you find anything more about the Hessian horseman or the Neville family."

"I bid you good day, m'lady." Virgil tipped his hat at us, and we hurried back into the van. The sun was getting low in the sky.

"Wow," Stacey said. "I didn't think he was going to stop

talking."

"At least we learned something." I started up the van and eased out onto the road.

"We learned way, way too much," Stacey said. "I'm going to have to watch hours of *Real Housewives* to scrub my brain empty after that. Nothing else is vapid enough."

"Maybe we should replay everything he told us," I said. "Start your recording from the top."

"You're kidding."

"We might have missed something. If you look down on this spot from Google satellite, you'll see that you only have to travel a couple miles through the riverside marshes to reach our client's farm. The battlefield might matter to our case."

Stacey groaned, then plugged her portable voice recorder into the van's sound system. She covered her eyes as Virgil's voice regaled us once again with the story of the long-ago battle and all of the musket calibers involved. Lucky for her, we arrived back at the client's house in just a few minutes. Jacob was on the way for his psychic walk-through, which would hopefully settle our questions about the ghosts and put us on the path to a proper spiritual extermination.

Chapter Ten

Stacey and I sprinted around the farm as the sun sank and the sky grew dark overhead, making a last check of our gear before nightfall. We spent as little time back in the woods as possible, giving the cameras and microphone in the old cemetery only the most cursory examination before leaving.

We did spend a little too much time just outside the cemetery, shovels in hand, digging out the earth around the old iron gate. The dirt looked sandy and soft, but turned out to have its share of rocks and gravel, and overall it took a lot longer than I'd wanted to spend on it.

Happily, we managed to dig the gate free before the sun went down. The old hinges were reluctant to budge, but I'd brought a can of WD40 to help with that. I soaked them thoroughly. The last thing I wanted was to snap off a critical piece of the gate while attempting to close it.

We managed to ease it shut, and I closed a shiny new stainless steel padlock into place. We both let out a deep breath when the gate was securely locked. I hadn't even been aware I was holding mine. There was a gathering thickness and coldness in the air, and I imagined I could feel the resentment of the spirits in the cemetery, watching me as I sealed them in for the night. At least, I hoped that was what I was doing.

Then we fled the swampy cemetery, sprinting to put that overrun hive of ghosts behind us.

We moved into the corn maze through the broken back row. We'd detected cold spots in the area each night, and broken cobs and stalks still lay strewn all over the path, but we were glad to be out of the woods, at least. Stacey checked the night vision camera plus the remote temperature and EMF sensors, while I changed the batteries in the microphone.

The hoof beats began as the sky went dark overhead, the last licks of sunlight having finally sputtered out.

The sound of hooves rumbled past, a few rows away. I swung my flashlight toward it, but all I saw was something dark flicking by before it was out of sight altogether.

Stacey and I looked at each other. Her eyes were wide.

"Do you think it's him?" she whispered. I motioned for her to stay quiet.

The hoof beats faded, as if the entity were galloping away. Stacey gave a relieved smile when they fell silent.

"It's gone," she said.

Then the sound returned, faster now and growing louder as it approached, the rapid thumping of a galloping horse. It was definitely coming toward us.

We spun and pointed our lights as the horse-mounted figure turned a corner and thundered our way, a dark blur in the night. The rider was solid black, faceless, a dark cloak flaring out behind it as it rode us down. It had the shape of a large man, tall with broad shoulders, one who could probably pick me up and toss me aside with one of his black-gloved hands.

The figure let out a deep, angry roar that sounded more like a wild beast than a human. It raised one hand that gripped something long and narrow—a sword. Virgil had said the Hessian horsemen would have carried one while alive, the better to convince travelers to hand over their coins and jewels.

Stacey and I blasted the entity with the searing white beams of our tactical flashlights.

It kept charging toward us, though. Our lights were not slowing it down at all.

Stacey and I dove to opposite sides of the path as the horse-mounted entity swept past. I heard the whoosh of its sword overhead, and severed cornstalks rained down onto me.

The horseman rode on until he reached the corner at the end of the path. He turned to face us, swiping his sword in midair, and his horse reared up.

In the moonlight, I could see that his cloak was pinned at his neck, but there was nothing above the high, stiffly starched black collar. This horseman was, indeed, headless.

Despite lacking a mouth, it began to laugh—a harsh, deep, grating laugh, not unlike what one might expect from, let's say, a psychotic German soldier returned from the dead.

On the other hand...I'd seen the ghost, heard it, and even *smelled* the horse as it raced past. That was a lot of senses for an apparition; typically you just get one or two. Also, the little blast of wind from the passing horse had been warm, not icy cold as one would expect from most ghosts.

Now that the horse had finally stopped for a moment, my flashlight showed me that it was spotted brown and white, with a big starburst on its head—not exactly the black shadow-horse I'd been led to expect.

"Corrine?" I asked, pointed my beam at the black-clad figure. Then I shouted the name louder to be heard over the harsh, grating laughter.

The laughing sound ended abruptly, as if a recording had been cut off. The black, headless figure regarded us silently for a moment, then laughed again. This time, it was a clearly female voice, and not particular scary or German or anything.

The giggling rider pointed one gloved finger at Stacey, who'd crashed through a row of corn and tangled in the plastic netting on her way down to the ground. Now Stacey got to her feet and glared up at the headless horseman while dusting sandy red dirt off her jeans.

"Ellie," Stacey said. "What if the horseback ghost is female?

Have we even considered that?"

"That's not a real ghost, Stacey. That's a teenage girl in disguise."

"I totally tricked you!" Corrine's face emerged from somewhere inside the coat and cape.

"Huh? No, I know that's her, it just made me think—" Stacey began.

"Yeah, right, whatever!" Corrine jeered. The black-clad figure unbuttoned its coat, revealing the rest of Corrine's face inside. "That was so much fun. I miss doing that."

"Somebody could have gotten hurt," I said.

"Like me, for example," Stacey added.

"You're fine. I know what I'm doing. Starburst and I ride through here all the time."

"Do you trample many people?" Stacey asked.

"Y'all don't think it was even a little bit funny?" Corrine asked. She was approaching us again, slowly, her horse moving at an easy walk.

"We don't," I said.

"It's just payback for springing that ghost trap thing on me," Corrine said.

"We didn't spring it on you," I said. "You walked into it."

"My mom's still mad at me, and all I did was go for a glass of water. 'Gee, sorry I forgot to use the back stairs because the ghost hunters were here, Mom.' I mean, get over it already."

"We'd appreciate it if you would just kind of avoid attacking or threatening us while we're here," I said. "You should understand there's real danger around. You said the horseman chased you...or was that a lie, too?"

"I'm not scared of him." Her expression turned hard and angry. "He chased me once, but if I see him again, I won't be scared. He's dead and I'm alive. I'm not going to be afraid of him."

"So you're sticking by that story, then," I said.

"He *did* chase me. But I've come out here since, to show him I'm not afraid. I yelled that at him, even, and he still wouldn't come out and show his face. I think he's scared of me now." Corrine bared her teeth, but it wasn't quite a smile. "I'll show him who's scary."

Stacey looked at me and raised one eyebrow. It did sound like Corrine might be cracking up a bit, maybe from the stress of living on haunted land, maybe for other reasons I didn't know about.

"Is that how he looked when you saw him?" I pointed to the costume that surrounded her.

"No, I *told* you," Corrine said. She opened a few more buttons around her face. "*He* was a black shadow. *This* is *my* costume. We made it before I ever *saw* the ghost. My friend Bianca helped, but she doesn't come over anymore. Everybody avoids me now, like it's my fault that I have creepy dead ancestors walking around in my woods. I didn't want them here. I didn't *invite* them here. Why does everyone have to treat me like a freak now?"

"Your friends encountered something strange and scary out here," I said. "If they're avoiding you, that's probably their way of avoiding thinking about what they saw. It was pretty bad that night, wasn't it?"

"Sure. But it was kind of fun before all that happened. My friends would come over on Friday and Saturday night, we'd do make-up and costumes, we'd run around the woods and corn maze scaring people."

"I hope you didn't trample customers with your horse," Stacey grumbled.

"Mom wouldn't let me ride as the headless horseman in the maze, but I always wanted to. That would really send them screaming."

"To their lawyers, most likely," I said. "So you rode around in the woods, acting like the ghostly horseman?"

"I'd also ride out into the dirt road and chase after the hayride, you know, waving my sword and playing my evil laugh. Dad worked out this gag—he uses the tractor to pull the hayride, right? So when I showed up, he would act all scared. He'd speed up the tractor and pretend he was trying to escape the ghost as fast as he could, like I was a real ghost, you know, and he was really scared. He would wear a straw hat and overalls and totally played the freaked-out farmer role to the hilt. I mean of course he could do that, he's seen a zillion horror movies. He's always watching obscure Japanese zombie movies and stuff. He's the one who decided to start the whole haunted-woods thing. My mom wanted more of a cheerful, crafty fall-festival kind of theme, so they kind of each got part of what they wanted."

"How did your friends describe the figures they saw?"

"Well, they knew right away these weren't just people in costumes," Corrine said. "Some of them weren't much more than like gray stick figures, kind of. They were just barely there, maybe you could only see a piece of a face. They weren't like romantic ghosts in sweeping ball gowns and top hats, that's what I'm saying. More like old bodies, like the walking dead. From, you know, *The Walking Dead*. Freaky, huh?"

"That's freaky," I agreed. That matched the apparitions I'd seen in the road outside the cemetery the previous night. "Where exactly did your friends see them?"

"Wherever they were performing," Corrine said. "Bianca was painted all in white, you know, in this cheap white dress and then total zombie-face. She was haunting outside that first overgrown shack on the side of the road. She had some wind chimes she would ring to sound all ghosty. And Sahiri, that's another girl, she did more of a weird vampire-with-cobras thing. A lot of blood on her face. And Kep tried to look all tough like a zombie with spiked chains, but he just kind of looked like a biker reject..."

"These are all people who saw the ghosts?"

"Yeah." Corrine turned to look through the break in the corn and into the swampy woods beyond. "I wish we could just cut down those woods. And, I don't know, move the graveyard or bury it under concrete or something." She shivered. "I wish we could move back home. Any chance you could just tell my mom that?" She looked back at me, a glimmer of hope in her eyes.

"Tell her what?" I asked.

"That you can't get rid of the ghosts. That we have to move out of here and never come back. Can't you just tell her that?" Corrine asked.

"If it's true, then that's what I'll tell her," I said. "But if we can clear out the problem, we'll do it."

"Sure. 'Clear out the problem.' You people don't have any idea what you're dealing with out there." Corrine turned her horse and trotted away.

Stacey and I stayed quiet until she was gone.

"I think that girl's losing her mind," Stacey finally whispered.

"You might have a point," I said. "The ghost is having a psychological effect on her. Maybe deliberately. She's the only one in the family who's seen the horseman so far."

"So you think the horseman's stalking her?"

"Could be. Maybe she reminds him of the girl he killed."

"And that's the bloody girl who's crawling up into the house at night?" Stacey asked.

"She might be," I said. "Let's finish up this gear and go wait for Jacob. Maybe he can tell us if we're on the right track."

Chapter Eleven

We stood outside the little shop near the front of the farm, amid the burning jack o' lanterns and paper witches, since it would be the first building Jacob would see as he drove up the curving dirt road. With no street lights, or even actual pavement, the farm was difficult to navigate at night.

He finally arrived, his gray Hyundai looking out of place way out here in the country amid corn and scarecrows, as if some suburban soccer mom had taken a wrong turn and ended up on Death Murder Farm. Not that our old blue cargo van fit in much better.

If we'd been in a joking mood, we might have grabbed a couple of the Halloween masks on sale inside the shop, maybe tried to scare him or at least startle him as he drove in. We were still not very amused at how Corrine had done that to us, though. Plus, there was a risk of Jacob swerving into a ditch and bending an axle on his car, which he probably wouldn't have appreciated, especially since he does his psychic readings for free. They're part of his therapy for adjusting to his fairly new and completely unwanted ability to speak with the dead.

We waved him down from the brightly lit front porch. He turned into the gravel parking lot next to the store and gave the place a look-around as he climbed out. Stacey hopped down the steps and greeted him with a kiss.

"So we're looking for He Who Walks Behind the Rows, huh?" Jacob asked, squinting through his glasses at the high corn maze.

"Or maybe She Who Walks Behind the Rows," Stacey said. "You never know."

"We should keep an open mind where gender roles and agricultural demons are concerned," Jacob said, nodding. "So are we searching a particular area here? Or should I just wander?"

"We'll start with the house," I said. "The family's gone for the evening...well, *most* of them are gone." Jeremy and Amber had arranged for their son to spend the night away at a friend's house, and they had taken little Maya to the nearest movie theater, which was half an hour away. Corrine had refused to go with them, or to go anywhere else, and instead locked herself in her room. "Once we're done with the house, then we can wander outside all we want."

Jacob looked down the dirt road toward the woods, and he shivered. "We'll be going that way eventually, won't we? I can't say I'm looking forward to meeting whatever's lurking in those woods."

Stacey nodded, glancing at me. Jacob, as usual for him or any other psychic consultant, had no advance knowledge of the case before visiting the property. He'd immediately detected the source of the problem, or at least the site with the heaviest ghost activity.

Stacey and I shouldered our backpacks, heavy with gear in case we needed it.

"Nice Halloween decorations," Jacob commented as we walked to the house. He pointed to a cluster of four miniature scarecrows in the pumpkin patch, dressed in black wigs and dark sunglasses like the Ramones, giving a concert with their gourd and corn-cob instruments. "So we're talking about a low-end tourist trap here, perfect for passing a boring fall day. Just an hour from two major cities."

"You weren't supposed to research," Stacey said.

"I didn't. It's...pretty obvious." Jacob pointed to a wooden booth, currently shuttered, with a brightly painted sign reading

FIRE THE AMAZING PUMPKIN CANNON! $3 per pumpkin. "Plus, all the roadside signs leading up to the place. I'm guessing those woods turned out to be more haunted than they realized." His smile faltered as he again glanced into the darkness ahead.

Jacob stopped as we reached the house's driveway, standing in the middle of the dirt road, and he laid one hand across Stacey to block her from taking another step. He stared at a seemingly empty patch of dirt. She raised an eyebrow, looking somewhere between amused and confused.

"Is it just me," he finally said, "Or is there a trail of blood spots starting right here, in the middle of the road, and leading..." He turned his head and pointed. "...across the lawn...to the front door?"

"It's just you, buddy," Stacey said. Jacob was indicating the path by which Bloody Betty—or possibly Bloody Mildred, if Virgil's story was accurate—made her nightly trips into the house.

"This is a well-worn path," Jacob said. "Right through here, a groove worn by years and years of repetition." He crossed the lawn slowly, holding out both hands palm down, as though warming them by a fire that kept crawling away from him. "She's not here now, but there are traces all over..."

Jacob tucked his glasses into his shirt pocket and proceeded with his eyes closed. He didn't trip as he ascended the wooden steps to the porch, hands out in front of him. Then he knelt near the front door and ran his fingers over the porch floorboards. He didn't quite touch them; it was more like he was checking a stove burner to see whether it was hot.

"She crawls across here, bloody, pale, in pain...everything in her lower body is just pain. Crawling is like dragging her legs over piles of knives." Jacob winced.

"What does she want?" I asked.

"Sanctuary," he said. "Safety. She wants to go home."

"Did she live in this house?"

"She wants to retreat here, but she can't quite do it, or can't quite find peace..." He shook his head. "Let's go inside."

We passed through the front door into the dim house, lit by moonlight from the windows and a small lamp over in the reading room off the foyer. Jacob didn't turn them on or state any particular desire for more light.

Stacey and I followed a few paces behind him as he moved slowly, slowly over the floorboards. He moved toward the stairs, his fingers gradually reaching over the lip of the first stair in a way that reminded me of the tendrils of fog.

"Her trail is stronger as you go," Jacob said. "Her desire is to return here and find safety, but safety is never found." He crawled up the stairs on his hands and knees, eyes closed. I could imagine the ghost climbing the same way, just as Maya had described her.

"Can you tell us what happened to her?" I asked. "Why is she covered in blood?" That seemed like a useful thing to know.

"She died in pain." Jacob moved a little faster now, thankfully, like he'd finally fixed on a scent and was ready to follow it to its conclusion. He stood and jogged up the stairs.

I wasn't shocked when he led us directly to Maya's room. He opened the door and surveyed the room, dimly illuminated by a nightlight shaped like a wacky snowman.

Jacob stopped just inside the door.

"This is it," he said.

"What is what?" Stacey asked.

"That's the end of the trail. She reaches the room, crawls through the door...maybe she crawls to the bed occasionally, looks at whoever's sleeping there...I'm guessing by the size of that pink panda-bear chair in the corner, we're talking about a small girl."

"What does she want from the girl?" I asked.

"I'm not sure what she wants," Jacob said. "I just know she ends up disappointed. And angry."

"That's how she ended her life?" I asked. "Feeling disappointed and angry? Or is that how she feels now that she's haunting the house?"

"It's usually the same thing, isn't it?" Jacob walked into the middle of the room, avoiding the pink plastic clutter all over the floor. "I think the house is too different now, and of course the people are different, they aren't the people she knew in life. Maybe this isn't even the same house. Was there another one that used to stand here?"

"There was," I said.

"She's not finding what she's looking for," Jacob said. "She's caught in a loop, night after night. If we stick around and wait, I might be able to communicate with her."

"We can catch her outside, if she comes," I said. It was possible that closing cemetery gate had sealed her inside the cemetery walls, but time would tell. "I'm trying to steer her away from the family. Clients kind of like it when I can stop the ghosts from terrorizing their children in their sleep."

"I see how that might be a priority." Jacob clapped his hands, as if to say he was done with the room. "That takes care of her for now. Let's see what else this house has to say..."

Stacey and I followed him through the rest of the rooms. We avoided the locked door to Corrine's room. I could hear voices in there, probably a movie.

"The house is full of residuals," Jacob said as we reached the back stairs. "A lot of generations have lived here, most of them related to each other. It's like a close-knit family. Like a pack of wolves."

"You said wolves?" I asked.

"Yeah. There's violence in their past. But the ghosts aren't really here, are they? They come and go here, but they're much stronger out there." Jacob stopped at the bottom of the back stairs, which had landed us in the family's living room, and pointed through a small window toward the woods. "That's where they really are."

"Do you think she's out there, too?" I asked. "The girl who crawls into the house at night?"

"It's worth checking." Jacob shook his head. "I wouldn't want to live here. The spirits of the dead are very present. They come out to patrol the house and land. And they look at the living at night. I can see them looking in through windows while the living sleep. Sometimes they slip into the house and just stand over the living, watching. For hours. I suppose they don't have much else to do."

"Are any of them here now?"

Jacob shook his head. "Maybe later."

"Can you get any names?" I asked. "Specific identities?"

"Names, no. The ghosts I'm talking about, the ones who come out to kind of patrol the property, they're mostly male, and they're definitely family. They're led by the oldest male among them, a really strong personality. He must be a couple of centuries old. Maybe he was the first one to haunt the property, but he's assembled a number of his heirs and descendants around him over the years. Great-Grandpa Ghost. He's definitely the one in charge."

"What does he look like?" I asked.

Jacob shook his head. "If they were here, I could tell you more. What I'm getting is like traces of gray, little glimpses."

"I think you'll get plenty more than that when we go outside." I checked the time. "We should go. I want to be out of the way before the clients get home."

We did a quick walk-through downstairs, but Jacob didn't have anything new to add, so we finally stepped outside.

We toured the farm on foot, exploring the gardens more closely, then heading for the stables where the horses were dozing. Jacob stopped to look over each one of the scarecrows that Amber and her family had made to decorate the farm. I had a feeling he was trying to put off going into the woods as long as possible.

"Ellie, what's your costume for the Halloween ball at the hotel tomorrow night?" Jacob asked as we approached the stables, following the sandy red-dirt road past another scarecrow, three of us walking abreast, the whole situation momentarily resembling a low-rent *Wizard of Oz*. I wasn't sure which one of us was Dorothy, but I would say Stacey, because I'd rather be the Tin Man, wielding an ax and shielded by metal armor. Stacey seemed a little more prone to skipping and singing. We hadn't brought a dog, but there wasn't much need for Calvin's ghost-sniffing bloodhound Hunter. The ghosts on this farm were quite active and strong, not hard to sniff out at all.

"I haven't decided on a costume," I said. I grasped desperately for inspiration. "Um, maybe something from *Wizard of Oz*?"

"Stacey and I were going as C3P0 and R2D2 until she rejected the idea," Jacob said.

"Yeah, I'm not crouching inside a rolling trash can all night," Stacey said.

"I told you, I developed a workaround—" Jacob began.

"Don't care."

"You could also go as Chewbacca—"

"Now you're just getting weird," Stacey told him. "I agreed to Supergirl. I already have the costume. You can be Superman. Perfect couple's costumes."

"Superman and Supergirl are cousins, so I have to disagree. I'd rather be...Blue...Beetle..." Jacob seemed to lose focus at the entrance to the stable. He swung open the wooden gate and stepped inside.

We followed him. The stable was dark, naturally, and smelled of hay and manure. I noticed Corrine had returned her horse to its stall. Most of the other stalls were empty.

"Who is Blue Beetle?" Stacey whispered to me.

I shrugged. No idea.

"He's usually paired with Booster Gold," Jacob whispered from a few feet ahead.

Stacey and I looked at each other, and this time we both shrugged. This was no time for nerd trivia, anyway. It looked like Jacob was picking up on something. He approached the stall holding the smallest horse, the golden one named Pixie. She trembled, but took a small step toward him.

"These horses are nervous, don't you think?" Jacob looked at Stacey. "Not just normal horse-nervous, either. I feel like they spend a lot of time getting spooked."

"By what?" I asked.

Jacob looked along the dirt floor as if studying the layers of overlapping hoof prints there. "Something restless passes through here at times. Something fast."

"Like...I don't know...a horse?" Stacey asked.

"Seems plausible," Jacob said. "A horse ghost. Or a ghost that presents itself as horse-mounted. It comes from the road, maybe the woods." Jacob fell silent, looking at the wall of the stable closest to the woods.

"Why can't you just be Batman or something?" Stacey asked after the silence grew long enough to be uncomfortable. "Why do you have to get all obscure?"

"Lots of people go as Batman," Jacob said. "I'll be the only Blue Beetle in the room."

"Yeah, for good reasons," she said. "Like how nobody will have any idea what your costume is. How about the Flash?"

"You want me to wear a skintight red suit? In public?"

"Um...Spider-Man?"

"Not if you're Supergirl. You can't randomly mix Marvel and DC universes like that. It'll be anarchy." Jacob led the way out through the opposite side of the stable. The three sleepy horses looked happy to see us leave.

Our next stop was the corn maze. We lingered at the entrance for a moment, looking at the archway that curved overhead, made of old shovels, pitchforks, and other tools twisted together with the help of Amber's blowtorch.

"Are y'all sure you know the way through here?" Jacob asked, waving his own flashlight along the first path.

"It's pretty complicated. We should go around instead of through," I said.

We eventually reached the opposite side of the maze and walked into the narrow pass between the last row of corn and the woods beyond. Jacob stood and looked at the broken area with the hoofprints for a minute.

"Same feeling here as in the stable," Jacob said. "Something came through here, maybe more than once. Still, it's vague to me. The presence isn't as strong as the family of dead guys that haunt the farm. It's not part of that group, either, but definitely has a separate identity. I do see somebody on horseback, somebody old. Maybe centuries old, like the old-man ghost who rules that other group. But this one is definitely independent, maybe antagonistic to the other ghosts."

"Can you tell us anything else about the one on horseback?" I asked.

"It's hard to scrounge up details," he said. "It's like the ghost wants to keep itself hidden. The other ones, they aren't so secretive—this is their place, they belong here, they don't really care for the living. The horse one could well be wearing a mask or an invisibility cloak for all the information I'm picking up about him. I guess we need to head for the woods. Maybe my Spidey senses will find more there."

"See? You should be Spider-Man. It's perfect," Stacey said.

"Different universes!" Jacob countered. "You're playing with fire, Stacey."

"Says the guy who's leading us into the haunted woods late at night," she replied. As we followed the road into the dark cover of the trees, approaching the cemetery, she started to reach for his hand. Then she stopped herself and dropped back to walk beside me, staying out of Jacob's way while he poked and prodded the woods with his mind.

As before, the air became noticeably colder the moment we entered the woods, even though it had been nighttime for a few hours and the shade of the trees shouldn't have been a factor anymore. Our flashlights showed us the same dirt road, overgrown on either side, that we'd seen by day, but the feeling of apprehension was much deeper now, as midnight approached. The temperature dropped even more at the cemetery. A low bank of fog obscured the ground, reaching up from the swampy little creeks that divided the woods into muddy islands.

Jacob looked back over his shoulder at us. His face had lost any hint of humor. He seemed very uncomfortable on that nearly-forgotten old road with the canopy above us blocking the starlight and moonlight, with our three flashlights barely scratching the darkness. Our footsteps were the only sound, as if the crickets and owls were holding their breath, waiting for something.

I shivered, both from the physical cold alone and the emotional darkness I could feel waiting ahead. I might not have psychic powers of my own, but you don't have to be Edgar Cayce to sense a haunting that strong.

"The horse and rider you're so interested in," Jacob said quietly. "This is his road. He rides from here, from somewhere up there..." He gestured northward along the road, in the direction where I knew it faded and vanished among swampy land bordering the Savannah River. "He might be along later. But the real action is over here, and you already know that." Jacob started toward the front gate of the cemetery.

"Could you try keeping it closed?" I asked him. "Just to start with?"

"Okay..." He stopped short, looking at the brick and rusty wrought-iron fence across the weedy ditch. "I'm seeing a lot of dark figures boiling inside there. There's a barely-contained rage. They feel trapped. They're restless and they want to come out."

"So they *are* contained?" I asked, feeling a glimmer of hope. Maybe our simple remedy had worked for the family ghosts. We certainly hadn't encountered any of them tonight, even though we had our psychic pal with us. They hadn't been shy the previous two nights, not at all. "Jacob, are you saying they can't leave the cemetery?"

"If they could, they'd be out here by now," he said. "They're agitated. But, you see, the walls and gates of a cemetery have a certain powerful importance to the dead. Sacred ground in general...it can be used to bind them in place."

"Yeah, I'm pretty sure we're the ones who taught you all of that," Stacey said.

"There's a lot of ghosts in there," Jacob said, stepping closer to the cemetery wall. "They're kind of stalking back and forth like a pack of tigers."

"An ambush," Stacey said.

"Where?" I asked. My hand flew automatically to my utility belt, ready to blast some holy sounds or extra light if needed. I swept my flashlight across the foggy cemetery and the dark road, looking for shambling gray figures, or Hiram Neville, the rotten-faced guy with the Thomas Jefferson wig. From what Jacob had said, Hiram and some of his heirs lingered here, watching the land, maybe resenting the living.

"That's what a group of tigers is called," Stacey said. "An ambush. Not a pack."

"Oh." I moved my hand away from my belt, placing it casually on one hip as if I'd just been planning to do that all along.

"An ambush of tigers. That makes sense." Jacob stepped closer to the rusty gate, as close as he could without crossing the weedy ditch at the edge of the road. "What do you call a group of ghosts, then?"

"Oh, that's a..." Stacey hesitated, then glanced at me. "A fright? Right? A fright of ghosts? I've heard that somewhere."

"If you heard it somewhere, it must be true," I said.

"What else could it be? A gaggle of ghosts?" Stacey asked.

"That's geese," Jacob said. He reached across the ditch and touched the old wrought-iron gate. He inhaled sharply and drew his fingers back. "It's cold. I can tell you this particular posse of poltergeists is not happy about being trapped in there. Is that a recent thing? Were they free to roam around at some point?"

"We just closed and locked the gate earlier tonight. It had been standing open for years," I said.

"Like, maybe a hundred years," Stacey said. "We had to dig it out of the ground to close it."

Jacob flicked the shiny new padlock on the filthy, rusty gate and nodded. "Very recent. That would explain the intensity of their anger. You've just rounded up one furious flock of phantoms."

"Now that we're up close with them, can you tell us about any individuals?" I asked. "It would really help to know who we're dealing with. And anything about why they're here and what's stopped them from moving on."

"At the risk of sounding chicken, I really don't want to go in there if I don't have to. Ghosts tend to be drawn to mediums like me, and these are particularly angry right now. If they have telekinetic powers...I'd just rather not be torn apart by a weyr of wraiths."

"What's a weyr?" Stacey asked.

"That's what you call a group of dragons," Jacob said.

"I see." Stacey nodded, then held her fist to her mouth and coughed, *"Nerd!"*

"You're just embarrassed you don't know more about dragons," Jacob said. "It's okay."

"I'm embarrassed for both of us. Hey, what are you doing?" Stacey frowned as Jacob stepped across the ditch and stood on the recently churned earth where we'd dug the gate free.

"Just trying to get a closer look at this badelynge of bad-tempered spirits." Jacob reached over the rusty spikes topping the low, crumbling brick walls.

"Great," Stacey said. "What's badel...thing? A group of trolls holding hands with a group of elves?"

"It means a group of ducks," Jacob said. "From my SAT vocabulary workbook. I think it was called *Fun with Memorizing Massive Lists of Useless Words That You'll Never Possibly Need Again.*"

"Be careful," Stacey said. "Those spikes are sharp, and they look pretty filthy and disease-ridden."

I pointed my light at the ground and squinted into the darkness of the cemetery, searching for any sign of the apparitions. The darkness seemed thicker beyond the wall, and the fog had piled up thick on the ground, obscuring some of the smaller and toppled-over headstones.

"It's freezing in there," Jacob said, waving his hand back and forth over the wall. "Okay. These are definitely the guys who've been going out and visiting the house, stalking around the farm at night. They're extremely territorial. And they're burning up with rage about the intruders and outsiders around here. I mean, they're not screaming 'outlander!' like in the previously mentioned *Children of the Corn*, but—"

"Careful!" Stacey stepped over the ditch and stood close to him. Hopefully this wouldn't distract too much from his reading. She managed to get in the way sometimes, letting her concern for Jacob's well-being interfere with his need to concentrate on getting in touch with the dead.

"They want to get a message out," Jacob said. "A very strong, shouting, screaming sort of message about how much they resent the living."

"So they aren't overjoyed about having their resting place turned into a haunted wilderness for extra cash at Halloween?" I asked. I could understand that. It also reminded me of what Virgil had said, about Jeremy and Amber disrespecting Jeremy's family and heritage.

"They're territorial, like I said," Jacob repeated. "They won't be happy while the living are still here."

"I don't get it," Stacey said. "Jeremy and his kids are still their family, right? Why all the beef with their own family members? It's not like outsiders came and bought the farm after Jeremy's great uncle, you know, 'bought the farm' himself. Jeremy was the closest available blood relative, that's why he inherited it."

"Good question," Jacob said. Then his voice dropped low, as if he didn't want to be overheard. I was only a few feet away and could barely make out his words. "One of them is coming forward to address me, I think. He looks like the corpse of some guy who signed the Declaration of Independence...oh, yeah. He's in charge here." Jacob fell silent, his jaw slightly open and his eyes falling to half-mast as he stared out into the cemetery.

Stacey reached out a hand, as if to poke him in the shoulder. I grabbed her wrist and shook my head. This did not seem to please her.

Jacob's eyes closed and he bared his teeth.

"Get...out..." Jacob's lips didn't move as the voice hissed from somewhere inside him.

"Jacob?" Stacey glanced at me, eyes widened, hands balled into fists at her sides. She obviously wanted to try and help him, but had just enough discipline to keep her hands to herself.

"They all say that," I told Stacey.

"You...die..." said the voice from Jacob's lips.

"Do they all say *that*?" Stacey whispered.

"Are we speaking to Hiram Neville?" I asked.

Jacob's head turned toward me, following my voice with his eyes closed, like a blind man trying to zero in on the source of an unpleasant sound.

"Be gone from here," said Jacob, or the thing speaking through him. Stacey was clearly beside herself with concern over Jacob, casting me a scowl for chatting with the ghost instead of trying to exorcise it from her boyfriend's body. It wasn't normal for a spirit to speak through Jacob on a simple walk-through like this.

"We will leave if you keep yourselves inside the cemetery, and you do not come out wandering at night, terrifying the living," I said. "Do we have a deal?"

Jacob stood in an awkward position that no living entity would have chosen. One arm reached way too far over the fence, fingers splayed like some kind of satellite antenna slurping up signals from within the burial ground. This left his belly dangerously close to the sharp, rusty points topping the fence posts, practically an invitation for angry ghosts to gut him like a fish. Stacey hovered close, ready to grab him.

His head twisted around, looking up and back at me at an almost neck-snapping angle. Behind his glasses, his eye sockets turned dark, as if someone had injected them full of black ink, just in case we weren't sure whether he was really possessed.

"I'm not hearing a clear answer from you," I said. "The dead should stay away from the living. The dead should move on. You can all be free of this place, you can all move on to a much better existence. We can help."

"*Silence, wench,*" he hissed.

"Did you really just call me a—" I began, but then he lunged forward over the rusty iron fence, putting most of Jacob's vital organs in immediate danger, exactly as I'd feared.

Stacey wrapped her arms around Jacob, and she grunted and pulled to keep him away from the rusty spikes. It didn't look as though she was overpowering him, though. I was already moving, leaping forward and grabbing him around the waist to lend my own strength to the effort. I wasn't going to let some long-dead guy in a wig and a silly hat kill my friends.

"Let him go!" Stacey screamed.

Then Jacob came free with a sudden ease, shoving backwards from the wall. Stacey cried out and fell into the dirt road.

He shoved me, too. I managed to keep some of my balance, but I was still pinwheeling my arms when he punched me in the face.

I went down on my back, landing in the weedy ditch alongside the road, my face just inches from the bulging, uneven brick of the low wall that supported the spiky iron fence. I'd barely had time to register what had happened—I'd gone from pulling hard to protect Jacob's life to crashing into the dirt in three seconds.

Jacob approached me, his glasses missing now, his eyes gone unnaturally dark. There was a stiffness to how he moved, almost an exaggerated formality, and for a moment it wasn't hard to see him as an eighteenth-century man in a powdered wig, marching briskly toward me in what looked like clockwork, military-drilled steps.

Jacob himself usually walked with more of a relaxed shuffle, and kept himself stooped a bit rather than square-shouldered and rigid. The spirit wasn't just speaking through Jacob anymore; he'd hopped right inside and made himself at home with a full-blown possession. If he had complete control of Jacob's body, then he could do anything he wanted to Stacey and me, and to anyone else he might encounter.

He stopped and looked down at me, while I waited for the ringing in my head to subside. I pointed my tactical beam at his face, but that didn't seem to deter him. He trailed his fingers over the rusty spikes topping the fence, carelessly cutting and slicing Jacob's fingers as he approached me. He was not smiling. His face was taut, he lips pressed into a thin line.

"Leave my friend's body now," I said, doing my best to sound like the authority in this situation. "You've crossed a line. Go back where you belong."

"I belong," he said. *"You do not."*

I crawled backward through the ditch while he pursued me. Standing up would have been nice, but at the moment I couldn't stop long enough without him grabbing me, so I just continued my desperate backward scramble. He leaned over me, walking at a fast gait, eerily quiet.

Something sharp gouged into my fingertips. Several something sharps, in fact, like I'd placed my hand onto a porcupine's back. It was wild blackberry, an invasive vine with long, narrow thorns that bite deep.

The vine blocked my desperate backward crawl and gave the entity possessing Jacob his chance to grab me. Jacob's hand reached for my throat as he bent closer. I noticed his other hand remained on the fence, his fingers smearing blood across one rusty iron post.

I kicked his inner thigh, meaning to knock him away from the fence and the cemetery. Hopefully, that would break Jacob from the ghost's control.

He staggered sideways, but caught himself, tightening his grip on the fence rail. I winced to see Jacob's sliced fingers clutching the flaky, rusting iron.

His face remained stoic, as if it were also made of cold iron. He stomped one shoe down onto my leg, and then dropped closer and coiled his fingers around my throat. He pressed down, shoving my head back into the weeds.

This was not going well.

Stacey finally showed up behind him, raising her tactical flashlight, which she'd turned off for sneaking-up purposes. The military-grade anodized aluminum shell of the flashlight was just the thing for bashing an attacker in the head, but she looked understandably reluctant to slam the metal into Jacob's skull.

"*My land,*" Jacob whispered, squeezing tight around my throat. "*My blood.*"

My brain spun as I tried to figure out how to turn things around fast.

"Hiram," I croaked, because that's the sound I make when somebody's index finger is jabbing me in the voice box. "What side were you on in the war? Did you take up *arms* against your king or *arms* against your neighbor? Did you...uh...fight for your right to bear *arms*?" I was really hoping Stacey would take the hint here.

Stacey looked from the back of Jacob's head to the arm he'd extended over the cemetery fence, then looked down at her flashlight. Good girl. Before your possessed boyfriend chokes me to death, please.

"*I have no king,*" Jacob said. "*I am sovereign.*"

She raised the flashlight as if to crack it down on Jacob's arm, then hesitated. Then she dipped it under his arm instead. He glanced back and opened his mouth just as she yanked the flashlight backward, hooking his arm away from the iron fence, as if prying him loose from electrified chain-link.

Jacob roared, his mouth stretched unnaturally wide, as if the live human body just couldn't contain the old ghost's fury.

Not taking any chances, Stacey whacked him hard in the shoulders with the flashlight. He collapsed toward me, but I managed to catch his weight with my arms and knees, just enough to roll him to the side, so he landed in the road rather than on top of me. Stacey gave him an extra kick in the ribs, and I jumped on him and pinned his face to the dirt.

"Why?" Jacob shouted. "Why is everyone kicking me?"

His voice didn't sound like a demon from beyond the edges of the world anymore—in fact, he sounded very much like an accountant who has just awoken in the middle of the road being kicked by a couple of girls—so I backed off. Stacey did, too, and also threw an arm across me as if to stop me. I gave her an annoyed *Hey, I already stopped* sort of look.

Jacob's voice returning to normal could have been a trick, but I doubted it. The ghost hadn't had long to sink in, not long enough to start wearing Jacob's personality as a disguise. Only the really sharp spirits figure that one out, usually malevolent things with demonic tendencies.

"Trust me, you needed it," I told Jacob, while Stacey dropped down beside him and wrapped her arms around his shoulders.

"The ghost got inside you," Stacey said. "Are you okay?"

Jacob rubbed his head with both hands. "Ever had an ice cream headache? Where it feels like your brain is freezing?"

"Poor baby," Stacey said, rubbing his head.

"Did you get a glimpse of who possessed you?" I asked. I hated to be all back-to-business right away, but somebody had to do it while Jacob's memory was fresh. "Did you learn anything about him?"

"Sure," Jacob said, while Stacey tossed me a scowl for going right back into work mode. "He's a colonial, Revolution-era guy. He thought of himself as very important. Owned a lot of land, was a person of influence, relatively speaking, not that there were many people around for him to influence in those days. Ruled his little farm with an iron fist, expected to be obeyed....He had a few slaves, too, but their spirits aren't here. They've moved on..." Jacob swayed and reached for his head with his bloody fingers.

"We have to get him to the hospital," Stacey said.

"Do you have any idea what an emergency room costs?" he asked. "I'll wait until morning and see a regular doctor."

"On a Saturday?" Stacey asked. "You need stitches, you need a tetanus shot—"

"I'm current on my shots, thanks," Jacob said. "As many times as I've ended up scratched, bitten, beaten, and bloody from hanging out with you, I couldn't really avoid that. You two are extremely hazardous to my health, is what I'm saying."

"It's not intentional," I said.

"The things in that cemetery." He shook his head and pointed with one bleeding finger, just in case there was any doubt about which cemetery he meant. "They need to stay in there. If they don't, they will take over. They'll run off the living. This place will end up an abandoned ghost farm."

"Like...a farm where they grow crops of ghosts?" Stacey asked.

He stared at her. "No. I just hurt my head, don't try to confuse me."

"What else did you see?" I asked.

"They're like a pack of...I don't want to say wolves. What eats bones and dead things? Hyenas. A pack of hyenas."

"A clan," Stacey said, almost under her breath.

"Yeah, a clan of dead men. The restless from each generation, the worst of them. They aren't willing to tolerate anyone but their own family on this land."

"But it is their own family living here," Stacey said. "Isn't it?"

"I don't know, but these guys are extremely territorial. The only good news is they're kind of stuck in there for now."

"There's salt in my backpack," I said. "I was thinking of salting the place to encourage them to stay inside."

"Do that. Do anything that might help keep them in there."

"Not now," Stacey said. "We have to at least get you bandaged up, Jacob."

"I won't bleed to death in the next hour," he said. "We don't want these ghosts creeping out and wandering around. Salt the little monsters."

I surveyed the perimeter of the cemetery, at least as far as I could see before the walls on either side vanished among trees, fog, and darkness. Tromping around the muddy creeks behind the cemetery in the middle of the night sounded somewhat hazardous, especially with all the angry spirits bottled up inside the walls.

At the same time, I needed them to see us putting down the salt. Salt is traditionally believed to have protective properties against wicked spirits and other evils. I don't know if this has any actual chemical basis, so it was best for the ghosts to see it for symbolic reasons. Even if the salt didn't provide a true barrier in an electromagnetic sense, it might provide a psychological barrier.

"We'll just do this front wall for now and see how it goes," I said. Stacey and Jacob nodded. Nobody rushed to insist that we walk the entire perimeter of the cemetery right away.

"Let's make it quick," Stacey said, sounding resigned. She was still eyeing Jacob's injured fingers.

I plonked down my backpack and opened it, relieved to be free of the pressing weight. I'd been lugging two heavy things in there: my thermal goggles and a five-pound bag of Dead Sea salt. Aside from the body of water's location in the Holy Land, the mineral content of the Dead Sea was a rich, dense mix of exotic salts like magnesium chloride, not just the tasty sodium chloride you find in most seawater or in a glass shaker on your table. If you're trying to salt restless ghosts into place, you might as well go big on both the symbolism and the physical reality.

"We can come back at first light, when it's safer," Stacey suggested.

"I need them to watch," I said, nodding toward the cemetery. I couldn't see anything but shadows, twisted limbs, headstones and fog, but I couldn't deny the deep chill in the air, or the feeling of being watched. I could imagine old Hiram lingering behind the fence, just at the spot where Stacey had broken his contact with Jacob, his dry skull of a face regarding us from underneath a crumbling wig and tricorner hat.

Stacey, Jacob, and I all stood together. I passed Stacey the thermal goggles. "Watch out for any creepers creeping up on us," I told her. "You, too, Jacob."

"I don't feel anything out here with us," he said.

"Good." I approached the cemetery gate with the big bag of salt open in one hand. The darkness beyond the gate was silent except for the distant, soft sound of slow-moving creek water.

I crossed the ditch to the gate, tense. When nothing jumped out at me, I dipped my hand into the bag, scooped up salt, and sifted it along the ground in front of the gate. Emboldened by the lack of violent supernatural response, I moved even closer to the gate so I could salt the rusty points and cross-bars, the broken nub of an old latch, and the new padlock I'd added, just for good measure. You can't oversalt a gate, as they say. Okay, nobody says that, but the gate was clearly the weak point here, the portal through which the ghosts had been coming and going for years, so I wanted to lay it down nice and thick.

"That's stirring them up," Jacob said from somewhere behind me.

"I can see a lot of cold spots on thermal," Stacey added. "They're clustering in close to you, just on the other side of the fence. Don't let them grab you."

"You're making them angry," Jacob said.

"Good. That means it's working." I scattered another handful of salt over the gate. The feeling of being watched had grown stronger, though that could have been the effect of what Stacey and Jacob were reporting to me. The air was certainly cold along the fence, and growing colder, creating fog along the bottom rail.

I spread more salt as I walked alongside the fence. It felt like a glacier had parked itself on the other side, with a palpable cold leaking out between the gaps in the iron spikes. The lower portion, the brick wall that supported the iron fence, looked even more buckled and broken than I remembered. Either it had developed an alarming number of new cracks over the past two days, or I was just much more aware of them now that I had some idea of the awful things within the walls.

Jacob and Stacey kept pace behind me, staying on the road across the weedy ditch, since there wasn't a lot of room on this side. I didn't want anyone crowding the narrow, crumbling dirt ledge where I walked.

When I reached the sunken brick corner of the fence, I hopped out onto the road and walked the opposite way. All indications were that the ghosts were hovering close, watching with resentment as I further sealed them into their proper resting place. I didn't get the feeling they'd be resting peacefully anytime soon, but at least we had made the farm a safer place by locking them in. They wouldn't be free to menace the living at night.

Chapter Twelve

Stacey grabbed the first-aid kit from the van, and we crept quietly into the house so we could clean and wrap his wounds until the nearest urgent-care place (a twenty-five-minute drive) opened up in the morning. We used the filtered water spigot at the kitchen sink to rinse Jacob's wounds. The farm drew its water from a well, and my confidence in the hygienics of the outdoor spigots was low.

While Stacey helped Jacob, I walked into the foyer to check our gear at the front stairs. The family had already come home and gone to bed while we wandered the farm.

According to our instruments, the 'ghost burglar alarm' we'd set up had not fired while we were away. The motion detector, thermometer, and EMF meter hadn't sensed enough combined activity to activate the white spotlights and holy sounds.

"Did you stop her?" a voice whispered behind me, making me jump. I turned and was happy to see a live, flesh-and-blood human being instead of something dead tiptoeing up behind me.

It's a little crazy, having a job where this is a major problem. I usually deal with only the worst ghosts, too. Things have to progress pretty far before people will even admit to themselves that their house is haunted. They have to get even worse, truly scary or dangerous, before they're willing to call in outside experts. Nobody likes to be thought crazy, after all.

This time, it wasn't a cold fog or a pale girl in a blood-soaked gown. Maya, the six-year-old, stood in her pajamas, which followed a fuzzy pink bunny theme right down to the puffy slippers. She stared up at me, her hair in thick red clumps around her face, a small box of apple juice in one hand.

"I'm not sure yet," I said. "We may have helped."

"She didn't come tonight," Maya said. "I can tell."

"We didn't detect any visits from her tonight, either," I said.

"Is she gone forever?"

"We can't be sure yet, but I think it will stay quiet tonight. Even if it doesn't, we're standing guard."

"Will you tell Lucy there's no ghosts?" Maya whispered. "She's scared of them."

"Who's Lucy?"

Maya raised one fuzzy bunny slipper. The fake pink fur around the bottom of it was worn, frayed, and dusty. The bunny's plastic googly eyes bounced as Maya waved her foot back and forth.

"Lucy's the scaredy one," Maya said. She pointed to her other foot, where the fuzzy bunny slipper sat quietly. "Lucky is not scared."

"It's going be okay...Lucy," I said. "We'll watch out for you."

"Thank you," Maya replied in a high, squeaky voice while bobbing the bunny slipper up and down. Its eyes bounced crazily again. Then Maya turned and ran away down the hall. I heard her footsteps thump away up the back stairs.

"Who was that?" Stacey asked, emerging from the kitchen. "Were you talking to somebody?"

"Just a small pink rabbit," I said. "Looks like no ghosts bothered the family tonight."

"Does that mean Bloody Betty is trapped inside the graveyard, too?" Stacey asked.

"Could be," I said. "We don't want to jump to any conclusions, but we can be cautiously optimistic."

We rounded up Jacob, with his hand wrapped in thick, fresh

gauze, and headed out to the van before we could disturb any more family members. I didn't want to be forced to apologize to any more items of footwear, not that night.

The farm stayed quiet for hours, thankfully. Stacey and I even took turns napping. Jacob, drained from his rough encounter of the supernatural kind, slept on one of the van's drop-down cots as soundly as if the painfully thin mattress were a princess's bed made of silk and goose feathers.

I dreamed of Anton Clay again, pursuing me into the dark basement of Michael's building, toward the furnace room where the old well served as a portal, a thin spot where spirits can easily cross back and forth. Demonic spirits had come and gone there for thousands of years. It had been known as a place of cursed water.

In real life, we'd sealed it off with lead and steel, and a dash of unauthorized magic from an ex-Jesuit, after dealing with a particularly dangerous entity in Michael's building. There was always a danger of something breaking out.

In my dream, though, fire billowed up and out from the well. Anton held me in the basement as the house burned down around us.

I awoke sweaty and trembling, and found myself lying in the shotgun seat of the van, the back of the seat reclined as far as it would go. All my muscles felt stiff, and I was still panicky from the nightmare.

Stacey and Jacob were both asleep on the cots. I'd dozed off during my watch, but now it was well past sunrise anyway, and the van's cab was full of light.

I grabbed the thick bag of salt and climbed out of the van, eager to stretch my legs, move around, and get some distance from the bad dream. My brain felt exhausted, but I was restless. Salting the cemetery wasn't a task I wanted to leave half-finished, and I'd had obsessive thoughts all night about the need to go back and wrap it up.

Since there was plenty of daylight and I wasn't going down into any dark, claustrophobia-inducing basements, I didn't bother waking the others. I wanted some fresh air and a chance to walk off my nightmares.

My last big non-dream encounter with Anton Clay hadn't been with the ghost himself, but with a fearfeeder or "boogeyman" ghost living in Michael's building. That ghost could take on the form of a living person's worst fear—in my case, that was good old Anton. It made sense that I would dream of encountering him in Michael's building again.

I checked my phone as I walked. I'd texted Michael earlier to remind him about the Halloween ball at the Lathrop Grand, but the message still hadn't gone through. No signal. I would have to borrow Amber's landline or wait until we returned a bit closer to civilization.

Only small spills of early-morning light trickled into the woods, burning holes in the low ground fog. The air felt warmer than it had for the past two days, and my Mel-Meter confirmed that the temperature in the shady woods was at the highest I'd seen it, no different from the temperature outside of them.

I braced myself for anything strange as I approached the cemetery. The gate remained closed, the little spills of salt on and around it completely undisturbed. Again, there was no shift in temperature or spike in electromagnetic readings. I let myself relax a little. The spirits really did seem locked up, and now that it was daytime, I didn't even sense them watching me from within the walls.

With my trusty bag of Dead Sea salt in hand, I crossed the weedy ditch at a front corner of the cemetery and began walking along the side wall. Like the rest of the cemetery's perimeter, it was a low brick wall topped with rusty spikes, as though designed to keep out medieval invaders.

I salted the uneven bricks and the muddy earth outside the fence. My walking space narrowed as I approached a creek, and soon I was walking carefully along a muddy ledge overhanging slow, dark water a few feet below. It was precarious, but it held my weight, and nothing scary lunged through the fence trying to grab my ankles, so overall it went fine.

The back side of the cemetery offered no more trouble. I spread salt along the high bank overlooking the creek, and I had a closer look at the rotten foot bridge that spanned from the back gate of the cemetery to the next marshy, tree-filled creek island. The bridge looked even less sturdy on closer examination, all the boards rotten or missing. It would probably collapse if anyone heavier than a child tried to cross. A small, thin child who hadn't eaten in a few hours.

Across the bridge lay marshlands. Tromping through them in a northern direction, you'd eventually reach the swampy battlefield where hundreds had died, many of their bodies lost forever to the deep mud. I didn't have any direct sign that spirits from that old battle were part of the problem on the clients' farm, but surely such violence had left restless ghosts or residual hauntings behind, helping to create the haunted atmosphere.

I turned away from the creek and gave the back gate some special salty attention, especially the latch and hinges. Despite its thick layers of rust, the old iron gate had held firm for many decades, but it couldn't hurt to reinforce it.

Through the iron spikes, I saw the fallen tree and the pit into which I'd stumbled. With the temperature higher and the fog depleted, a few more of the mossy old headstones were visible. One of them tilted near the spot where I'd fallen. I'd been lucky not to crack my head on it.

Moving as quickly as I dared on the slippery weeds and mud overhanging the creek, I spread the salt along the back of the cemetery and then up the other side. I breathed a sigh of relief as I reached the corner. The entire perimeter of the cemetery was now salted, reinforcing the power of the cemetery walls to contain the ghosts.

The ground was clear of any lingering fog, and the sunlight was brighter than the past two days, as if a heavy shadow had lifted from the cemetery. The crickets and birds weren't shy about filling the air with their music anymore.

I hesitated in front of the gate, then drew out my key to the new padlock. With the spirits gone to ground for the day, it seemed safe to have another look around. The family's encounters with these ghosts had happened at night, at sunset or later, never in the morning. It's rare to find a ghost who's a morning person.

The plan for the day was to get Jacob some stitches if needed, then head back to Savannah, sleep in our own beds, attend the Lathrop Grand Halloween ball with the guys, then spend a night at our own homes. We'd collected a lot of data, and the troublesome ghosts seemed to be contained. There wasn't much need to run up our motel bill—which would be passed on to our clients—while we reviewed what we'd learned and planned our next move. The stale-perfume air of The Old Walnut Inn was starting to bother my sinuses, anyway.

Before we went home, I wanted to see if I could corroborate some of the things Virgil had said. It would only take a few minutes inside the cemetery.

I unlocked the gate, slipped inside, and quickly latched it behind me. I didn't sense anything strange—no sudden drop in temperature, no feeling of being watched. My Mel-Meter picked up nothing. Still, I left the shiny new padlock open in case I needed to leave in a hurry.

The area seemed momentarily safe to me, though I wouldn't have set foot inside the cemetery at night. Even going in the day might have seemed foolish, when Hiram had just possessed Jacob the previous night, but I wasn't a psychic medium with my feelers out, just a cynical girl with my guard up. I've developed a thick emotional shell. It's handy.

Hiram's granite obelisk was one I'd already identified in our first survey of the cemetery. I stepped close to it now so I could read the faded inscription. It was deep in the shadow of an old cypress tree, so I clicked on my flashlight and leaned close.

1736-1823. Beloved father, Patriot, deacon, servant of God and liberty.

"I guess that answers what side you took during the Revolution," I murmured. Several feet below my boots lay the bones of the spirit who'd accosted me and briefly possessed Jacob. I shivered to think of his decayed face, his dead eyes staring from beneath his wig.

I wasn't there to see him, though, so I moved on, checking for headstones that I'd missed earlier, or inscriptions that had been too faded to read on their own, but might suggest the name I was trying to find.

I found it near the pit below the fallen tree, the same stone I'd just noticed from outside the back gate, the one on which I could have bashed my brains out if I'd fallen a little differently. I remembered the roots digging into my legs and back like skeletal hands.

Mildred Neville, 1764-1781. I couldn't have read the badly faded inscription the first time I'd been here, but now that I knew what name I was looking for, it was clear enough.

"There you are," I said. "Are you the one who's been crawling over to the house at night?"

I imagined the girl—seventeen at the time, by her headstone—lying in the wagon, belly and legs slick with blood, just as I'd seen her in the vision. And the hard-faced man walking alongside the wagon, in his waistcoat and powdered wig, carrying a sizzling pitch torch—had that been her father Hiram?

The haunting was starting to make a little more sense. The poor girl had been killed by an ex-Hessian vagabond on the highway, according to Virgil, with either a sword or a crude eighteenth-century pistol. I imagined the father seeing his daughter that way, her lower half soaked in blood, dying as she lay in the wagon.

The girl's tragic and violent death could have stuck her here all these years. If the ghost of the horseman still traveled up and down the old dirt road, that could have caused Hiram to stick around as well, trying to protect his daughter's spirit against that of the Hessian horseman. All of them could still be caught up in the drama—murderer, victim, victim's family. Once the farm was so deeply haunted, it would have begun to accumulate more ghosts over the generations.

I could imagine old Hiram gathering the roughest, most disturbed spirits of his descendants, the ones who stuck around after death instead of moving on, and pulling them together into a family group built around his obsession with protecting the farm and his daughter. He'd failed to protect her in life. The guilt might have haunted him, keeping his spirit earthbound after he died.

"There must be some way to release you all," I whispered.

More words were engraved low on Mildred's small, sunken headstone. I had to peel away moss before I could make out the letters—and even then, it took a little time.

After a minute, I was pretty sure it read *Infant Neville, 1781.*

I blinked, tracing the remnants of the inscribed letters with my fingertip.

"Infant?" I asked, as if poor Mildred could have answered me. "Virgil didn't say...did you have a baby with you? The horseman killed your baby, too?" I curled my lip in disgust, thinking what a monster he must have been.

The baby didn't have a name, though. Perhaps Mildred had been in advanced pregnancy when she was killed, enough for the family to mention it on their shared headstone. Mother and unborn child interred together.

Then again, maybe Virgil was wrong altogether. His story about the Hessian horseman killing Mildred had been based on an oral history, after all, that might have been no more than local folklore. There might have been no horseman at all. Mildred might simply have died in childbirth, as so many did in those days. The gravestone offered no clues about how the young mother and her baby had found their way into the earth so early, both of them at such tender ages, sharing a headstone.

Horse hooves sounded, distant and soft, moving at a low trot. I wasn't immediately worried, since I knew Corrine woke up by sunrise to attend the horses. Still, it was a little unnerving, given the stories of the murdering horseman.

I hustled to the gate, having completed my mission of finding Mildred's grave. The girl had indeed existed, though the circumstances of her death remained murky. I had a strong feeling she was the one who'd touched me with her cold hand.

Anyway, the ghost had left her psychic mark on me, regardless of whether either of us had really wanted that to happen. I could feel pain in my lower body from the moment I found her headstone until the moment I stepped outside the gate and closed the padlock again. Then it was gone. I can't say for sure whether it was the horrible pain of a childbirth gone awry, or of a sword having ripped its way through my stomach, or getting gutshot with a primitive ball of lead. I'm not familiar with the finer distinctions among those different forms of excruciating pain, and I'd really rather not become too familiar with them if at all possible.

Outside, I took a deep breath. I'd been more nervous than I'd realized while inside the cemetery, and stepping back onto the road felt like fresh air and freedom.

The hoof beats returned, still distant. I turned slowly, trying to find the source. They weren't coming from the Neville farm, but from somewhere farther up the road, toward the place where the riverside marsh eventually swallowed it. It was possible that distant neighbors used the road for horseback riding, since it was virtually guaranteed to have no auto traffic on it.

Still, I didn't waste any time hustling down the road. The hoofbeats sounded closer, definitely on the approach.

I watched over my shoulder. The trotting sound seemed just around the curve now, on the cusp of emerging from behind a stand of interwoven old oaks thick with poisonous vines. My body tensed up in expectation, ready to fight or flee. Or wave, I suppose, if it turned out to be Corrine or just some neighbor happening by.

The hooves fell silent. I waited, and continued to wait, but nothing emerged from around the bend. There weren't any sounds of retreat, either. It was as if something had come to a halt behind the stand of trees, and now waited there silently.

I crossed the road so I could see a little bit farther around the bend. Then I approached the place where I'd last heard the sound, feeling more tense with every step.

Around the bend, there was more dirt road, lots of weeds in the ditches on either side, and nothing else. Light spilled through the canopy above in a hundred little sunbeams.

There was no sign of a horse or rider, except for the fresh-looking hoofprints in the dirt. They ended abruptly, just where the sound of the approaching horse had fallen silent. It was as though the horse had evaporated, just like we'd seen in the corn maze. And I hadn't seen any sign of a choppa.

I turned and hurried back to the farm, eager to leave the woods behind.

Chapter Thirteen

"So that's it? You're all done?" Amber asked. Stacey and I stood with her in the little shop near the front of the farm, while Jacob snoozed in the van. The shop was already open for Saturday-morning business, and a couple of elderly early-bird customers studied the small baskets of fresh produce with sour looks on their faces.

"I wouldn't say we're all done," I said. "You'll want to keep the gate locked and never allow anybody in there again, for starters. We're going to study all we've learned, see if we can learn more, and develop a strategy for making the whole area safe again." I was trying to speak in some kind of vague, coded language, since I doubted she wanted us talking openly about ghosts and ghouls in front of visiting customers, even if it was almost Halloween.

"So much for Jeremy's prized Haunted Woods attraction, then. Y'all want some hot cider?" Amber asked the two customers, indicating the warm urn that filled the air with a sweet cinnamon. The elderly couple muttered under their breaths, as if competing to see who could sound the most bitter and the least coherent at the same time. Amber shrugged, then lowered her voice to a whisper, leaning toward us across the counter. "What about the corn maze? Is it safe now?"

"Wait a couple of days," I said.

"We'll miss Halloween." Amber shook her head, looking crestfallen. "This was all a bust. All our work to make this some kind of fun place, to turn around the bad memories..."

"The bad memories?" I asked.

"Well, the time or two Jeremy came here as a kid, his uncle was pretty mean to him," Amber said. "Called him a city-sissy, threatened him with a gun when his parents weren't looking. Made Jeremy help skin a deer when he was a kid, which gave Jeremy nightmares. The poor thing was still breathing when they dragged it off the truck and hung it up on the deer stand. Bleeding all over, shot through the ribs, but still alive."

"That's awful."

"It's kind of ironic that Jeremy ended up inheriting the farm, considering how much old Uncle Tyrus hated him," Amber said. "But then, Tyrus should've been a nicer person if he wanted to have some kids of his own, you know? Jeremy was the closest relative."

"So that could be why the..." I paused as the elderly couple left without buying anything, muttering sourly to each other as the entrance bell jangled happily on its ribbon overhead. "...why the dead ancestors don't like Jeremy. Because his great-uncle, the last owner of the place, thought he was weak, thought he didn't belong."

"Jeremy was always kind of a reject among some of his family," Amber said. "I guess because he was adopted."

"He was? Why didn't anyone mention that?" I asked.

"Does it matter?" Amber looked perplexed.

"That could explain why the native ghosts are so hostile," I said. "Jeremy isn't a blood relative. That means your kids aren't, either...none of you are. The family ghosts might see all of you as outsiders."

"There's not much we can do about that." Amber shook her head. "Maybe this was all a bad idea. Jeremy was right when he wanted to sell it. I was the one who had to get crunchy and New Age about it. Hey, let's move our family out into the country, let the purity of nature clean up our souls and clear out our problems...or at least put some serious distance between Corrine and her druggie friends back home..."

"It sounds like a nice idea," Stacey said.

"It might still work out," I said. "Just leave the cemetery alone."

"This year's a bust, anyway." Amber sighed. "I'm glad you were able to help. I can't say how much it means." She looked a little bit relieved, at least, but clearly still had plenty of worries and fears on her mind.

"There may be more ahead," I said. "But I'm glad there seems to be some progress. You and your family should rest easy tonight. We're taking most of our gear with us, but we've left the ghost burglar-alarm arrangement set up on your front porch, and another one on the front stairs, in case the crawling girl returns. The lights have been effective in driving her off before. Let us know if anything sets them off, or if you see anything else. You call my cell anytime. I'm a night owl."

"Thank you," Amber said. "Are you sure you don't want some fresh-brewed apple cider?"

"No, thanks," I told her, but Stacey eagerly accepted a to-go cup.

It was nice to leave the farm behind and begin our journey home. We stopped by the Old Walnut Inn long enough to check out.

"I'm going to miss this place," Stacey sighed, looking over the concrete-plugged pool surrounded by grimy furniture. I assumed she was kidding.

We stopped at the first urgent care that was open on Saturday. It was in the small town of Rincon, about half an hour outside of Savannah. Jacob's injuries weren't so bad. He received two stitches in his middle finger, and that was about it. We had a late breakfast at a local spot called Debbie's, which was a small house tucked into a sandy corner lot next to a trailer park. The food was basic but tasty —eggs, grits, and mushrooms for me. Filling. I was ready to sleep after that, but we still had to drive back home.

After dropping off the kids—okay, Stacey and Jacob are only a couple years younger than me, but sometimes they seem like kids to me—I finally returned to my own apartment. Bandit, my cat, hadn't seen me in a few days. He responded to my return home after this long absence by opening one eye where he lay on the couch, then closing it again and going back to sleep.

"Nice to see you, too, pal," I told him. I refilled his water and dry-food dispensers before adjusting the blackout curtains, showering, and heading to bed. My apartment is nothing special, just a narrow brick-walled studio in a refurbished factory, but at that moment it seemed nicer than any five-star hotel. The Old Walnut Inn couldn't compete.

My sleep was filled with nothing but intense, fiery nightmares and Anton's smiling face, just as it had been for the past few days.

Calvin called me into the office that afternoon. Stacey wasn't there yet, but Calvin was at her big three-screen video editing station, looking through footage and images she'd earmarked for him. Cold spots and dark figures from around the farm looked back at us from the screens.

I caught him up on the case so far.

"What are the odds that Virgil got the girl's name right but was wrong about how she died?" I asked. "It seems just as likely she could have died in childbirth. Any kind of death certificate or news article would help right about now, but it's hard to scrape up documentation from the seventeen-eighties."

"You should contact Grant at the Historical Association," Calvin said, without looking up from a still image of the cold front that had crept across the foyer, the one that represented Bloody Betty—or Mildred, as the scarce evidence was beginning to indicate.

"He's in the loop. And he'll be at the Lathrop Grand ball tonight, hopefully with something new to add. And you're still invited."

"I'm not interested in balls, thank you," Calvin said. "You and Stacey make better representatives to the public than I ever could."

"I don't know about that. What are you looking at?" I gestured at the screens.

"Have you contained the haunting?" Calvin asked.

"Sure, but I'd call it patched, not fixed," I said. "If you have any suggestions about draining the swamp, you know, getting all the ghosts out of that cemetery so that even the most sensitive mediums can walk through there at night without getting harassed and possessed, I'm definitely all ears."

"Determine what's keeping them here," Calvin replied. "The natural course is for us to move on, not to linger around poking at a life we've outgrown and need to leave behind." He didn't look at me at all, just kept his gaze fixed on the screen. It seemed like he was making an effort to avoid eye contact.

"Are you talking about the Neville case, or something else?" I asked.

"I forgot to offer you coffee." Calvin gestured at the coffee maker on the worktable—the old-fashioned green coffee maker that looked like it dated back to 1982, not the newer espresso machine I'd added more recently. The pot was full of something that looked like black tar. "I made coffee," he added.

"I've had your coffee before, and I'd rather not watch my heart explode out through my chest, but thanks."

He didn't even give a fake smile for my lame joke, just kept looking at the screens as if there were something new to see there. He hadn't looked at me since I'd arrived, in fact.

"Calvin?" I said. "What are you not telling me?"

He finally did look at me, his eyes wrinkled and tired behind his glasses, his hair thin, gray, and unkempt, nothing like the crisp and formal look he'd always had as a cop. He wasn't yet sixty but looked older than that, his thin body slumping in his wheelchair.

The look he gave me was one of resignation...and maybe apology.

"No," I said. "No, Calvin, come on."

"You know I've been wrestling with this for weeks. It wasn't easy."

"That's why you wanted to speak to me before Stacey got here," I said.

"I thought it might be a little more personal for you. She is still relatively new."

"While I've been at this since I was fifteen. Not that it ultimately mattered to you, did it?"

"Lori was five when the divorce happened," Calvin said. "Then they moved away. I missed most of her childhood, Ellie. Neither of them wanted anything to do with me, the crazy man who spent all his free time in the haunted attics of old houses, wrestling with spirits of the dead. Sometimes things followed me home from work."

"Not puppies, I'm guessing," I said, thinking of all the protections Calvin had insisted I hang around my apartment.

"My daughter wants me back in her life. This baby she's having...it's like a second chance for me. There won't be a third."

"Do you really have to pack it up and move?" I asked.

"I don't want to see her only in pictures. I had enough of that with Lori's childhood. And, let's be honest, it's not as if I've been much help here lately. You operate independently, Ellie. You haven't needed me in some time. Or hadn't you noticed?"

"I hadn't noticed because it's not true. I depend on everyone around me. Jacob, even Stacey a little bit...but mostly you. You taught me everything. You're still teaching me. Even right now, I'm not sure how to handle this case."

"You know how," he said. "You always do. Lower your head and keep pushing until you find a way. That's the only answer there is."

"Tell me you're not really moving away." I tried to look calm and not as mentally unbalanced as I was beginning to feel. "You can't just leave out of nowhere."

"I've been preparing you for weeks," Calvin said. He was staring at the screens again, not facing me.

"You were always planning to do it," I said. "From the first time they offered to buy the agency."

"I'm doing what's best for all of us." He finally looked in my direction. "You'll still have your job, and I'll be paying you a bonus as soon as the sale goes through—"

"Forget the bonus. You're obviously more desperate for money than I am." I turned away and left the room, passing through our ratty little lobby on the way to the broken, uneven parking lot outside. My eyes were burning, and I didn't want him to see it.

After my parents died in the fire, Calvin had been the one who'd told me the truth. He'd encountered the dark side of our city a number of times during his time as a homicide detective. He discovered the name of my parents' murderer: Anton Clay, a handsome and wealthy cotton trader who'd first burned down a house in the same location in 1841. It had been a sizable plantation house, and Anton had an affair with the young wife of the older man who owned the house. After she ended the affair, Anton had slipped in one night and burned down the house, killing her, her three children, her husband, three slaves, and himself.

Since 1841, five more houses had been built in the same general location. The last one was my parents' house. I'd barely survived the fire. The lot had been abandoned, which meant Anton was trapped and contained in the earth there. Calvin had assured me it was too dangerous for me to face Anton.

I still visited the place occasionally. It had become a weedy lot barricaded behind a saggy wooden fence, without much sign of my parents' house left to see. Sometimes I could sense Anton's presence, though. Sometimes I could see him, watching me through the fence.

If we caught a dangerous ghost, the best we could do was bury the ghost trap in a distant, abandoned graveyard with the ghost still inside. If the ghost managed to eventually slip out of the trap, the psychological force of the old walls or fence would keep the spirit inside with the dead, where it belonged. As long as the site of my old house remained undisturbed, Anton Clay was just as trapped. The place was a graveyard itself, after all, the earth full of the remains of all those who'd burned to death there over the years. The ashes of Anton and all his victims, including my parents, were mixed deep into the soil by now.

I burst out through the front door, passing Stacey, who was just arriving to spend the afternoon sorting through the hundreds of hours of video and audio we'd captured from around the farm.

Stacey was scowling.

"Jacob wants to be Martian Manhunter," Stacey said. "Do you even know who that is? Because I don't. He says it goes with Supergirl, but I think..." Stacey trailed off, noticing that I was ignoring her and stalking toward my car, trembling with too many emotions. "Ellie? What's wrong?"

I didn't answer, because answering would mean letting her hear my voice break; it would mean letting everything out. I had to keep all of it inside or none of it. There was no middle way.

I climbed into my Camaro—a black 2002 model, a present my dad had bought for himself not long before he died. I was going to drive that car until the wheels fell off. The fire hadn't left much to remember my parents by. Everything had been consumed, from photo albums to Christmas decorations, everything that had meant anything to us as a family. The car and what was left inside it were all that remained.

My car was pointed downtown, but I didn't have any specific destination in mind. My mind was spinning.

I had a degree in psychology, but you didn't need one of those to see that Calvin had taken on a surrogate father role for me in the intervening years, teaching me to become a ghost hunter. Now I was losing him, too, just as I'd lost my real parents. Only he wasn't being killed by some evil ghost with the power to start fires, or anything beyond his control. Calvin was choosing to go.

Of course he was. I wasn't his real daughter, after all, and I'd more or less forced him to accept me into his life with relentless persistence over the years. After my parents died, I lived in Virginia with my aunt Clarice and her family until I finished high school. Then I'd returned to Savannah for college. Poor Clarice was dismayed—my grades had led to acceptance at University of Virginia and a few other places where she'd made me submit applications. I didn't care, because I wanted to go home. Calvin had started his own detective agency by then, specializing in the paranormal. As soon as I moved back, I started showing up every day, pressuring him into taking me on as an apprentice.

I thought we'd grown close over the years, but I suppose blood is thicker. He was leaving, and I would be completely alone.

Almost.

When I reached a long red light, I picked up my phone and called Michael. I wanted to forget about my problems for a while, and he had comfort and strength to offer. I needed him.

Chapter Fourteen

Michael picked me up for last-minute Halloween shopping. When I opened my door, he smiled and lifted me from my feet, giving me a fairly high-pressure and hungry kiss, like he'd been missing me. I wrapped my arms around his neck, kissing him back twice as hard. Maybe I'd been missing him, too, or maybe I was just desperate for contact, affection, whatever he could offer.

"It's good to see you," I whispered as he lowered me, almost reluctantly, to my feet.

"It's been a long time," he said, brushing his fingers along my cheek. His fingers almost glowed with heat, or maybe his touch summoned it from inside me...more likely, though, it was just residual fever from his illness.

"Just a few days," I said. "You don't have to be so dramatic about it. You're the one who was avoiding me."

He stared at me, his green eyes smoldering. I thought he was about to say something, but actually he kissed me again and drew me tight against him. I could feel his muscles through his thin cotton shirt, his scratchy denim jeans, and for a while I forgot everything outside that moment.

It was a while later when we finally emerged from my apartment.

"I thought of an amusing costume for you," Michael said as we descended through the brick stairwell away from my apartment, down one story to the parking lot.

"Oh, 'amusing'?" I asked. "That's an amusing word choice for you. Are you making fun of me?"

"You could dress as one of those Ghostbuster ladies."

"How creative. And you could dress as a firefighter."

"I already have the attire."

"Right. The attire. Weirdo." I climbed into his truck as he held the door open for me. He drives a shiny red Chevrolet pick-up from 1949 that he restored himself. The truck has a curvy, bubbly old-fashioned shape, complete with running boards, and is kind of adorable. As with the mechanized clocks he repairs and refurbishes, Michael's mechanical talents seem to incline toward things that are very old.

"Don't worry," he said. "We'll be going to a place where nothing's weird: the Halloween store." He closed my door and walked around to the driver's side.

I was glad to be with Michael, since he was one person who wasn't leaving me. Calvin's news had stirred up painful thoughts of my parents, but I hadn't even begun to think about the other consequences—strangers owning the agency.

My future would be in the hands of those people I'd briefly met from the bizarre and multifaceted corporation Paranormal Solutions, Inc. In order of how much they seemed to dislike me, from most hateful to least, they included: Kara Volkova, a waify-looking creature who hated me for ruining her important assignment while resolving a case; Octavia Lancashire, the sour-looking older woman who'd been introduced to me as a 'general director' of the company; and Nicholas Blake, a psychic investigator who was dangerously close to charming at times, and certainly had been effective at helping me against the particularly violent hive of ghosts that had inhabited the top floor of the Lathrop Grand Hotel. He'd even asked me out. I'd declined; I didn't trust any of them, even if they'd helped me clean up the supernatural mess at the old hotel.

I tried to refocus my thoughts on the short term. Tonight, we would go to the Lathrop Grand and have fun. I would be with Michael and Stacey. I'd known each of them for less than a year, yet they were now the two people who were closest to me in my life. That's kind of sad. It certainly doesn't say much for my overall social skills.

We drove to one of those pop-up Halloween stores that appear in strip malls around September and vanish again in November, as if by some sort of retail black magic. This particular shop inhabited a large vacant area that had obviously been a supermarket in its past life, and now it was a shopping maze approaching Swedish-furniture-store levels of complexity. Past the brightly colored kiddie costumes lay a dark, twisting warren of aisles hung with masks and murder weapons. Bats on wires and skeletons on chains swung from the high ceiling.

"Superheroes are out," I said, my gaze lingering on a Chris Hemsworth-as-Thor life-size cutout guarding one aisle with his massive hammer. "That's what Stacey and Jacob are doing."

"And what would you prefer? Something terrifying? Guaranteed to induce nightmares?" Michael pointed to an impish figure chained behind fake prison bars in what had once been a produce display. The bars and the figure's ragged clothes glowed green under a black light. Its face was a buck-fanged Nosferatu mask, positioned to stare at us as we walked by.

"Something classic," I said. An Egyptian sarcophagus opened inside what had once been a glass meat-counter display at the old grocery store. A pretty gross green mummy rose halfway out of it, greeting us with a tinny recorded scream. Then it dropped back into place.

"It doesn't get much more classic than mummies," he said. "They're ancient history. Or I could dress as a Trojan." He indicated a plastic suit of golden armor with a big red mohawk on the helmet.

"Nope."

"Here's a thought." Michael lifted a detailed latex face from a pantheon of ancient gods and heroes hung along one side of the aisle. It was the goat-god Pan, with a thick, curly beard and dark latex horns. Michael drew it over his face. The god's tongue leered out through open jaws, waggling obscenely in my direction.

Michael's eyes glinted within the god's eye holes, reflecting the glowing plastic torches around us. The aisle was momentarily empty of other shoppers, leaving us alone with masks of Medusa and the three-headed hellhound Cerberus.

"Pan's coming for you," Michael rasped, making his voice hoarse and deep. The god's permanently open mouth seemed to amplify it like one of those big masks used in ancient Greek drama. Michael moved toward me, raising both arms.

"Stop it," I said.

"You can't stop a goat-god who knows what he wants..." He stalked closer, forcing me to grab a big plastic trident from the Neptune-and-mermaids display and jab it at him to stave him off.

"Get back!" I snapped. "Bad primitive deity!"

He charged, and I turned and ran, feeling annoyed with him but also weirdly giddy. I rounded a corner into what looked like the Ye Olde Renaissance Faire section. Crowns, jester hats, princess dresses, shields and two-person dragon costumes hung on display walls topped with cardboard castle-wall borders. Red battery-powered torches lit the way.

Michael grabbed for me again, heedless of the little cluster of startled middle-school kids over by the Harry Potter knockoff costumes. I ducked under Michael's swinging arm. My kickboxing lessons took over and I landed my sneaker in his side, which sent him stumbling into a rotating rack of medieval weapons. Battle axes and spiked maces spilled all over the floor. One of the middle-school girls decided to scream, then they all screamed, boys and girls, and ran away round the next corner of the mazelike arrangement of aisles. We couldn't have been that scary. The kids probably just wanted an excuse to scream and run.

Michael seemed to snarl beneath the mask. While he was still stumbling and regaining his balance, I grabbed the Pan mask by both horns and yanked it off his head.

"Ow!" He scowled at me and grabbed at his head. "You ripped out some hair with that."

"Sorry, but you're evil when you're disguised as a horned god."

"And you're pretty violent when you're shopping," he said, rubbing his ribs where I'd kicked him.

"Beating you up was just a quick reflex," I told him. "I couldn't help it."

"Because I scared you so much?" He smiled.

"I've faced much scarier things than you," I said. "And defeated them. I'm pretty sure I sent a few of them right to Hell, assuming it exists."

"You won't take me so easily," he said.

"We'll see."

I watched him suspiciously, not entirely sure whether I was playing or actually feeling suspicious. He was acting odd today, but maybe he was just trying too hard to be funny. Off his game. Or maybe I was off my game and failing to behave like a normal person in a normal social setting. That seemed pretty likely.

I didn't want to think about it too much. I just wanted to enjoy my day off and pretend that my life wasn't full of problems. Was that really too much to ask? It would be great if my brain would stop working overtime in search of problems—analyzing and criticizing every single interaction between Michael and me, for example, looking for signs that I was running him off, or that he was going to leave me, as people so often do. Fifteen or twenty minutes of mental peace every now and then, that's all I ask.

We cleaned up the mess we'd made before moving on. The next aisle offered an array of science fiction masks and costumes, from *Star Wars* knockoffs (I saw "Chawbacco" and "Hans Sulu") to huge masks that looked like the aliens from *Alien* and the predators from *Predator*. Motion detectors activated strobe lights, *pew-pew* laser sound effects, and weird wormy extraterrestrial creatures that hissed as we walked by. Flying saucers hovered overhead.

"There's no choppa to rescue us," I said, looking up at the tiny spaceships.

Michael nodded, looking puzzled but not asking what I meant. At least he didn't try to insist on dressing as Flash Gordon, or dare to point out the Princess Leia slave-girl outfit. I would have jabbed him with a light saber for that.

We passed through a narrow gap at the end of the aisle, thick with fake spiderwebs, and into a dim, cave-like dungeon environment. A werewolf head snarled at us from inside a cage. A sickeningly realistic corpse was chained to some kind of arcane torture device made up of wheels and spikes. Recorded screams played around us. Demon and devil heads watched from the walls, with small red Christmas lights glowing inside their slitted eyes. More red firelight glowed among black cardboard stalagmites and stalactites.

"This is pleasant," Michael commented. "Homey."

"Sure, if you're the devil," I said.

"Have you ever met him?" Michael asked.

"Who? The devil?"

"With your job, I thought it might have come up."

"I've seen weird stuff, but never a devil. I've met some ghosts who seemed like devils, though—"

A pale, glowing blue shape emerged from the shadows above, cackling with high-pitched laughter. Its empty black eye holes and formless black smear of a mouth reminded me of many specters I've seen.

I gasped as I stepped back, my hand reaching for the tactical flashlight on my utility belt, except of course it wasn't there. I don't go out in public wearing a utility belt equipped with flashlight holsters and other ghost-related gear, and that way people don't stare at me like I'm a lunatic.

Michael caught me from behind, slipping his arms around me. I felt him shaking, and then I realized he was laughing.

The glowing blue sheet-ghost, suspended on a thin cable that wasn't visible in the darkness overhead, turned and rolled back the way it came, still cackling. It was just another decoration activated by a motion detector.

"Is that one of those much scarier things you bragged about defeating?" Michael asked.

"The face was realistic. For a second." I tried to pull away from him, but he held me firm. I smiled, and my head was turned away from him, so I didn't bother trying to hide it. "I saw a dead man just the other night with eyes like that."

"Should I be jealous?" he asked, and I laughed. I was feeling a little giddy now, between the momentary scare and getting trapped in Michael's arms.

A couple of teenagers rounded the corner and gave us disgusted looks as they passed, as if they'd just left the Victorian age and found our embrace to be an affront to society itself. More shoppers followed, so we moved on, trying to behave more like adults.

The next aisle was brighter, and the costumes more densely packed, as if the store were growing desperate to sell you something, anything, before you reached the check-out counters. All kinds of costume sets were jammed together—clowns, police officers, prisoners. The costumes offered for women included the obligatory sexy-cat and sexy-nurse costumes, but also some head-scratchers like a "sexy" Darth Vader with a black miniskirt, and a "sexy" Richard Nixon outfit with a mask, tie, and hot pants. Weird. The pickings for anything decent as well as inexpensive were pretty slim.

"How do you like this?" Michael grabbed a Founding Father costume, with a colonial-era wig and plastic waistcoat. It looked like something Hiram Neville would have worn. All he needed to add was a skull mask.

"That's a definite no," I said quickly.

"There's also this." He picked up another costume nearby, a basic pirate outfit with a hook, sword, and Jolly Roger hat. "I could be a pirate, you could be my captive princess. Look, we can get you some chains with this prisoner costume."

"I can't say I'm excited about playing the damsel in distress, even if it does involve chains," I said. "I'd rather be a pirate with you. A co-pirate."

"Co-pirate?" He seemed to puzzle over the word for half a second before nodding. "We could conquer the savage seas together."

"That's what I'm saying." I lifted a different pirate costume, though it was also from the men's side of the aisle, since I couldn't see myself wearing the skull-print plastic microskirt and Jolly Roger tank top offered as the only female pirate-costume option.

The pirate costume I picked came with a neat plastic telescope with a skull-and-bone design, which tucked into a holster on the black plastic belt. There was also a sizable stuffed parrot to mount on my shoulder, but it looked ungainly and I figured I would leave it off. The weapons included both a cutlass and a long-nosed plastic pistol.

"I can work with this," I said. "I'll just have to go home and get my boots."

We stood next to each other, looking at our reflections in the nearby mirror and holding our plastic-wrapped costumes out in front of us.

"We'll terrify high society tonight," Michael said with a smirk.

"I think they'll understand we aren't really pirates."

"Not after we swoop in and burn the place down."

"Not funny. At all."

"With charm, I meant. Metaphorically."

"So we're going with the pirate costumes, then? Because I can finally see the exit."

"Yes," Michael said. "And we'd better get out of here before the decorations scare you again."

"Ha."

"I think I see a roll of crepe paper sneaking up behind you."

"You did realize that my last laugh was sarcastic and not genuine, right?" I asked.

"We should just forget the ball," he said. "Spend the night together, away from everyone else."

"Be antisocial rather than go to a crowded party? Don't tempt me." I headed for the cash register with the shortest line. Michael stood close, his hand on the small of my back, seeming a bit more possessive than usual. After missing him for a few days, it felt reassuring.

Chapter Fifteen

The exterior of the Lathrop Grand hotel glowed with jack-o'-lanterns arrayed along the brickwork and the wrought-iron balustrade on the second floor. The pumpkins weren't carved with scary or silly faces, but incredibly elaborate little scenes depicting statues and landmarks from around the city. The hotel must have hired professionals to create them, or maybe students from the art school.

We passed through the lobby, toward the sound of a live jazz band in the ballroom. One doorman in a top hat, tails, and a simple skull mask took our invitation, which was printed on silky paper; a second identically dressed man opened the door to the ballroom for us.

The ballroom was crowded and loud with music and chatter. Lighting mostly came from actual candles in actual black candelabras, keeping the room full of shadows. The crowd dressed at the formal end of the Halloween spectrum, men in devil masks and black ties, women in fanciful ball gowns and feathered masks.

Plenty of jewelry glittered out there. I hoped I wasn't underdressed. I wore the plastic props from my store-bought costume—hat, sword, pistol, and even the ridiculous bird—but I'd replaced the cheapo plastic pirate coat and thin polyester pirate pants with real trousers and a blousy shirt from the thrift store.

Michael laid a hand on my back as he escorted me into the room. He looked down at me, one of his eyes hidden behind a black patch.

"Co-pirates," he whispered, and I smiled. I felt glad to have someone to lean on while going out into this crowd. I wasn't in the mood for small talk, chitchat, chewing the fat, or otherwise pretending that Calvin hadn't collapsed the world beneath my feet. Part of me, a very large part of me, wished I'd jumped on Michael's idea about forgetting the whole thing and staying home.

"Why, Ellie Jordan!" gushed a voice with a distinctly Texan accent. Madeline Colt, general manager of the Lathrop Grand and our former client, emerged from the crowd. She wore a black cocktail dress and a very realistic-looking black tarantula clip in her platinum blond hair. "Aren't you just the prettiest little buccaneer in the room?"

"I think that title might go to my date. Do you remember Michael Holly?"

"Oh, yes." Madeline took his offered hand but held it rather than shaking it. She looked up into his eyes in a very friendly way. Get yourself a hot firefighter boyfriend and you can deal with that look from other women every time you go out somewhere, too. "How could I forget that night? And the aftermath has been so hectic."

"Are the fourth floor renovations coming along?" I asked. The top floor of the hotel had been closed for a century, and I'd more or less burned and then flooded that area in the course of clearing out the wicked ghosts up there. It wasn't entirely my fault, because it was a pyrokinetic ghost we were facing. That's my absolute least favorite kind, considering one of them murdered my family. I'd rather deal with a shapeshifting demonic—even one that takes the form of my best friend or my cat so it can get right up close before it claws my face off—than a fire-starter.

"We're remodeling it into six top-flight suites," she said. "They should be ready before Christmas, and they will be the very best accommodations in town."

"No more supernatural troubles?" I asked.

"If there are still any ghosts here, sugar, they're quieter than a church mouse at a golf tournament. Our only complaints have been from guests who want to see ghosts but don't. The news stories have drawn so many people."

The Lathrop Grand had made a big splash in national news for a day or two. We'd found a concealed room filled with grisly evidence of the hotel's secret history. The bones and antiquated rusty implements hauled out of the old luxury hotel by the authorities made for prime news footage, especially accompanied by tales of ghosts and old murders, especially when the story broke at the beginning of October as Halloween season was creeping in.

"It sounds like business hasn't suffered much, despite the dead bodies and everything."

"Oh, no, sugar. We've got more ghost tourists than ever, coming in from all over the world. We had to raise the ticket prices for the Halloween ball just to stem the demand. I don't have the heart to tell the guests all the ghosts have gone. Who knows? Maybe Abigail will come back for a visit. Her room's still here if she does." Madeline winked.

"I'm glad it's going well." I couldn't say the same about my own job. I almost asked her whether the Lathrop Grand was hiring. It had to beat whatever was coming at the detective agency with the new ownership.

"Oh, look, it's George Fountain," Madeline said, her voice hushed. "He's one of the Black Diamond bigwigs. If you'll excuse me just jiffy-quick while I speak to my boss..."

"Of course. It was nice to see you, Madeline." I almost called her *Mildred* after the bloody-girl ghost we were investigating.

"Oh, you, too, sugar. And you, honey." She patted Michael's bicep and walked away toward a rotund man in a Brooks Brothers suit and elephant mask.

"So that was half the people I know here," I said to Michael. "Let me know if you see Grant Patterson. And what's taking Stacey so long?" I checked my phone, but there was no message from her.

"I don't know about Stacey and Jacob, but I think I see

Liberace over there." Michael nodded toward a man in a glittered, gilted, powder-blue coat and huge white wig not dissimilar from the one worn by the ghost of Hiram Neville, only much larger, cleaner, and curlier, tied with a giant blue ribbon that matched the blue coat.

"Grant!" I approached with a smile of relief. I felt like a complete stranger here, although with everyone wearing masks, it was hard to tell.

"My dear," Grant said, looking over my costume and then Michael's. "You look like a dangerous pair of ruffians."

"That's exactly what we are," Michael said, drawing out the *are*, in dorky pirate fashion.

"And you look ready to attend a ball far more extravagant than this one," I said.

"If only one were available," Grant said. He indicated the man beside him, dressed as Zorro, who looked to be around Grant's age or younger, maybe somewhere in his late forties or early fifties. It can be hard to estimate around a black Zorro mask. "Have you met my friend Jack Taylor? You may not recognize him in his traditional vigilante attire. He's fresh from protecting innocent Mexican peasants against their avaricious landlords."

"I'm usually found playing the avaricious landlord instead of the hero, sadly." Taylor shook my hand and Michael's. I did know Taylor, or at least his family, and they did indeed own a great deal of real estate around the city. He must have heard of me, too, because he added: "So you're the one who's inherited Calvin Eckhart's position, defending the city against all that goes bump in the night?"

"That's me."

"I may need to call you," Taylor said. "We have a few properties that could stand to be less haunted. And who is your pirate captain?" He looked at Michael with interest.

"We're actually co-pirates," Michael said.

"The young gentleman is Michael Holly," Grant said. "One of Savannah's finest."

"I'm with the fire department, actually," Michael said. "Not the police."

"I have often found fireman to be a bit finer than police officers, in my experience," Grant said.

"And you've had plenty of that," Taylor said to Grant, who narrowed his eyes just slightly in response.

"I'm so glad you're here, Grant," I said. "I feel a little out of place at these society things."

"Society? What society?" Taylor looked around as though I'd just mentioned that a wild, rabid wolf was stalking through the crowd.

"Not Savannah society, certainly," Grant told me. "The attendees I've met are mostly tourists, in town for the haunted holidays. They may be high-dollar tourists, but this ball is far too new and well-advertised to attract the old families."

"Present company excepted?" I asked, looking from Grant Patterson to Jack Taylor, both of them belonging to lineages that could be traced back to eighteenth-century Savannah.

"Oh, yes, we have come precisely to escape the tedium of the usual crowd and embrace the joys of anonymous celebration with strangers," Grant said.

"Really?" I grew more comfortable as I saw the crowd in a new light. They weren't a society where I didn't belong. They weren't a society at all, just an accumulation of travelers who didn't know anyone here any more than I did. I might as well have been a tourist from out of town myself. That thought made me smile, maybe at the idea of going on an actual vacation, which I hadn't done since my parents died.

"I like this party," Taylor said, looking over the crowd with their masks and pricey clothes. Some danced near the stage, where the jazz band played a tune so fast I was amazed the dancers could keep up with it. Others cruised the buffet, where servers in formal black and white attire and animal masks served shrimp and oysters on silver. The ballroom's heavy curtains had been drawn over the floor-to-ceiling windows to create a darker and more private environment.

"It's very *Masque of the Red Death*," Grant said. "Let's be sure to leave before thirteen o' clock."

Michael accepted two champagne flutes from a passing waitress in a unicorn mask. He passed one to me. I sipped and tried not to wince at the intensely sugary taste. I didn't want to look too uncultured if I could avoid it.

"Did you have anything else for me, Grant?" I asked. "Something to do with colonial-era farmers or horsemen?"

"Ah, as a matter of fact...you owe a debt of gratitude to one Ethel Wisenbaker of the Georgia Salzburger Society. She is in charge of the group's genealogical research. For a ninety-one-year-old, she's quite feisty. At any rate, she has been in communication with librarians at Franklin and Marshall College in Pennsylvania, which has an archive of Hessian-related materials, as well as the Hessisches Staatsarchiv in Germany...and we may have tracked down a name for your horseman."

"No! How?"

"The Hessians occupying Savannah naturally developed relationships and communications with locals over time. These particularly included the Salzburgers who created the town of New Ebenezer—German immigrants. The town lay inland from Savannah, north along the river."

"Close to where my clients live?" I asked.

"Your clients are a bit farther inland," he said. "However, New Ebenezer, as a town full of Germans, would have been a natural stopping point for German deserters slipping away from Savannah. Many Hessian soldiers were impressed into service, you understand —young men drafted into the armies of their German princes back home. They weren't necessarily eager to die for any cause."

"And our horseman was rumored to be a deserter," I said. "The war was still in full swing when he was robbing people on the highways, and when he killed Mildred."

"There was a particular detail that might be of interest. Colonel Friedrich von Porbeck, as you perhaps already know, was the Hessian commander in charge of Savannah. He wrote frequent reports to his masters in Germany, which have been archived. I have here one that may interest you." Grant reached into his voluminous powder-blue coat and drew out a few sheets of paper neatly folded together.

I opened the pages eagerly, then frowned. They looked like faxes of photocopies of pictures of faded old handwriting. I had some difficulty reading it, and eventually determined that my difficulty stemmed from the fact that they were in German.

"Um," I said. "Thanks?"

"Here, the officer recounts a case of a certain deserter," Grant said. "Josef Bracke, a private who deserted along with others while out on patrol in 1780. The commanding officer listed six names besides Bracke's. Two were caught and executed, and four were never seen again by the Hessian officers, but Bracke was a special case. His body appeared some months later, dumped in a bag on the road outside the German settlement of New Ebenezer, with an unsigned proclamation that he'd been a thief and a murderer on the roads of Georgia and South Carolina. That was believable enough, as the roads had their share of bandits during the war, with no stable government to control them.

"So, in that missive you hold, the officer naturally derides the deserters and cowards, and he sheds no tears for Josef Bracke or any of the others. Bracke was identified by the other Hessians. His body had bullet holes and more than a dozen stab wounds; someone had really gone to work on him. Eventually he was buried with no marker, most likely outside the walls of the church cemetery in Ebenezer. Many people were hastily buried there during the war."

"*Outside* the walls?" I asked, and Grant nodded, looking amused by the intensity of my interest. "And who brought Josef's body to the town? Why?"

"Whoever killed him, presumably," Grant said. "As for the why—well, the Hessian was German, so the body was left at the only German town in the area. It could be as simple as that. Perhaps those who killed him hoped the body would be interred with some semblance of piety, but did not wish to foot the expense themselves."

"Why? To keep the ghost from coming back and seeking revenge on his killers?" I asked.

"That is a possibility. You're the expert in supernatural matters."

"What else do we know about Josef Bracke?"

"There doesn't seem to be a great deal to know. He was a peasant child in Germany, probably drafted into military service. He was nineteen when he died. The officer comments on the unusual nature of the situation. Hessian deserters, if not caught and killed, typically hightailed it out of state, usually trying to reach the much larger German community in Pennsylvania, where they could hope to blend in. But Josef was still in the area six months later."

"Robbing travelers," I said.

"So claims the note pinned to his corpse. The Hessians in the area were focused on maintaining the British occupation and patrolling the state in search of Patriot activity. Josef and his friends may have become well-acquainted with the roads, plantations, and traffic prior to their desertion."

"Information that would have been useful during his later career as a highwayman," I said. "So we might have identified Bloody Betty's killer, finally."

"Pardon?" Grant asked.

"Mildred Neville," I said. "We called her something else before we learned her real name. All of this fits with what the local history buff told us." I winced as I heard the word *buff* escape my lips. "After Josef killed Mildred, Hiram Neville and his sons and neighbors and so on formed a posse and searched the roads until they found Josef. Either he resisted or they just killed him on sight."

"Such a posse would have been easily created in those days," Grant said. "Landowning males were expected to participate in regular patrols, primarily for the purpose of catching runaway slaves, sadly. Mr. Neville had only to rouse the existing local patrol to his cause if he needed assistance finding Josef."

"Are all their conversations like this?" Jack Taylor asked Michael, with an amused smile curling under his Zorro mask.

"Yes, it's mostly stories of murder, betrayal, and war," Michael said.

"How dramatic," Taylor said.

"Ghosts can be total drama queens," I told him. To Grant, I said, "I think this really helps complete the picture. Thanks. I just wish I could read German..." I frowned at the pages Grant had handed me.

"Oh, yes. There's another debt you owe Ethel Wisenbaker of the Salzburger Society." From the interior pocket of his coat, he brought out two more folded pieces of paper. "Translated. And typed, on what I would guess to be an old Underwood typewriter, judging by the thickness and kearning of the letters."

"Thank you!" I pocketed the English translation, feeling happy to have made some progress on the case. I would have to write a long thank-you note to this Ethel Wisenbaker.

That happy feeling soon faltered, though, when Supergirl arrived alone. I went to greet Stacey, who just looked worried and confused.

"Jacob had some kind of family emergency, but he said to go ahead to the party and he would catch up." She looked around the crowd. "He's not here, is he?"

"Not unless he's hiding from me," I said. "What kind of emergency?"

"I don't know. I hope it's not serious."

"It can't be too serious if he's still planning to come."

"I guess. He hasn't returned any of my texts since. It's been a few hours."

"He'll be fine. Hey, Grant's here, and he has some news about our Hessian horseman..."

The band played on, and we waited for Jacob to arrive. Michael somehow convinced me to go out onto the dance floor. I don't know how; he must have slipped something into my champagne. I didn't really know what I was doing, but he guided me at every step, keeping time with the band, and he even spun me and somehow I didn't crash to the floor.

"What are you doing?" I asked.

"Dancing?" he asked, looking puzzled.

"Yeah, exactly. Did you go to dance camp or something? Since when can you dance like this?"

"Have we ever danced before?"

"That's not the point."

"I had dance lessons years ago," he said.

"I can't see you signing up for that."

"They weren't entirely my choice," he said. "I would have rather been out riding horses, or shooting rifles..."

"Right. Because you grew up on a dude ranch."

When the song ended, I sent him to dance with Stacey instead, since her date still hadn't arrived and she was more into dancing anyway. Something was still off about Michael, but it wasn't something I wanted to dwell on tonight. He was recovering from a fever, I reminded myself.

I decided life might begin to feel more normal if I took a break and ate something. At the buffet, I picked up tiger shrimp, ultrathin slices of rare beef, and slivers of baby carrots cooked in butter. I don't know why they bothered to sliver the carrots; they were small enough to begin with.

Michael and Stacey remained on the dance floor, both of them looking cute and happy for the moment. I watched them as I stood and ate in a comfortable little shadowy nook where a tall potted plant kept me company. I didn't want to be here, but definitely didn't want to be alone with my thoughts, or my dread of Calvin leaving and throwing me to the sharks on his way out.

It slowly dawned on me that I seemed to be crawling toward a new low, between losing the people I had and feeling distant from those who remained. I had an urge to visit my parents' grave site—not so much the official one with the headstones, but the real one, where our house had once stood. I'd seen glimpses of their murderer, but never of my parents. I supposed it meant they'd moved on. That was always for the best, of course. Still, of all the ghosts I've seen, it would have been nice to have encountered one of theirs—maybe just once, long ago, before they'd left forever.

Watching Stacey in her red cape and high boots, I thought about how Supergirl, like Superman before her, had access to a couple of holograms of her dead parents so she could speak to them whenever she needed advice. Sounds pretty great to me. When I have difficult questions, all I have is my cat, and he never has any answers for me.

A cute-looking guy in devil horns and a tuxedo took my arm and tried to escort me toward the dance floor. I pulled away, mumbling something about having a horrible case of leprosy. He gave me an annoyed look but left me alone.

Chocolates were available at the end of the buffet, several varieties, slivered into thin leaves like everything else. I made my way there and accepted some nearly transparent slices of dark and white chocolate, and a little bit of truffle.

"You've had so much to eat tonight," a voice said behind me. "You must have been starving."

I recognized her accent, originating somewhere far east of Berlin. I turned to see a waify girl with big blue eyes and sharp cheekbones—Kara Volkova, an investigator with Paranormal Solutions, who did not like me at all. Her eyes seemed to coldly assess my hair, costume, and shoes, and one side of her lip curled in a slight sneer. While I wore a thrift-store blouse and plastic sword, her own outfit looked like it cost a thousand bucks, a black cocktail dress accented with gold and diamonds at her fingers and ears. She held a white, expressionless porcelain mask painted with pastel flowers on one side. The disdain was clear on her face.

"It always impresses me how much American women can eat," Kara continued, clearly not trying to endear herself to me tonight. "Is this your third trip to the buffet?"

"Second," I said, forcing a smile and hating that I could feel my cheeks flush with embarrassment. I had nothing to be embarrassed about, I told myself, but the sardonic twist of her lips and the knowing look in her eyes made me doubt it. "I didn't know you would be here tonight," I said, hoping to shift to bland small talk and then make my escape.

"We thought it would be amusing," Kara said. "We were in town, anyway. Preparing to take over your agency, you might remember."

"I'd almost forgotten," I said.

"And shopping for a flat." That was another voice that I recognized, too, even though it came from a boxy, metallic-looking monstrosity that enclosed the head of a man in a classic black tuxedo. It has a British accent—Nicholas Blake, also from Paranormal Solutions, and from whom I'd very reluctantly accepted help on the Lathrop Grand case. "We may rent a house instead. They're remarkably inexpensive in this city."

"Because most of them are haunted. So the two of you are...?" I waggled my eyebrows.

Kara looked at me with even more disdain, if that were possible. "We are *not* involved with each other."

"You don't have to look so offended about it. You might hurt his feelings." I watched as Nicholas turned an oversized screw in the gray monstrosity of a torture device he wore over his head. "And who are you supposed to be? The Terminator after his face burns off?"

"The Man in the Iron Mask," Nicholas said, pulling the mask apart in two large pieces to reveal his own face, haughty as ever, unable to smile without it coming across as a condescending smirk. Or maybe he just never smiled and always smirked. His eyes seemed to momentarily darken as he looked at me.

"You're a Dumas fan?" I asked.

"This time next year, we might all come as the Three Musketeers," he said. He glanced at Stacey across the room. "Of whom there were four."

"Yeah, I don't know about that," I said. "So PSI is sending both of you to, uh..." I looked from him to Kara.

"Transition your firm into a fully functioning subsidiary, compliant with all company standards," Nicholas finished with a wink. His gaze drifted down over me, taking in my costume, in a way that at least seemed less judgmental than the looks Kara had given me. Last time we'd seen each other, I'd ruined Kara's work and then turned down Nicholas's attempt to take me on a date. I expected some resentment from both of them, but Kara really seemed to have it in for me. I could see that in her icy stare. She was going to love having me under her thumb.

"I advise you to do exactly as you're told during this process," Kara said. "You do not want to make the situation difficult for us."

"Maybe I do want to do that," I said. "You don't know my motives."

"If you become an obstacle, we can make *your* situation difficult," she said, her accent sounding very Russian now. "We can punish you in ways you've never imagined—"

"Let's not begin with so much conflict," Nicholas said. "We've worked together well in the past. We can do it again. For the greater good, wouldn't you agree?" He took my hand in his, holding it just a little too tight for me to escape without difficulty. His fingers were soft, not rough with calluses like Michael's. "Perhaps we can discuss this more privately, Ellie. I can apprise you of the many changes we'll be bringing to your agency—all of them improvements, I promise."

"I can't wait to see what you're going to do to us," I said, laying on the sarcasm good and thick so it couldn't possibly slip past him.

"What's going on?" Michael asked as he arrived. Stacey was threading her way through the crowd behind him as he stalked toward us. Michael glowered, his jaw tight, definitely noticing that Nicholas was still gripping my hand. I couldn't tell whether his anger was directed mostly at Nicholas or mostly at me, but I was definitely getting some share of it.

Michael grabbed my arm as if to pull my hand from Nicholas's. For a moment, it seemed like they were going to play tug-of-war with my forearm. I could think of countless other places and situations where I would rather have been at that moment. Crawling into the sub-basement of an old mansion in search of a murderous ghost would have been more pleasant.

Michael and Nicholas glared at each other like a couple of primates ready to fight for alpha status. It was incredibly embarrassing for everyone involved, I think.

Then Nicholas let my fingers slide free as Michael pulled me away from him.

"We were having a friendly conversation, nothing more," Nicholas told him, smiling. "I will be Ellie's direct supervisor for the foreseeable future."

"Maybe you're not foreseeing clearly." Michael stepped closer to Nicholas, one hand balling into a fist at his side.

"Michael," I said. "Come on." There wasn't much point in them fighting, and I wasn't ready to lose my job this way. Not yet, anyway. So, for the moment, Nicholas did have a tight grip on me, whether he was actually touching me or not.

Kara gave me a sardonic little look, as if reading my mind and seeing my helplessness. Maybe she was. She'd been chosen by PSI to be voluntarily possessed by a spirit that was very important to them. That sounded like a job for someone with strong psychic ability. I suspected Nicholas was psychic, too, just by the way he looked at me, like he could see right through. Plus, I was pretty sure I'd seen different hues in his eyes, sometimes dark and sometimes light.

Maybe he just wore colored contacts. He seemed vain enough.

"She's mine," Michael said, with enough anger that I wondered if he'd been drinking a lot of alcohol while I wasn't looking. He didn't seem drunk, though. Just angry.

Nicholas backed away from him, looking amused, holding up his palms in surrender.

"My mistake," he said. "She is all yours, friend."

My phone rang. Grateful for the interruption, I fished it out of my woven-net purse, which looked like a small woven rope net. I had picked it as my most pirate-y purse, since it sort of looked like something you could catch fish with if you really had to.

It was the Old Walnut Inn, where Stacey and I had stayed. I frowned. We'd paid in full at checkout, and we hadn't done any damage to our rooms. Why would the motel be calling?

"Hello?" I said.

"Ellie?" The woman's voice on the other end trembled, and she seemed to have trouble catching her breath.

"Yes, it's Ellie. Who is this?"

"Amber. Whatever you did, Ellie, it wasn't so good—"

She was cut off, as though she'd dropped the phone, and then Jeremy's voice replaced hers.

"Whatever you did made it worse," he said, and his voice wasn't very steady, either. He spoke much more rapidly than I'd ever heard him. "They came after us. You provoked them, and they came after us."

"What happened?" I dashed away from the brewing confrontation—happy to do that, honestly—and hurried to escape the noisy, music-filled ballroom and found my way out to the enclosed brick courtyard behind the hotel. A number of guests had strayed out here, but the crowd was much thinner, and I could hear Jeremy more clearly.

"They wrecked our house," Jeremy said. "They drove us out."

"Mr. Neville, please tell me *exactly* what happened."

"It threatened the girls, right in her rooms."

"The bloody girl from the stairs?" I asked, drawing strange looks from a small group of partygoers. I moved into a little arbor to get away from them.

"No. The headless horseman. He's not headless, though—"

"Nobody ever said he was headless," Amber interrupted in the background.

"—he was a big black shadow. We all saw him. He went into Corrine's room, then into Maya's. The girls were screaming," Jeremy said.

"Is your family safe now?" I asked.

"We're all at the motel. The house is destroyed."

"I'm so sorry. Was anyone hurt? The kids? Amber?"

"Not physically. If there's anything you can do, now's the time," Jeremy said. "If you can't fix it, we're never going back. We'll just move. We'll lose everything, but I don't care."

"Hold tight. We're on our way."

As I hung up, Michael and Stacey reached the courtyard. Nicholas and Kara weren't with them, thankfully.

"You left in a hurry," Michael said, standing close and cupping my face in his hand, as if to show concern, or maybe possessiveness. His eyes burned into mine; he still seemed angry and uncharacteristically jealous. I wanted to be mad at him for treating my new bosses that way, but I couldn't. I mean, I hated them, too. He just needed to tone it down around them.

"I got bad news from the client," I said. "Stacey and I have to run."

"That wasn't the plan." Michael pulled me closer.

"Believe me, I preferred the original plan of spending my night off with you. I've been looking forward to it all week, but..." I turned to Stacey. "The horseman went on a rampage. It looks like those cranky, bad-tempered ghosts of Hiram and family were holding the Hessian in check."

"A Hessian?" Michael asked. "Interesting."

"I'll let you know how it all wraps up," I said.

"You aren't leaving without me," he said. "I'd like to see this haunted farm and this dangerous ghost on horseback. I could help."

"I promised myself I wouldn't drag you into my work anymore, Michael."

"Who's dragging? If anything, I'm dragging you. Let's get to work." His hand gripped my arm, making it clear that we'd be sticking together. Despite my protests, this made me happy. I was also happy to have any excuse to leave the ball right away—the presence of Kara and Nicholas had completely soured it for me.

Though it wasn't yet midnight, Stacey, Michael, and I fled the ball as if we were Cinderella expecting our coach to revert to pumpkin form. If Cinderella dressed like a pirate, or like Supergirl. I wondered if Stacey had picked the costume just as an excuse to buy the super-high red boots.

"So how are we going to stop the horseman again?" Stacey asked.

"Josef," I said. "His name is Josef Bracke. A Hessian mercenary, murderous highwayman, and an apparently angry and powerful ghost. And I have no idea how we're going to stop him."

Chapter Sixteen

"Just when we were finally getting some time away from this place," Stacey sighed as the Old Walnut Inn appeared, slouching on the side of the dark, desolate highway. The concrete building and paved-over parking lot looked as depressing as ever. The Circle Q convenience store beside it didn't look much more inviting, the outdoor fluorescent bars flickering and stuttering like a bug zapper in a swamp.

"Hopefully the family's overreacting," I said, slowing the van. "Clearly something happened, but it doesn't sound like anyone was seriously hurt. A quick glimpse of something supernatural can be enough to drive rational people into a panic."

"They said their home was wrecked."

"So the horseman can send out psychokinetic energy. Maybe just unfocused shockwaves. We don't know whether he can really focus it."

"But we know it means he's dangerous and could be strong enough to kill us," Stacey said.

"Yep, we definitely know that." I checked the side-view mirror. The round lights of Michael's antique truck glowed behind me. He'd seemed angry at me, maybe for getting distracted with work when it was supposed to be our first night together all week. I'd thought I had secured the clients' home, at least for the short term, but clearly I'd been way, way off about that.

Stacey and I had grabbed the cargo van full of gear from the office, but Michael had driven separately, mostly because nobody in their right mind would ride in the back of our cargo van for an hour.

I pulled into the motel parking lot and Michael parked alongside me, a little too close, as if he meant to pin me into place. I was barely able to open the driver-side door and wiggle my way out.

"Hey, great parking job," I told him. "You should work as a valet. Seriously."

Michael gave me a cold little stare, for just half a second, before breaking into a smile. Whatever. I would not apologize. His parking was undeniably sloppy.

"Yet he can be trusted to maneuver a fire truck?" Stacey asked.

"Those don't have to fit into parking spaces," I said. "They can park wherever they want."

We approached the motel room door in front of the family's big gray Suburban. In our rush to meet up with them, we hadn't had time to go home and change clothes—there had been enough stops along the way as it was, such as picking up the van and gear. Michael and I looked pretty absurd in our blousy pirate shirts, but Stacey had it even worse in her bright red and blue Supergirl costume. She'd borrowed a jacket from Michael that covered her to her hips, but there wasn't any hiding those thigh-high red boots.

I knocked, and Amber opened the door, leaning heavily on it. She looked exhausted. Her hair hung in a loose, careless ponytail, and her eyes were puffy and red as if she'd been crying.

"We came as fast we could," I said. It was a little past one in the morning. We had sped all the way to the motel, to the extent that the van was capable of speeding.

Amber nodded and led us inside. The rest of the family looked as bedraggled as she did—unkempt and upset, dressed in pajamas and tennis shoes. Little Maya huddled on one of the motel room's two saggy beds, leaning against her father with her face buried in his shoulder, her hair matted into red clumps. The boy, Castor, sat on Jeremy's other side, staring intently at a game on his tablet, as if desperate to escape into a world where angry birds were the biggest problem he had to face.

Corrine paced the room, dressed in checkered pajamas and a Nirvana t-shirt featuring a smiley face with the eyes X'ed out. Unlike her traumatized, quietly shaking siblings, Corrine seemed furious and ready to smash things, baring her teeth as she snapped at her mother.

"Did you tell them about the horses?" Corrine said. With eight people now crammed into the motel room, she had to truncate her pacing a bit. She pointed at me. "Who's going to save the horses? You? They're helpless. They're locked in their stalls and can't even run away if they want to. We should have let them out. Who's going to protect them?"

"What happened with the horses?" Stacey asked, looking almost as concerned as Corrine.

"Oh, nothing," Corrine said. "They were just screaming like, I don't know, somebody was out in the stable *attacking* them, maybe *torturing* them. But did we go to help them? No, Dad just made everybody get in the car and leave. I mean, who cares what happens to the horses, right?"

"Corrine, we're going straight to the farm after this," Stacey said. "I promise I'll check on them."

"We all care about the horses, Corrine," Amber said.

"Then why did we just leave them there? They're probably dead by now—"

Maya let out a little yowl as if in pain, and Jeremy hugged her close and scowled. "Corrine!" he snapped.

"Well, it's true! I'm going crazy in this stupid tiny hotel room. How long do we have to stay here? I have to get out of here, I feel bottled up," Corrine said.

"Why don't you run over to that convenience store before it closes? You could get us some snacks and drinks. And blow off some of that steam while you're at it," Amber said.

"Fine. I'll go get some stupid Doritos while nobody helps our horses." Corrine pulled on a shirt, jeans, and boots over her pajamas, then accepted some cash from her mom.

"Don't get anything with caffeine," Amber added while Corrine walked out, slamming the motel room door behind her. The place instantly felt calmer, as though a whirlwind had blown itself out.

"She's very worried about the horses," Jeremy told us, as if to clarify.

"I understand, and we will check on them for you." I briefly introduced Michael, and nobody complained about having a firefighter on board. Then I asked: "Can you tell us exactly what happened tonight?"

"It was late," Amber said. "About eleven. The kids were exhausted, because we took them over to Sylvania for trick-or-treating. The little shops downtown were giving out candy. This should have been our big weekend at the farm, you know, with Halloween and everything. There should have been hayrides, we were going to have a bonfire...instead, we're closed and out of business."

"We heard the crashes downstairs," Jeremy said. "They woke everybody up. The thing broke down our front door, wrecked some stuff down there, then came charging up the stairs. You know that system of bright lights and music you set up for us? Yeah, that didn't slow it down at all. It trashed everything in its way, broke all your lights. Then it rode into Corrine's room and threatened her. It had a big black sword in its hand. Then it went into Maya's room and threw her bed aside. I have to say, I think you failed to remove the threat from the ghosts."

"I'm really sorry. It sounds like locking up all the others may have cleared the way for the horseman," I said. "The horseman had never come near your house or done anything so destructive before, so we had no idea—"

"Is it ever going to be safe for us to go back?" Amber asked.

"We have a plan," I said. "We think we've identified the Hessian horseman; the way he died fits with an historical person named Josef Bracke. We stopped by where he's believed to be buried, which is just outside the graveyard walls in a ghost town called New Ebenezer. It was on the way here from Savannah. We collected earth from his burial site. Our plan is to set ghost traps around your farm and bait them with candles, the horseman's grave earth, and a couple of old silver coins that might attract him, either as a mercenary or as a thief. If we can lure him into a trap, we'll seal him inside and remove him from your property."

"And what if you can't?" Amber asked.

"Then we'll develop another plan of attack," I said. "And we'll keep at it until the horseman is gone." This last was delivered with more certainty than I really had. It was entirely possible we'd fail and the farm would end up as yet another abandoned, deserted property overrun with restless spirits. There seems to be at least one in every town. In many small towns, the ghosts are the only residents left, drifting among crumbling porches, sagging roofs, and empty roads.

Still, I wanted to inspire a little hope. If it turned out to be false hope, we could deal with that later.

The four family members looked up at me, all of them a little pale and desperate, shivering like animals who'd just managed to find shelter from a cold rainstorm. Maya stared at me mutely. Even Castor was looking up from his video game, and I had a sense he'd been listening more closely than he'd let on.

I felt the weight of my responsibility toward them—and more than a little guilt for mistakenly thinking we'd settled things for them, and attempting to enjoy a night off to myself.

I couldn't help thinking of my own family. At fifteen, I hadn't had the knowledge or skills to protect my parents from the vicious ghost of Anton Clay. Now that the horseman had shown off his well-hidden psychokinetic abilities, I knew I had to stop him.

It's my calling to stand at the border between life and death, sometimes helping the better spirits cross over, but more often trying to stop the evil ones from coming back. This family needed protection of a kind few people could offer. Even if they left the land, the ghost would remain to menace others, to claim more victims.

I thought of the violent crimes over the past couple of centuries on that stretch of road, and the various members of Jeremy's family accused and sometimes convicted of senselessly murdering travelers. I wondered whether the horseman had killed some or all of those travelers himself, on the road near the Neville farm, and Jeremy's ancestors had been blamed for them. From the cases I'd read about, Jeremy's ancestors usually pled not guilty, though that wasn't exactly clear evidence of anything.

Maybe the men of Jeremy's family weren't actually murderous at all, but haunted by a curse. The horseman Josef Bracke, having been killed by Hiram Neville, could have stayed close to the Neville farm over the generations, occasionally murdering people on the road, as he had in life. The descendants of his enemy Hiram were accused of these crimes and punished. The horseman was carrying out a centuries-old vendetta.

And over the years, Hiram and those who'd been wrongly accused had remained in and around the cemetery, perhaps waiting for justice, perhaps doing what they could to keep the dead Hessian horseman away from their living descendants.

On the other hand, I couldn't count on the dead Neville men as allies, either. They'd strongly indicated that they didn't consider Jeremy and his wife and children to be their family members at all.

"We should get going," I said. "Hopefully we can catch the ghost while he's still active tonight."

"He's angry," Maya said, speaking for the first time since we'd arrived. "The man on the horse. He's angry at somebody."

"Do you happen to know who he's angry at?" I asked.

Maya shook her head. "Can you make him go away?"

"We're going to try," I told her. "I promise."

The family didn't look as though they had much faith in us as they watched us leave the motel room. I couldn't say I blamed them.

Stacey and I were subdued under the weight of the task ahead and the family depending on us to get it right.

"This farm sounds like an adventure," Michael said. He seemed in better spirits than us as he walked to his truck. I waited for him to back out so I didn't have to wriggle in between his truck and my van again.

Soon we were driving again through dark pine barrens, past overgrown remnants of houses and fallen fence posts, toward the farm and the host of unhappy souls waiting there.

Chapter Seventeen

The farm had a charged feeling that was palpable as soon as we turned off the paved road and began meandering past the pumpkin patches and the gardens. A strong gust of wind moved some of the decorative scarecrows, which were cutesy by day but a little ominous by night, reminding me of the restless dead who inhabited the farm.

I thought of ancient idols, statues built to be inhabited by the spirits of strange pagan gods who fed on blood sacrifices. Amber had told me that she'd often felt watched while she was out in the gardens in the evening, and she would look up to see one of the scarecrows, having momentarily mistaken it for a shadowy person staring at her from a distance. I wondered if the ghosts sometimes stirred the scarecrows or looked out somehow through their cloth-patch eyes.

These thoughts made me shiver, and I tried to push them away.

We checked the stables first. The horses seemed jittery but unharmed, so we doubled back to the house.

We parked in the gravel driveway at the main house, and Michael pulled in close beside us again. Jeremy's old Corolla sat on the other side of our van, waiting in the driveway like a faithful old pet abandoned in the family's hurry to leave.

I sat for a moment, taking in what I saw in the van's headlights. The house was completely dark, without a single external or internal light shining. An orange mash of broken pumpkin was scattered over the porch. The front windows, downstairs and upstairs, were all cracked, some of them smashed out entirely, with only a few jagged pieces of glass clinging to the window frame.

"Well, they wanted a haunted farm, didn't they?" Stacey said.

"Yeah, very funny," I replied.

"Just trying to lighten the mood. Which, to me, is a little heavy and thick right now. Do you feel that? It's like something's waiting for us in there." She nodded at the house.

We stuffed our backpacks with thermal goggles and extra tactical flashlights, plus a few floodlights with batteries. The horseman might still be in the house, lying in wait to attack, if we were lucky. If we were unlucky, he'd already gone for the night.

"Should we grab a trap?" Stacey asked.

"First we'll have to figure out where to set it up. Let's see where the horseman's been active tonight." We had only two stampers, the heavy devices that could slam the traps shut either by remote control or automatically, whenever a ghost was detected inside the trap. We had to pick the two most likely locations to trap him.

I pocketed a Ziploc baggie of earth that we had collected from the area where Josef Bracke had been buried. Sometimes the dirt from a spirit's grave can ward it off. I wasn't holding my breath for this to help very much, though, since we couldn't be sure exactly where he'd been buried, just a general area of unmarked wartime graves outside the old cemetery wall in New Ebenezer. It was better than nothing. Or maybe it wasn't.

We advanced toward the front porch, Michael just behind us. The porch stairs showed signs of damage, the wooden steps cracked and splintered in an alternating pattern, as if the horse had been so heavy that its hooves had bashed and broken the wood.

We made our way up carefully. The floodlights we'd set up lay shattered on the higher steps and on the porch. Stacey found the motion detector and other sensors off to one side, as if they'd been kicked away.

The front door had been vertically ruptured, broken in half. The doorknob and deadbolt remained locked, holding a splintered fragment of the door in place.

I nudged open the half of the door that was still attached to the hinges. My flashlight revealed the wreckage of the foyer beyond. Chairs and lamps were overturned, pictures were shattered on the floor.

The light switch did not respond when I jiggled it up and down. It was like walking into a house after some natural disaster had knocked everything off-kilter, like an earthquake or a flood. I'd never experienced the Neville house when it was truly silent and empty like this—even a house where everyone is asleep still feels alive, with whispers of small movements behind the walls and doors. Now it felt abandoned and cold, just the way the ghosts of Hiram and his heirs seemed to prefer it.

"I'm reading a degree or two colder than outside," Stacey said, circling the room. Michael stayed close to me. I could feel his warmth.

"EMF is slightly elevated but nothing special," I added, after checking my Mel-Meter.

In the front parlor room, paperbacks and old album covers were heaped all over the floor. The big armchairs lay overturned.

Looking the other way, I saw that the dining room chairs had been toppled, the table was shoved out of place, and broken dishes and glassware lay strewn in front of the old china cabinet.

"Watch for glass," I said. We took a quick look around the first floor. Everything was moved, fallen, or simply shoved aside.

"It's like some kind of tornado blasted through here," Stacey said.

"This spirit is a real strongman," Michael said.

"He's definitely got a temper." I led the way back to the front stairs. Every few steps, a deep depression had been gouged into the front lip of a stair, roughly the size and shape of a horse's hoof. It echoed the damage to the porch steps outside, like some unbelievably heavy beast or monster had smashed its way upstairs. "I'm not looking forward to facing this guy."

We started up toward the second floor. I had to give another broken-glass warning when I saw all the family pictures had been knocked off the wall and shattered. This is a common tactic of highly territorial ghosts. They don't like new people, living people, coming in and marking their territory. Family pictures are emotionally charged markers, the cheerful gang tags of the reasonably happy and domesticated.

The hardwood floor upstairs was dented heavily in a left-and-right alternating pattern, again like the prints of some impossibly heavy creature. Plaster was cracked along the walls.

We followed the deep hoof prints up the hall. They led directly into Corrine's room, where most of the furniture had been smashed or overturned, the windows shattered from the inside. A galaxy of glow-in-the-dark green stars and planets decorated her ceiling.

The hoof prints continued into Maya's room, the same room into which Mildred had crawled. The Mel-Meter ticked up as I entered the little girl's room, and the temperature sank. I could feel the coldness as the thermometer numbers dropped on the meter's display. I tried to imagine what it must have been like for the family as the entity had charged through the house just a few hours earlier, a huge shadowy thing that destroyed all it saw.

The deep hoofprints in the damaged floor led right to Maya's bed, or to the place where it had been. The bed now lay on its side against one wall, one bed post driven deep into the plaster there.

The prints crossed the floor where the bed had been and ended at another wall, into which a sizable hole had been bashed, like a small cave or an animal's burrow. Plaster dust and a trampled-to-shreds Winnie the Pooh poster lay on the carpet around the ragged hole. I could see an old wooden beam within it, crossed with a horizontal wooden timber like a hidden shelf. A heap of yellow paper lay amid broken slats of wood inside the hole.

"So where did he go?" Stacey asked. She blew a long piece of blond hair away from her eye. "Did he just ride away into the wall?"

I stepped closer and knelt in front of the hole, half-expecting something furry to leap out and bite me. The papers were old and fragile, and I had to carefully pick away broken splinters and chunks of wood to look at them. I had the impression the papers had been tucked inside some kind of old box, maybe a jewelry box, that had shattered around them, probably around the time the horseman had broken the wall open.

A chime sounded in the silent room, making me jump.

"Sorry, that was me." Stacey drew her phone and looked at it, her face glowing eerie blue in the light of its screen. "Oh, it's a voicemail from Jacob. He finally calls me back, and of course I'm too far out in the sticks to get a signal..."

I ignored her as she stepped out into the hall. Picking the broken pieces of wood away from the fragile old paper was delicate work.

A necklace lay coiled in one corner of the shattered old jewelry box. I lifted it slowly in case it was broken, but it seemed intact. It was simple, a strand of red coral beads with a tiny silver clasp.

I pocketed the jewelry and continued quietly excavating the papers. Dried chunks of leather lay among them like puzzle pieces. It looked as though the pages had originally been bound together.

I lifted out one page after another, laying them in a row across the carpet. They were scrambled and out of order, some of them broken into fragments. The ink was faded, and the handwriting wasn't great, but at least they were in English.

With my flashlight, I searched among them, looking for the most legible portions. I read:

...cannot understand each other so well, but in place of words we have gestures, and laughter, and smiles, and touching. He heals and he hides, and if Father or the others knew where he hides in the forest, he would be dead. I bring what food I can. He is fond of peaches and salted meat...

...think of him always, and wish I had the courage to go with him. He is not safe here, yet daily and nightly risks his life to be near me, to wait, to again insist we should be together. He is stronger now, with a fine horse. He will not say how he purchased the horse nor the sparkling jewels he gives me, and I know it cannot be honest work, but what man is honest in times of war?

The truth is growing obvious. I cannot long hide it from Father, even less from Mother or my sisters. They will know. They must suspect. I fear the day when the truth must come forward, more than I fear illness or wild beasts, or death itself...

My heart was thundering. If this was what it looked like, it would completely change our case.

"It has to be her," I muttered under my breath. I shuffled through the pages, one after the other, just looking for a name. His or hers. "Why else would Josef be interested in this?"

I finally found one of them: *Joseph*. The English version of *Josef*, naturally. The author of the pages had written how deeply she loved Joseph, how it pained her that her family would never approve. The Neville family had been Patriots and certainly wouldn't have wanted their daughter getting intimate with a Hessian soldier, even if he was a deserter. He would have been considered a foreign rough, a mercenary, and a dangerous killer.

"Come on, come on..." I whispered to myself.

Then I found it—a page where Mildred Neville had written her own name several times, in slightly different styles, as though trying to develop a trademark fancy signature for herself.

"Hey, Stacey," I said. "What if...Mildred was secretly having an affair with the runaway soldier, the highwayman? And she was carrying *his* baby?" I turned to see Stacey's expression at this saucy, gossipy new possibility. I expected her to be somewhere between gobsmacked and jaw-dropped.

Stacey wasn't there at all. Neither was Michael.

I'd been alone in the room for—who knows? No more than a few minutes.

"Hey, guys? Way to leave me stranded in the middle of a violent ghost's path of destruction here." I stepped out into the hall and swung my flashlight around, but I didn't see either of them, not even a glimmer of a flashlight from either of them. "Hello? Michael? Stacey? I'm not in the mood for a prank or anything. Not funny."

I walked up the hallway, certain that they must have heard me by now. Something creaked ahead—maybe a footstep on a floorboard, maybe the house settling. I followed the sound to a closed door. Just a linen closet, or a small storage closet, if I remembered correctly. Of course, that's exactly the kind of small, dark place where the nasties like to hide, ready to leave you scratched and bitten with their invisible nails and teeth.

So I approached the door with caution.

I opened it with one hand and jabbed my light ahead with the other. Soft shapes and deep shadows lurked within, but these were flowery hand towels and folded quilts, nothing more.

"Stacey? Michael?" I called out again. No response from the dark house around me. "Stacey, if this is a joke, it's very unprofessional."

I did a quick room to room search upstairs. They weren't anywhere, and I was breaking into a cold sweat. At this point, it had dragged on much too long to be a joke.

I couldn't imagine an entity capable of sneaking into the room and physically removing both Stacey and Michael in complete silence from just behind me. I'd been pretty focused on looking through the remnants of the old journal, and I do tend to wear blinders and just zoom all my attention onto one thing at a time, but it seemed pretty far-fetched that the horseman could have grabbed up two people without either of them making a sound.

It quickly became apparent that Stacey and Michael weren't going to come popping out from behind a door or a piece of furniture just to laugh at the look on my face.

It was possible we were dealing with a psychotropic ghost, one who could get into my head and make me *believe* I was alone when I wasn't, but I didn't think that was happening. There wasn't any other distortion or hallucination, no sense that the floor was sliding out from under me or bugs were crawling underneath my skin, no blood-red haze falling over the world while all the corners of the room melted like an Escher painting.

There was literally no reason for them to sneak off together. What was the last thing Stacey had said? Something about finally getting in touch with Jacob. Maybe she'd gone outside in search of a better signal, but again it seemed like somebody would have mentioned to me they were leaving.

I shouted their names again as I reached the front stairs, hearing the panic creep into my voice. I ran down the steps as quickly as I dared, avoiding the damaged steps and the broken glass.

Nobody answered. I was alone in the house.

Chapter Eighteen

I made a quick check of the downstairs, but at this point it was obvious that Stacey and Michael were gone. Either that or they'd both suddenly turned invisible and lost the ability to speak. Maybe Jacob's message had caused them to flee for some reason, but it didn't make sense that they would leave me behind. Unless, of course, this was their way of telling me that they'd secretly hated me all along and hoped a ghost horseman would put me out of my misery.

Outside, I stood on the porch and searched the front yard with the iris of my flashlight wide open to create a sweeping floodlight.

All three vehicles still remained in the gravel drive. I pointed my light inside the windshields of Michael's truck and the van, and even looked inside Jeremy's old Corolla, where I saw some bowling shoes and a battered Heinlein paperback on the floor, but not much else.

I opened a back door of the van but wasn't surprised to find it empty. I would've been much more surprised to find Stacey and Michael hiding in there with the lights off. Still, it's best to be thorough when the people you care about suddenly vanish.

Calling their names again, I circled the outside of the house and checked the little dirt crawlspace beneath the front porch. Nothing.

It was hard to ignore the fear spreading all through my body with every heartbeat. I have encountered some weird stuff in my time, but nothing like two people instantly vanishing in silent, alien-abduction fashion.

A horse whinnied in the distance. Lacking any other direction, I started toward the stable, leaves crunching under my boots. It was past midnight and officially Halloween. The gates to the world of the dead now stood wide open, if you believed the lore.

That thought did not place me in a calm frame of mind as I approached the stable. I couldn't see any of the horses from the outside, nor did I hear any of them whinny again.

"Stacey? Michael?" That was me, drawing attention to myself as I wandered toward the dark old building like a soon-to-be-stabbed-to-death character in any horror movie. I really have to stop treating horror movies like how-to manuals for life, but they're just so relevant to the problems I face.

I lifted the thick horizontal board that latched the wooden door to the stable. The horses shied back from my flashlight as I entered.

The footsteps began just overhead, as though someone were watching me from the rafters. At first, it was just a creak, not necessarily anything more than the old timbers settling, no different from the insignificant sound that had drawn me to look for monsters in the house's linen closet.

I've learned not to ignore such small noises, though. I pointed my light up at the ceiling above, made of boards with significant gaps between them. It might have been okay for storing bales of hay, but it didn't look like the hayloft up there was exactly child-safe. There was plenty of opportunity to trip and fall while you walked, and maybe even slide right through and free-fall onto the ground.

A thump sounded farther along. I moved my beam quickly across the ceiling to follow it, just in time to catch the fleeting edge of a shape as it passed over a gap between the boards.

"Hello?" I said, just in case a psychotic killer ghost was stalking around up there and wanted to know exactly where I was so it could pounce on my head.

Another noise followed. It sounded like a foot-fall, like a boot clomping on wood. There was another thump, and then another. I tracked along underneath, pointing my flashlight up through the gaps, but I saw nothing except the dust and strands of hay that came trickling down toward my eyes.

"Is somebody up there?" I asked.

There was silence, as though the entity were hesitating, and then the boot-steps started up again. They were moving toward the steep wooden stairs tucked into the corner. A variety of leather implements hung on nails near the stairs. I assumed these to be horse-related.

The top stair creaked, and then a dark form began to descend toward me, the sound of boots creaking on every step. My flashlight revealed, not a murderous dead mercenary, but the pale face of a girl who looked back at me with guarded suspicion.

"Corrine?" I asked, knocked completely off-guard. She moved so softly as she descended the narrow stairs that she could have been a ghost herself.

"Hey," she finally said as she reached the bottom step.

"Where...how did you get here?"

"Hid in the van," she mumbled. Then, with a little more confidence, she added, "*Somebody* had to check on the horses, you know?"

"We told you we would do that," I said. "And they all look okay to me. They aren't hurt."

She just shrugged and walked over to one of the stalls. She petted the big brown horse with the white forehead.

"We need to call your parents and tell them where you are." I drew my phone, but the little satellite graphic had no bars. "Do you have a signal?"

"Of course not," Corrine said, after the briefest glance at her own phone. "There's never a signal. You have to walk around in a big circle trying to find one."

"Maybe we can use the landline at the house. The power seems to be out, though..."

"It's this stupid place. No phone signal, power conks out for no reason, we're lucky there's running water," Corrine said. "There's no reason to tell my parents I'm here. They'll just worry."

"You don't think they'll worry that you were last seen going to the convenience store, and then you vanished?"

Corrine shrugged.

"You'd better stick with us," I said. "It could still be dangerous around here."

"Where are your friends?" she asked.

"Um..." Here I was acting like the responsible, experienced adult who could keep her safe, when I'd just failed to accomplish the same thing for Michael and Stacey. "They're around. I was just looking for them."

"Around?" Corrine walked to the wide stable door through which I'd entered and looked up toward the house. "Did they get lost or something?"

"Something like that," I said, and a high-pitched scream tore through the night, making us both jump.

"What was that?" she whispered.

"That was Stacey," I said. I knew her scream pretty well. I tried to act calm, resisting the urge to sprint toward Stacey's voice for just a moment, because I didn't want Corrine coming with me. "Stay put. I'll be right back for you." I bolted out the door. It was a tough call to leave her, but it seemed even more foolish to drag the clients' kid right into the thick of the danger. Neither option was a great one.

"It sounded like it came from the woods," Corrine said.

I rushed out from the stable, along the wooden rail of the corral and toward the dirt road.

The scream came again, and I began to run.

"Stacey!" I shouted. "Stacey, where are you?"

Her voice cried out again, fainter, as if she were losing energy or consciousness.

I sprinted across the yard and into the dirt road. The voice came from ahead, from somewhere within the acres of corn that made up the maze. I began to run toward the maze entrance, the high archway made of old shovels and pitchforks twisted together, with the scarecrow beside it holding the plastic sign with the maze rules. I called out again, but Stacey didn't answer.

I paused to slide my thermal goggles out of my backpack and

place them on my forehead, ready to drop them over my eyes when I needed them. Normally, I use them to search for abnormally cold spots and shapes that indicate ghosts. This time I'd be looking for warm reds and yellows, searching for the living instead of the dead.

A rhythmic thumping approached on the road behind me—heavy hoof beats. Terrified, I turned back, ready to face the horseman.

It was only Corrine, though, riding after me on that big brown horse with the white spot.

"What are you doing out here?" I snapped. "I told you to stay inside the stable."

"Who says it's really safe in there, either?" Corrine asked. "And it'll take you forever to search on foot. The horseman will have killed your friend by then."

"Why do you assume the horseman took her?"

"Because he's scary."

"Go back to the stable," I said. "You're not putting yourself in danger for me."

"Who says it's for you? Anyway, I'm in danger as long as I'm here. The whole stupid place is haunted."

"Then maybe you should take your dad's car and leave." I turned and shouted Stacey's name again, toward the woods and the maze, but I didn't get any response. I needed to get moving.

"And *maybe* my parents should have let me get a license, but they didn't. They probably thought I'd just go get high or something."

"Would you?"

"Probably not." She shrugged. "So do you want my help, or..."

Corrine fell silent and gaped at me. I was feeling the same shock. More hoofbeats approached—heavy, slamming thuds, as if the approaching beast were impossibly huge.

I looked up and down the road, but didn't see anything.

"Hey, Corrine? You didn't happen to let another horse out of the stable, did you?"

"It's him." Corrine held out a hand. "Come on up. You'll never outrun him on foot."

The hoofbeats sounded louder and closer. It didn't even sound like a horse, but something much larger, like an elephant. Or a brontosaurus. The ground rumbled.

"I don't think I can. I don't have much horse experience." I looked doubtfully at the big brown mare and the girl on top of it. "You should go on. I'll deal with the ghost."

Then Stacey screamed again—weaker and fainter this time—and I thought it might be better to keep everyone together, or else I could find myself following Corrine's screams a little later if something awful happened to her.

"Last chance," Corrine said.

An immense black shape erupted from the woods, formless, like a thundercloud rolling over the dirt road and rushing directly toward us, swallowing up what little light was in its path. Though it was more than a hundred yards away, I could feel a sudden press of frigid air from that direction.

The horseman was back. He clearly wasn't done for the night.

I took a deep breath and did my best to jump onto Corrine's horse, just behind Corrine. I landed awkwardly, of course, draped over the horse's back like a carpet. Fortunately, the horse was gentle and remarkably calm, especially considering the cloud of supernatural evil rushing toward us. Most animals would have bolted already.

With Corrine's help, I barely managed to arrange myself. As soon as I was in place, the horse started to move. I held on tight to Corrine.

The horse trotted toward the corn maze, then broke into a run as we passed under the archway. Corrine steered her down the path. High rows of cornstalks formed walls on either side of us, reinforced by plastic mesh.

As we twisted and turned, I had to admit I was glad to be moving so fast, with somebody who knew her way and wouldn't accidentally run us into a blind alley where the horseman could trap us. It was up to me to keep Corrine safe, even she maybe happened to be rescuing me at the moment.

I drew my thermals down over my eyes and looked out over the maze. Mounted on the horse, I could see much farther than I could have on foot, peering across several rows at a time. I searched desperately for a warm sign of life. The corn maze sprawled over five acres, so there was a lot of searching to do. We hadn't heard a thing from Michael, either.

Cold air pressed against my back like a giant hand. I turned and saw a deep cold swallowing up the trail behind me, engulfing the high stalks and corn cobs in a deep blue. A dark purplish figure rode at the center of the wave of cold—I could discern the basic outlines of a man on a horse.

He was close, and drawing closer. His ghost horse was faster than ours. The hoofbeats sounded loud as thunder now.

"Corrine, he's close!" I shouted.

She urged our horse to race even faster, but the poor mare was burdened with the weight of two riders and racing against a phantom made of nothing but energy and fury.

We rounded another tight corner. There would be no shaking the horseman, no losing him in the endless twists and turns of the corn. He was much too close for that, and much too fast.

My thermals bounced askew, so I nudged them up and off my eyes with my shoulder.

I no longer needed them to see the horseman. With all the heat he'd just sucked out of the air, he was beginning to manifest as a visible apparition, giving me my first real look at him.

He was tall, narrow, and shadowy, his eyes lost under the pointed brim of his black tricorner hat. I could see his pale lips, drawn back in a tight little smile. The smile unnerved me more than anything—the dead don't usually greet you with a grin.

He wore a long black outer coat and matching waistcoat, both adorned with rows of brass buttons. I could see white just below his throat, maybe lace ruffles. I was more interested in the long, narrow blade he brandished in one hand, swiping it through the air as if to demonstrate what he intended to do to my throat.

His horse was wiry and fast. It seemed much thinner than ours. After a moment I realized it was a running corpse, its eyes missing, its flesh dried and shriveled, its stiff dark hair barely covering gaps in the skin through which I could glimpse the bones beneath.

The horseman moved in. He raised his ghostly sword, which was really a psychic projection on his part, based on the memory of the blade with which he'd killed men on the battlefield and later robbed travelers on the road. In another moment, he'd be close enough to plunge the blade into my heart. With the kind of power and energy he'd demonstrated while wrecking the family's house, I had no doubt he could kill me.

I clung as tightly to Corrine as I could manage with one arm, while trying to reach inside my jacket with my other hand. It was precarious. One extra-hard bounce from the horse would have sent me sprawling on the ground, and old Josef could have had some fun trampling me a bit before he skewered me with his sword.

The Ziploc bag inside my jacket pocket was reluctant to open, especially since I was blindly working at it with two fingers while trying not to fall off a rapidly moving animal. I managed to open a corner of it and dipped my fingers into the soft, sandy red dirt.

Ghosts can have a range of reactions to encountering the earth from their own graves. Many are entirely indifferent. Some of them, seeking solace and rest, may move into it. Others, resisting against their state of death and their need to move on, will desperately avoid that soil.

I didn't know what effect it might have on the horseman ghost, but this seemed like a worthwhile time to test it out.

I pulled the open bag from my pocket. I meant to toss just a pinch of it at him to see how he responded, but I was holding the bag in one hand and holding on for dear life with the other. All I could do was wave the open baggie in his general direction.

All the dirt spewed out at once, leaving only trace amounts inside the bag. Gone to waste, really. Regardless of how he responded, I now had none left to use, either to draw him into a trap or draw a defensive line he couldn't cross.

The thin, dead horse let out a dry, rasping whine. I could see its teeth through the rotten remnants of its nose and mouth. It was a dry rot, and what remained of the horse's flesh had a shriveled texture almost like beef jerky.

The burial earth puffed out in a thick red cloud across the path. This seemed to bother the horse, who slammed into the cloud of dirt as though it were solid brick. The horse reared up, kicking its long, stick-like front legs in my direction. I ducked aside as best as I could. The horse's limbs might have looked withered and brittle, but I'd seen the damage they had done to the stairs and walls inside. They could easily cave in my skull.

The highwayman held onto his reins with one hand, still brandishing the sword with the other. His horse remained high, up on its rear legs, as if it couldn't break through the haze of dirt.

The highwayman was no longer smiling at me.

Then we pulled away, around a corner and out of sight, because Corrine was still urging her horse to run as fast as she could. We'd delayed the horseman momentarily, but at the cost of probably my best weapon against him. The dust would settle, or he would find another way through the maze.

We didn't have much time, so I immediately pulled the thermals down over my eyes again.

Another turn of the maze, and I glimpsed a slice of glowing red through the corn many rows away. I nudged Corrine and pointed toward it, though I wasn't sure if she would be able to see where I was pointing.

She managed to get us closer, whipping back and forth through the rows of corn. I could identify a fairly Stacey-shaped red figure, now much closer. Several other warm spots glowed nearby, like tiny light bulbs.

"There!" I shouted. "Stacey! Stacey, can you hear me?"

The glowing red form didn't answer. I pushed up my thermals to get a better look at her.

Corrine's horse slowed as we emerged into one of the larger clearings within the maze, where several paths came together. This was the one decorated with the row of three scarecrows styled as the butcher, baker, and candlestick maker.

The butcher remained just as I'd seen him before, a butcher knife in one hand and a meat cleaver in the other, clad in his apron stained with fake blood. His cloth bag of a face was literally expressionless, with no features at all, yet he still seemed to be watching us.

At the other end of the row, the candlestick maker was lit up, including the electric candles in his hands and those on the brim of his scarecrow hat.

The middle scarecrow had been removed. Stacey had been mounted in its place. Her toes dangled a few feet off the ground. Rope and torn strips of scarecrow clothing lashed her to the tall wooden framework that had previously held the baker scarecrow upright.

Stacey had been dressed in the puffy chef hat the scarecrow had worn, and its ratty old coat had been loosely draped around her. A strip of stiff, dirty denim was tied across her mouth.

"Stacey!" I shouted. I hurried to slide off the horse as it came to stop. It turns out that getting off a horse is not something you want to do in a hurry when you're not familiar with the procedure. I plunged several feet straight down and slammed into the dirt.

I pushed myself to my hands and knees, trying to catch my breath as quickly as I could. Then I stood, more or less, and staggered toward Stacey.

"Stacey," I gasped, hoarse because I was still short on air.

"Mmmf," she replied. Then she added: "Muh uhh uh go gah gy umf."

"I get it, you're gagged." I pulled the thick strip of denim from her jaws. "What happened to you? Where's Michael?"

"Jacob's message," Stacey said. "Michael attacked Jacob and locked him in the trunk of his own car."

"What?" I took the small Swiss Army knife from my utility belt and went to work trying to cut her free. Her arms and hips were bound into place by coils of rope, flannel shirt-cloth stripped from the scarecrow, and more of the scarecrow's ripped denim jeans. They were tightly knotted, with no hope of being untied, so I had to start sawing the material with my knife.

"Jacob called when he finally got someone to set him free." Stacey looked at Corrine on the horse. The horse looked tense, sniffing the air. "Why is Corrine here?"

"Long story. She stowed away in the van. What's going on with Michael?"

"He grabbed me when I said I got the message from Jacob," I said. "He carried me out here. Jacob says—"

"Someone's coming," Corrine whispered. She pointed toward one of the paths that converged on our clearing.

"—Michael's possessed by something pretty bad," Stacey finished, her voice dropping low.

At that moment, I could believe it. There had been some signs that things were amiss with him, but I'd been too focused on how I wanted our relationship to be something sound, how I needed Michael's presence to create at least the illusion of stability and connection in my life. They say love is blind, but I guess love can be blinding, too. Maybe love's just bitter about being blind and wants to blind everyone else, I don't know.

I thought of the imposing black clock Michael recently purchased for his little side business of restoring and reselling them. It had been taller than me, carved to look like a dark castle with parapets, steps, arrow slits, and other minute features rendered in careful detail. The spring-driven automatons that came out every hour were an assortment of hand-carved wooden chess pieces that gave me the creeps.

I'd urged him not to buy it from the antique store, but why listen to a professional ghost hunter when it comes to bringing scary old things into your home? He'd seen a major restoration challenge with a lot of potential profit. He was almost obsessed with bringing dead, delicate mechanisms back to life. I mean, there are easier ways to make extra money.

"Did Jacob say anything about who or what was possessing him?" I asked Stacey. That's my training, keeping me logical and functional on the surface while locking away my feelings down inside. I owed Calvin for that. Because honestly, I just wanted to collapse. It was too much, and too much of it all at once. The horseman was out there stalking us, almost certainly gearing up for another attack, and now Michael was around the bend, possessed by something malevolent enough to kidnap both Jacob and Stacey.

Even more frightening was how the entity possessing Michael had managed to stay mostly in character, wearing Michael's mind and personality like a costume. The costume may have been somewhat ill-fitting, with gaps here and there, but either I hadn't been looking closely enough or I hadn't wanted to admit to myself that there might be a real problem unfolding with him. It takes a strong ghost to possess living humans against their will, but it takes a very intelligent one to puppeteer that person from the inside and try to keep the possession hidden. Michael had been acting a little off, but it wasn't like his head had been spinning in circles while he yakked pea soup all over the room and threatened to see us all in hell.

"No," Stacey said, while I sawed desperately at her bonds. Someone had done a clever job here, braiding, twisting, and knotting the different materials used to tie her up, to make sure she couldn't be cut free too easily. It was as if some evil-genius Boy Scout had done the job, earning himself merit badges in both knot-tying and kidnapping.

"He's here," Corrine whispered, drawing her horse a little closer to us. The mare stamped and let out a nervous chuffing sound.

A tall, broad-shouldered shadow emerged from the corn, a handsome face smirking at us in the moonlight. It was Michael, but it wasn't. Everything about how he moved and held himself was wrong. He walked with the attitude of a tiger approaching its prey, a predator who had no doubt that the kill was his.

"Eleanor," he said, and everything inside me froze. I knew the voice. It was *him*. And that was impossible. He was supposed to be trapped in the ground, buried with the remnants of my childhood home and the ashes of my parents, and the ashes of all those he'd burned to death over the centuries.

Chapter Nineteen

"Keep cutting," Stacey whispered low, not moving her lips. My whole body had locked up at the voice of Anton Clay, as if I had no control over myself in his presence.

"Eleanor, step away from that other girl," he told me. "We will all remain here together."

"You can't be here," I said, my voice almost certainly too low to hear. I felt powerless in his presence. He'd taken everything from me, he'd ruled my life from that pivotal moment in my past. He'd stalked my nightmares. He'd made me into who I was.

And now, inexplicably, he was free of the spot where he'd been bound since his own death in 1841. I can't begin to explain how much that terrified me.

"I have waited long years for you," he said, approaching us. The row of corn directly behind him erupted into flames, as if they'd been drenched in gasoline and were just waiting for a match. The fire spread down the row, lighting up one of the paths out of the clearing.

"Corrine, go!" I said. "Now!"

"I don't want—" she began to protest.

"Someone has to protect the horses at the stable," I told her. I doubted the stable was in much immediate danger, but I hoped that would motivate her to get going. Although it was entirely possible that Anton Clay, my own personal demon, was about to engulf the whole farm in flames, and there was no hope for any of us.

Corrine nodded, trusting that I knew what I was talking about, and she started toward another path out of the clearing. Both rows of corn ignited, the fire spreading away in parallel rows that momentarily made me think of the DeLorean in *Back to the Future*. The flames grew thick on either side of the path, making it impassable for humans as well as horses.

The brown mare reared up in a panic, wisely refusing to plunge into the flames. Corrine managed to get her back down to four legs, but she was clearly trapped in the clearing with us. Every path out was lined with stalks of highly flammable corn.

"Let her go, Anton!" I shouted at Michael. "She's not a part of this. Neither is Stacey." I resumed hacking at the bonds that held Stacey in place.

"I instructed you to leave her tied there." He nodded, and the scarecrow candlestick maker burst into flames. The fire spread across his hat, scarf, and coat, and the electric bulbs cracked in the heat. The plastic pumpkin face began to melt at the corners of the jaunty triangular eyes and grinning mouth. "I could burn her just as easily."

"You came for me," I said. "Here I am, so let them go."

"The other girls will make lovely additions to my collection." Michael—*Anton*, I reminded myself, and surely Michael's eyes had never danced with infernal glee like that—took a moment to look over Stacey and Corrine, as if they were cuts of meat he intended to cook and eat. Veins of fire spread through the maze, out in every direction from us, setting the field ablaze and trapping us inside with the evil, crazed ghost.

I walked toward him, doing my best to conceal an obvious tremble in my knees.

"I should have trapped you years ago," I said.

"But you did not. Why?" He smiled, and it was all cruelty, the smile of a torturer or a hangman. He reached out as if to caress my cheek, and I halted.

I hadn't done it because Calvin said Anton Clay was too dangerous, and that he was already as good as trapped as long as the site of my old house remained undisturbed.

"How did you escape?" I asked him.

"A fascinating opportunity arose, and I took advantage," Anton said. Michael's face was like a thin mask now; I could almost see Anton through it. Certainly I could feel his presence, and I could smell his smoky musk, the scent of burning wood and smoldering flesh, death and cremation. "I've had much time to reflect on my peculiar condition, Eleanor. I refuse to remain a bit of lost memory, endlessly caught within myself. The truth of my current state is now clear to me. I am no pale shade, destined to fade like old smoke. All these years, I never understood, but now I do. Now I see I am something more like...a god." He smiled. He was less than a foot away, his pupils reflecting the growing fires all around us as he looked into my eyes.

"You didn't answer my question," I managed to say.

"What do we do?" Corrine asked. Her horse was shifting around nervously. The big mare had performed admirably, even heroically, but the growing inferno was going to make her panic.

"Stay calm," Stacey advised her, which didn't help much.

The fire had spread so far and so high that a strong wind, blowing across the flames and turning them sideways, could very well roast us all alive. I was sweating all over from the heat.

"Why don't you just die?" I asked him. "Just let go and move on. It's long past time."

"Let go? Move on? I have only now gained my freedom. Only now do I know my full potential." He took my hand and raised it to his lips. "You say I belong among the dead, but you belong there, too, Eleanor. You were meant to be with me. You've spent the years since thinking of me, looking across with longing at the far bank, at the land where the spirits dwell, because you know where you belong. You became a ghost the night we met, the night you were meant to die."

His hand tightened around mine. His grip was blistering hot. None of my usual ghost defenses would work now, while he commanded a living body. My only chance of survival was to defeat him physically, and between his pyrokinetic powers and the great strength of Michael's body, there wasn't much chance of that.

I was going to die. I could accept that—Clay had a point. Most of me had already died that night, long ago. This was the proper end for me, death by fire, joining my parents on the roster of Anton Clay's victims. Some part of me had always known it would end like this.

But I wasn't willing to let the others die.

"Let them go," I said. I didn't need to speak much louder than a whisper, his face was so close. "Let it be just you and me tonight. No other girls."

He stared at me, and I watched the irises of Michael's eyes turn to circles of glowing red. His hand gripped mine tight enough to make my bones creak, and his skin burned even hotter. I hissed in pain.

"Ellie, just get away from him!" Stacey said. "Don't worry about me."

I stared back at Anton Clay. "Let them go," I said again.

"No," he finally said. "I want you all. But don't fear, Eleanor. Your parents will be so pleased to see you again. They've missed you terribly." He bared his teeth, as he twisted that old knife right into my heart. Then he gestured toward a burning patch of corn nearby. "See them, Eleanor. See them all."

I looked, and whatever remnants of strength, courage, or tough-girl bravado I still had left instantly drained away.

For a moment, I could see them, and I could hear them screaming. It was a cluster of burning skeletons standing close together, maybe two dozen of them, fire rolling from their empty eye sockets and open jaws. Red-hot chains held them close together, like prisoners or animals. One such chain ran across the ground, up into Michael's hand, so hot that it seared and steamed the flesh there, though his face registered no pain.

Then the screaming, burning skeletons were gone, along with the coils of heavy red-hot chain. Michael's hand—the one that wasn't slowly crushing and overheating mine—was empty again.

"Did you see?" he asked.

I didn't answer. I understood. Though he was free of the patch of soil where he'd been rooted so long, he still had the power granted by the little slivers of soul he'd shaved off from all his murder victims over the years.

"Are my parents with you?" I whispered.

"Would you like to be with them?" he asked. With the screams gone, the sound of the swelling, growing fire roared in my ears like the ocean during a storm.

"Let my friends go." I gave him my best desperate, pleading look, which was easy to do because it was how I felt. I squeezed his hand back as tightly as I could, and then I moved my face toward his. Anything to keep him from noticing what I was doing with my other hand, which was digging into my pirate-trouser pocket as furtively as I could manage.

I moved even closer, as if I meant to kiss him. It was so strange to see Michael's face with another soul behind it. It was as if every muscle in his face had altered slightly, creating a different person inside his skin.

The fires all around us roared and rose again, as if my closeness inflamed him somehow, stoking up the acres of fire that he was creating to kill us all. Stacey would die, and Michael, and Corrine, and our violent deaths would leave some remnants of us in his control, fueling his growth into an ever more powerful monster. Now that he was free to roam, I knew he would become a living nightmare, burning new victims every night, if he could.

Perhaps he'd already claimed some victims, somewhere, before coming after us. He was more powerful than I'd ever seen him, and newly self-aware in a way that was dangerous. Ghosts can have all kinds of powers—moving effortlessly through walls, throwing objects with their mind, getting into your head to share their pain and horror with you. Usually they are just stuck in repetition mode, so they keep pacing the same ground, slamming the same doors, forming the same frightening apparition. A ghost who actually understood his condition and was ready to take full advantage of it presented a larger and more unpredictable threat.

Stacey watched me, silently, as if in shock. More likely, she was just being careful, waiting for her chance to help. I noticed her tugging with one hand, trying to finish tearing the bonds at which I'd been cutting. Corrine was somehow keeping the horse on this side of full-blown panic.

I had to try to save the two of them.

Anton Clay had to be stopped. If I died, that was a price I would pay to protect Stacey and everyone else from him...even if that meant Michael had to die with me.

While Anton's red eyes burned into mine, I held out my free hand and spread out my fingers a little. I struggled to hold onto the slippery necklace. My fingers were dripping sweat. I felt like I was standing in the middle of a bonfire.

According to the broken remnants of her journal, the antique coral necklace had been a gift from the highwayman to the farmer's daughter he'd apparently impregnated. Josef Bracke, Mildred Neville. If we'd gotten our research right, based on what loose and generally unconnected fragments of evidence we had.

If I was wrong, or my move simply didn't work, we would all be consumed by the corn-maze fire. Anton was stoking it higher and higher as he moved even closer to me. He embraced me with his other arm, in what almost felt like some kind of formal dance move.

"We burn together," Anton whispered.

Then he pressed his lips, Michael's lips, to mine, and did what he'd been wanting to do to me since I was fifteen. He surrounded me with heat even as he drew me close with his arm. My skin flash-dried and began to feel like it was cracking. I could smell my own hair beginning to singe. The air was so hot that it stung my lungs.

It was, in so many ways, the death I'd always expected.

The fires rose straight up—ten feet, fifteen feet, like tidal waves of flame preparing to roll in from all sides, turning us all to ash and bone. Everyone screamed. Stacey, who'd only managed to work one hand free. Corrine and her terrified horse, frantically turning in circles as if there were some way to escape.

Anton's lips lingered on mine. I was waving the necklace back and forth, clinking the beads together. A small sound, but a persistent one, at least.

The horseman had been trying to tell us something. Once we'd penned up the Neville family ghosts, the horseman's first act had been to reveal the box hidden inside the old wall, containing the relics of Mildred's life. It was in the same room, Maya's room, where Mildred's ghost liked to crawl at night, as if searching for her old belongings.

I hoped I'd understood his message correctly. If not, we were all dead. There was no time to devise a new plan, no other options left.

I swung the necklace back and forth, clacking the beads, as the surging heat began to bake me inside my blousy pirate shirt.

Just as the heat pressed in around me, on the verging of roasting me alive, the blast of cold air hit. It was more than welcome; it was salvation, a wall of icy air quelling the deadly heat.

I opened my eyes.

He'd carved a trench through the burning maze, soaking up heat as he rode toward the sound of Mildred's necklace, leaving darkness in his wake.

The horseman's eyes remained concealed in the shadows of his black tricorner hat. The lower half of his face was bone white. His smile had not returned.

He grew more visible as he rode toward us, feeding on the heat unleashed by Anton's fires. Stacey gasped at the sight of his decayed, shriveled black mount. Corrine's horse shied away from the specter, but overall seemed calmer as the wave of cold rushed out from the newly arrived ghost.

I pulled my face away from Michael's. With my one free hand, I drew the necklace over my head and down to my throat.

Then I pushed against Michael's chest—not very effective against his powerful grip, but at least I was putting up a struggle. And I screamed.

"Josef!" I shouted at the advancing shadowy horseman. "Save me!"

"Josef?" Anton turned Michael's head and looked. He glowered at the apparition that was sucking up a big swath of his fire and becoming more solid by the moment.

Anton turned to face the horseman, but he still gripped my hand tightly. In his other hand, he summoned a tall gout of flame. He smiled as the horseman bore down on him. With any luck, Josef would see me wearing Mildred's necklace and it would stop him from hurting me, maybe even motivate him to protect me.

Josef raised his sword—he looked very solid now, freshly fed on so much heat—and Anton raised his free hand, the fire floating above it like the flame of a candle.

Even as the horseman reached us, there was no telling whether he intended to attack Anton, or me, or just kill both of us as well as Stacey and Corrine.

Corrine, for her part, was making good use of the temporary rollback of the all-consuming deadly corn inferno. She'd gotten down off her horse and was freeing Stacey from her bonds, with help from the pocket knife I'd carelessly left behind.

Good. They had a chance of escaping. I wasn't so sure about me.

I did my best to push away from Anton/Michael as the horseman reached us. Between these two ghosts, my chances of survival didn't seem high at all. I sent up a sort of prayer, aimed generally in the direction of my parents, just kind of letting them know I might be joining them soon. And sorry again about that last fight.

The sword gleamed in the firelight. It swept down toward us, lightning-fast, almost too quick for my eye to follow.

I braced myself for the deathblow.

The tongue of fire hovering above Michael's hand, drifting close to his head like a mockery of the Pentecost, snuffed out all at once.

Michael's mouth opened and let out a horrible sound, somewhere between a shriek and a gurgling choke. I didn't know who was truly suffering in there, Anton or Michael. Maybe both.

The front of Michael's blousy pirate shirt ruptured in half as the ghostly sword sliced through him. The shirt fell open, revealing not a fresh, bloody wound, but a brand-new black scar that ran from his left shoulder, over his heart and across his chest, and down to his right hip. It looked as if it had always been there, but it definitely had not.

Michael fell to his knees. His eyes were no longer glowing and fiery red—and, in fact, the eyes and the face looked just like Michael again.

He gave me a look of hurt and pain as he fell to the ground. He looked at me as if I'd betrayed him, and I had. I had betrayed Michael. I'd been willing to sacrifice him to save Stacey, Corrine, and anyone else that Anton Clay might have killed.

What would bother me later, though, was knowing that I'd also saved my own skin by choosing to sacrifice him. Even if that hadn't been foremost in my mind, it was true, and there was nothing noble about that.

Michael landed in the dirt without a sound, and he lay there without moving.

The great walls of fire lowered immediately. The corn was flammable, but it also burned up quickly, and Anton's spirit didn't seem to be feeding the flames with his power anymore. The fires lowered, revealing a maze of glowing red ashes outlined all around, though we couldn't see far because of the smoke.

The smell of charred plants and ash filled the air, stirring terrible memories of the night my parents had died in the fire. Now Michael lay at my feet, unmoving, one more person that I cared about, taken from me by the ghost of Anton Clay.

I dropped to my knees and checked Michael's neck for a pulse, my fingers exploring only inches from his sudden new scar. He was feverishly hot, but I was having trouble finding any heartbeat.

At the burning edge of the clearing, the dead horseman twisted around and turned back toward me. For a moment, about halfway through his turn, he and his horse seemed impossibly thin, like looking at a slice of black construction paper edge-on.

Then he approached me at a trot, his eyeless horse sniffing in my direction.

Now I could see the horseman's eyes. They were gray and pale like the rest of him.

He pointed the sword at my throat, indicating the necklace.

"No, I'm not Mildred." I lifted the necklace up and over my head.

The horseman turned and eased his mount closer to Corrine instead. Stacey moved to block his way. Corrine looked up at him with some fear, but she didn't cower.

"She is not Mildred, either," I said. "Leave her be, Josef. You want Mildred, I'll show you where to find her. I'll try to help." *Please don't cut through me with that sword*, I wanted to add. *Me or anybody else.* I didn't want to say that aloud and risk putting the idea in his head, though.

The horseman stood in place, and Stacey tried not to tremble as she held her ground between the horseman and Corrine. The fires burned down low around us now, acres of maze paths etched out in glowing red stubble across scorched, sandy earth. It was a bizarre, hellish landscape, the air still full of heat and smoke.

Michael shivered under my fingers. His pulse returned, low and weak. His eyes did not open.

I stood and walked toward the north end of the maze, the section closest to the woods and the cemetery within them. I clicked together beads on the necklace, hoping that would keep the horseman's attention.

Slowly, the apparition shambled after me. The necklace would have made good bait for the horseman, had we gotten around to setting a trap for him.

"Stacey," I said. "Check on Michael. And tie him up."

Stacey nodded and went to his side, while Corrine stepped away from all of us to pat her nervous horse.

"Wait here." I told them. I continued walking toward the woods, stepping directly over the smoldering outlines of the maze. The corn and plastic netting had all burned down to the dirt, so we could move pretty freely, as long we avoided major fires like the one consuming the gazebo.

"Ellie?" Stacey called after me, clearly concerned about me heading into the haunted woods with Josef the Dead Horseman just behind me.

"I'll be fine," I said. I couldn't be sure of that, but after what I'd just survived, I was almost too shell-shocked to care. I just wanted to lead the horseman away from Stacey and Corrine before he turned violent.

I walked over fire and smoldering earth until I reached the pitch darkness of the woods. The horseman was close—a shadowy figure now, so dim I might not have seen him at all if I hadn't been looking for him. I could hear an occasional hoofbeat, but not a steady rhythm of them. I could feel him, though.

We entered the dark wilderness together, his cold presence making my flesh crawl.

Chapter Twenty

Within the woods, his presence remained inconstant, sometimes a shadow, sometimes a cold spot, sometimes a visible apparition.

"We're taking the long way around, going to the back gate," I whispered. I didn't know if I needed to explain anything to him, but I wanted him to stay focused, or at least remember that we were together and I wasn't some enemy he needed to strike down. "It's been closed so long that I doubt those who dwell inside give it much attention. And her grave, Mildred's grave, is near that back gate."

I seemed to be alone as I moved out into the marshy creek islands behind the cemetery. I had to use my flashlight to avoid slipping and falling into the creeks, but I kept it on the lowest, dimmest setting to avoid drawing attention.

Rumbles sounded in the distance, deep in the swampy woods. A light flared and faded in the distance, then another. They weren't exactly fireworks. I could smell gunpowder on the wind, and then I heard distant moans, the squish of boots tromping in muddy earth. Cries of pain echoed far away.

The battlefield. If we'd continued onward through the marsh, we would find the swampy intersection of Brier Creek and the Savannah River, where hundreds had died in the bloody battle, many of them drowned and lost while crawling away from the massacre, their bodies vanished into the marshy water.

Now, in the early-morning dark of Halloween, I could hear and see evidence of that long-ago fight. I wondered if Virgil, our helpful local history buff, knew that he could observe ghostly glimpses of it late at night, at least at the time of year when the veil between life and death was at its thinnest. They say you can see or hear ghosts almost any night at some battle sites, like Gettysburg.

As long as the restless dead soldiers didn't make their way over and interfere with us, I was glad they were out and active. Their noise and activity could help provide some distraction from the horseman and me making our way to the back gate of the cemetery. It would have been harder to sneak through a completely silent swamp.

On the other hand, I was not at all prepared to fend off hundreds of dead men if they decided I was the enemy, so I also had to keep a wary eye in that direction. I was in the company of a Hessian mercenary, after all, so the ghosts of hundreds of American militiamen would probably not look kindly on us.

"I understand Mildred loved you," I whispered. The horseman was nowhere in sight, and I hoped he was still with me. "I read her journal. Why was it hidden there in the wall? I'm guessing some relative who cared about Mildred kept them after her death, but hid them because of the scandal. Mildred having an affair with a runaway German mercenary. I'm sure her family didn't approve of that. Am I right?"

The night grew colder. The horseman was visible again, though he was only a thin, transparent shadow that followed just behind me. I didn't entirely trust him. I needed to keep watch on the horseman, on the distant hints of battle, and on the cemetery, too, but sadly I don't have eyes on all sides of my head.

"The real question is how you felt about Mildred, and what you did," I said. "We don't know enough. Did you love her? Did she die giving birth to your child? Or did you kill her? Because that's what everyone says—"

A groan sounded from him, not quite a human voice, like a tuneless echo from deep inside a cave or a well.

His apparition was much clearer now, so that I could see his bone-white lips and chin under his hat. His sword was out, pointed in my direction. Maybe I'd touched a nerve.

"Why are you still here, riding the roads for two hundred years?" I asked. "Are you pursuing her? Is she running from you when she crawls into the house at night? Is that why Hiram and the men of her family patrol the road by the cemetery? Are they trying to protect Mildred from you?"

The highwayman drew closer. I could smell the rotten-leather stink of the dried horseflesh that slowly crumbled from his steed's bones at every step.

"Or is she seeking refuge in her old home?" I asked. "That's not really her house, of course, but it's on the same site. Someone—I'm guessing a mother or a sister—kept Mildred's diary and necklace in that jewelry box and hid it inside the walls when the house was rebuilt. Someone who couldn't bear to destroy the girl's property, but wanted to keep it secret."

The horseman backed off a little, but kept his sword tilted at me.

"The other possibility is that you loved her, too," I said. "Her family wanted to keep you apart. Maybe she died in childbirth, or from miscarriage, and the trauma of that keeps her ghost here. You're trying to reconnect with her, but the men of her family won't allow it. Now that they're penned up in the cemetery, you're free to move around the farm...but now *she* is trapped inside with them, too. Mildred can't do her crawl from the cemetery to the farmhouse now that the gate's locked. If all this is true, then you're trying to rescue her spirit from this farm, and her dead relatives are standing in your way. Is that right?"

He was more fully formed now, to the point that I could see the brass buttons in his heavy coat glinting in the faint moonlight. He sat up straight, his posture less threatening, his sword fading from visibility altogether.

"That's what you wanted to do in life," I said. "You wanted to gather her up and take her away from here. But her family killed you instead, and they blamed you for her death. Is that right?"

The horseman was a solid apparition now, as solid as life, and the air around me was so cold that my ears and nose started to go numb.

"I'm betting on you," I said. "Based on what Mildred wrote. Don't disappoint me."

Having gone the very long and muddy way around, I finally approached the last leg of our journey. The rotten posts and other remnants of the footbridge spanned the last little creek on the way to the rear gate of the cemetery, the one that looked like it hadn't been opened in a hundred years or more.

I didn't trust the bridge one bit, so I took a running start and leaped across the creek to the slippery, weedy bank on the other side. I landed awkwardly, but managed to regain my balance without grabbing onto the fence. I didn't want to alert the ghosts within to my presence if I could avoid it.

Though the bridge was little more than a memory of rotten wood, held together by nothing but habit, the horseman crossed it easily. The hooves that had crushed floorboards and broken down a wall made no sound as they stepped over the old bridge.

The inside of the cemetery lay calm and silent. I didn't see the kind of heavy, cold fog I'd seen before, or glimpse any shadowy figures among the sunken headstones and mossy old trees. They might have been lying low, or they might have been slumbering altogether, resigned to their fate, but I wasn't ready to bet on the second option, especially not on Halloween.

"She's just inside the gate," I whispered. "We'll have to move fast."

The horse and its rider remained unnaturally still, as only the dead can be.

I took a deep breath, then grasped the latch on the cemetery's back gate. The latch was ice-cold, which could only indicate that at least some of the spirits were up and around.

I raised the latch, then pushed the gate. Unlike the front gate, it opened inward. The hinges squealed loudly, and I winced at the sound.

Carefully avoiding the big hole where I'd fallen on my first visit,

I approached the sunken remnants of Mildred's headstone. Nothing immediately lunged out from the shadows to grab me, but the environment felt threatening and hostile. That wasn't surprising considering our past experiences here.

I clacked the beads of the coral necklace back and forth as I touched it to Mildred's headstone. We had a connection from the time she'd touched me and I'd seen her memory. I could feel her rousing in the swampy earth beneath my feet.

Her apparition was faint, and her back was turned to me. She was pale, as they usually are, dressed in lace petticoats, her upper body held rigid by whalebone stays. I expected her clothes to be soaked in blood when she turned to face me, but they weren't.

Previously, I'd looked out through her eyes. Now, I finally saw her face, a girl of seventeen, frightened, eyes large and dark. She resembled Corrine quite a bit, probably enough to explain why the horseman had once pursued Corrine in the woods.

What caught me a little off-guard was the infant in her arms. It was wrapped in simple linen—a small burial shroud, I realized, not a cutesy baby blanket. The baby wasn't moving at all.

"Mildred," I whispered.

The horseman eased past me to stand over her. Mildred looked up at him, then she quietly wept. The tears were blood-red on her cheeks.

A shot sounded out, startling me. It wasn't a distant echo from the swampy battlefield this time, but close by, enough to make my ears ring. The horseman had a rusty pistol on his belt, but he hadn't touched it, as far as I could see.

Mildred looked at me. I saw the bright red bloodstain spread across the front of her white petticoat, centered on her stomach. The baby also had a bright bloodstain at the center of its blanket, as though it, too, had been shot through the stomach. For the first time, the dead baby stirred and let out a cry.

Shadows gathered behind Mildred. At the head of them stood a filmy apparition of Hiram Neville, face decayed beneath his own tricorner hat. He opened his hands, and they were stained in blood. Gunsmoke rolled from his finger tips.

"Oh," I said. I was shocked, and I hadn't seen this part coming, but I forced myself to hold steady. Hiram and his family members were rough ghosts. I was fighting down panic. I didn't want them to smell fear on me.

Hiram's shape became clearer as he moved toward his daughter, while Josef held out one gloved hand toward her. It was the same basic conflict they'd all been reenacting for years, but I'd rearranged things a bit, in search of a different outcome.

I let Hiram have it with both barrels, dual tactical flashlight beams, narrow and concentrated, searing white.

"You killed your daughter?" I said, still putting it together. "Because she slept with the enemy. You killed her for what? Immorality? Impropriety? Simple disobedience? The shame and embarrassment of her having a baby out of wedlock with a foreigner? You killed her, and the baby, too, either just before or just after it was born. And then you blamed Josef. You gathered up your slave-patrol buddies and hunted him down. You killed and dropped his bagged body at the town Ebenezer for burial...but that didn't quite work out for you, did it? Because Josef was buried *outside* the churchyard wall, leaving him free to roam the roads. To make his way back and try to rejoin Mildred after death. But you wouldn't allow that, either."

The shades of Hiram's heirs were growing darker and more distinct, as well as closer. Despite the intense light of my beams, they advanced toward me. I resisted the urge to turn and run. Letting the fear overtake me would just make me even more vulnerable to their attacks.

I heard a baby cry.

Mildred and the infant sat on top of the horse, just ahead of the pale horseman. The dead horse creaked as it turned, its beef-jerky muscles and tendons stretching over its dry bones. The family was together now, the horse taking them slowly back toward the open gate and the rotten old foot bridge beyond.

"It's over," I told Hiram. "Let them go in peace."

The horseman and his two new passengers passed out of the gate. There was a single clomp as they crossed the bridge. On the other side, the dead horse broke into a gallop, speeding them all toward the distant explosions and cries of the battlefield. Tonight, the entire swamp seemed like a wide-open gate to the underworld.

Then I was alone with Hiram and his descendants, all of them looking angry as they closed in around me.

"Wait," I said, but they didn't wait.

I backed away as they approached. As soon as I was outside the gate, I grabbed it and pushed it shut.

The freezing-cold rusty latch wouldn't quite close, though, as if something invisible were blocking it.

The shades approached, clearer than ever now—generations of dead men, some in waistcoats or frock coats, others in more modern business suits, all of them decaying inside their burial clothes, with pieces of their faces missing. Their dead eyes stared at me.

Hiram lifted his hand, and the gate flew open against me. It slammed into my chest, knocked me off my feet, and sent me tumbling into the shallow, muddy creek below the bridge.

The gate swung open all the way, one of the rusty hinges cracking at the impact against the uneven brick and wrought iron fence beside it.

I got to my feet as quickly as I could, but it was too late. The ghosts were escaping.

They crossed the rotten old foot bridge, one after another, heading toward the swamplands full of ghosts. They seemed to be pursuing the horseman, but he was well away, barely visible in the shadowy woods. I had the impression that they could follow and follow but never quite catch up. Not unless they found ghost horses of their own.

I stood in the creek, the water gurgling around my boots, and watched the shades of the Neville men grow distant and less distinct as they walked into the swamps.

Symbolism matters to ghosts. For countless years, they'd come and gone by the front gate, which led them to the road, to the farm buildings, to the land of the living. The horseman himself had ridden up and down that road, though the shades of Hiram and the others had blocked his way to the farm, even when he'd tried to sneak out of the woods through the corn maze.

The back gate, however, led out into a system of muddy waterways. Whether you're talking about the Styx or the Jordan, river crossings have long served as the symbolic boundary between life and death.

Tonight, the swamp itself stood for the land of death, with the doorways to the next world wide open. The old battlefield on Halloween was a place where the line between living and dead was temporarily blurred, at least for a night or two.

All of the dead, from Josef and Mildred to Hiram and his family members, ought to find it easy to cross over from there.

I climbed up the slippery bank, then closed and latched the gate as quietly as I could, blocking the shades from retreating into their burial ground. My symbolic message was clear, if they noticed it—they could not return, they had to move on. All of them.

Then I sat down by the gate, caught my breath, and watched to make sure none of them tried to return.

Chapter Twenty-One

By the time I emerged from the woods, things had changed pretty drastically.

Jacob, after escaping from his car trunk, had alerted the authorities on his way up to the farm. Blue and red lights flashed all over the little dirt road, and the local fire department was soaking the acres of smoldering ash where the corn maze had been.

Stacey and Jacob stood at the front of the house, along with a few local police officers. Michael was being loaded into an ambulance, so I hurried in that direction, but Stacey saw me and yelled that I needed to come over. The police were staring at me without a grain of trust in their eyes.

I didn't look forward to explaining any of this to the local cops. It was one thing in Savannah, where ghosts are all over the place, and anyway Calvin still had a number of friends on the police force.

On the bright side, Amber's Suburban was arriving, nosing its way down the dirt road, so at least the actual property owners would be there now. Otherwise, we looked like a few out-of-towners who'd apparently just rolled into the area for a little trespassing, vandalism, and arson.

"Ellie! Are you okay? What happened?" Stacey dashed a few feet in my direction as I approached, which drew a sour look from one of the cops, who obviously didn't want her running away.

"The horseman, Mildred, and their baby rode off to the other side," I said. "Just one happy dead family, I guess. Hiram and the others chased after them in fast pursuit. Well, not really fast, more of a lurching walk. But that obsession that's kept old Hiram here all these years, the determination to keep his daughter and the highwayman apart...he followed that obsession right on out of here, and he seemed to take his descendants with him."

"You'll have to catch me up on this," Stacey said. The cops were moving closer to us, wanting my information.

"Later," I told her. I looked to the ambulance again, but they were already closing the doors and starting up the lights to take Michael to the hospital. I'd missed my chance to see him.

The Suburban parked nearby. Jeremy climbed out on one side and Amber on the other, and from how they bickered, it was obvious they'd had some disagreement about who would go to the farm and who would stay at the motel with the kids.

Clearly, nobody had won that argument. The two kids were in the back seat, and six-year-old Maya began to open the door on her side.

"Stay in the car!" Amber and Jeremy shouted in unison. I guess they still agreed on some things.

"Looks like the corn maze is officially closed for the year," Jeremy said when he joined us. The fire department was rapidly turning what remained of it into mud.

"Where's Corrine?" Amber asked.

"Over at the stable," Stacey said. "She's fine. A hundred percent."

"How is Michael?" I looked in the direction where his ambulance had gone. "I didn't get to see him."

"He should be okay," Stacey said. "I mean, he was breathing, and he didn't even have any open wounds. Just a big scar. Other than that, he seemed okay physically. As for mentally, or spiritually..."

Stacey and I both looked at Jacob. The cops were momentarily busy jawing with Jeremy, still trying to figure out what was going on.

Jacob took in a deep breath, then blew it out, as if buying time to frame what he had to say.

"I don't think he's possessed anymore. I did have a chance to touch him before the medics loaded him up, and I think the ghost has left him."

"You *think*?" I asked. "I sort of need to know whether my boyfriend is still controlled by a mass-murdering spirit who wants to watch me burn to death. That's going to have an effect on our relationship."

"I *think* he's gone," Jacob repeated, more quietly, not looking at me. "That's all I've got, Ellie. It's not an exact science."

"Great. Okay, well, thanks for coming out and helping us. Sorry Michael locked you in the trunk of your car."

"It's fine, seriously," he said, while Stacey rubbed some grease from his cheek. "I usually end up burned or bleeding by the end of these things. Lying around for a few hours was a nice change."

"Sounds relaxing," Stacey said.

"It would have been, if not for all the kicking and shouting I had to do until somebody heard me."

The police came back with more questions. We just answered them truthfully, which only made the cops annoyed with us. They decided to wait for the county sheriff to arrive so we could repeat everything to him (or her, as it eventually turned out).

"Is it over?" Amber asked me later, while we stood on the front porch amid broken floorboards smeared with crushed pumpkin. I don't think she meant the police investigation.

"I think so. I'd say the horseman and the girl who crawls into your house are definitely gone, and those were the ones who caused you the biggest problems. I also believe we've emptied the restless ghosts out of the old cemetery, too, and moved them on to the next world. I'd still avoid that area at night until we can come back to follow up. Everywhere else on the farm should be safe."

"Thank goodness." Amber hugged me. "We just couldn't move again, not after we invested so much into fixing up this place." She glanced around at the damage. "It's going to take some work to clean all this up, and of course we'll have to plant a whole new maze next year..." She headed to the stable to round up her wandering daughter Corrine.

I took a final look at the dark woods. Nothing sinister or horrific waited there any longer. Daylight would arrive soon to seal up the doors to the land of the dead. For a while.

Jacob and Stacey stood near his car, embracing. Jeremy opened the Suburban door to let the kids out, so their family could join together, too.

Unlike everyone else, I'd be going home all alone, just me and my cat. First I'd stop by the hospital to see Michael, but he would probably still be out cold.

That was okay. Being alone seems to be my natural state. You eventually lose everyone, anyway, somehow or another.

Chapter Twenty-Two

"So Anton Clay is on the loose," I told Calvin, many hours later. I'd gone home to sleep, but hadn't slept. Too much on my mind. I'd been in touch with Michael's sister Melissa. She was at the hospital with her unconscious brother now. I'd be there again later, waiting to see who he was when he awoke. "Jacob doesn't think Michael is possessed anymore. Maybe the horseman's sword helped with that." I hesitated, then added, "I summoned the horseman toward us. On purpose. I knew he would attack Michael."

"You feel guilty about that." Calvin watched the road ahead. He drove his truck, a hefty green Chevy Blazer modified with accelerator and brake handles. His wheelchair lay folded in the camper-covered truck bed behind us.

"Of course I feel guilty," I said. "I should feel guilty. He could have killed Michael. Now Michael might be in a coma, and who knows if he'll wake up?"

"Why did you make the choice at the time?" Calvin asked.

"Because he was going to burn everybody alive. Not just me, but Stacey and the client's daughter, too."

"And Michael, too?"

"Right. Anton would have burned us all." My gut tightened as I turned past a boxy wooden sign that read RIVERSIDE POINT. Despite the name and the peeling sailboat painted beside it, the neighborhood was not located on any river, creek, lake, or pond. My mom had joked about that plenty.

I drove down the once-familiar streets, past little houses that were decades old. Some were charming and cute, especially near the front of the neighborhood, but many of the others had fallen into gradual neglect, the yards shaggy with weeds. A couple were for sale, according to sagging signs in their yards. The signs looked like they'd been there a while.

One brick bungalow stood dark and empty, an eviction notice taped to the front door. It had belonged to a grandmotherly lady named Mrs. Davis, I was pretty sure, who had given out marmalade cookies on Halloween. I wondered whether anyone from my childhood still lived in the neighborhood at all. I had certainly avoided the place as much as possible.

I slowed as I looked at the home of a girl I'd known—Alison something. She was a year or two older than me, but she'd been friendly, let me play on her swing set when we were little. Her house was a 1970's contemporary, asymmetrical with steep roofs pointing in different directions. I could see the rusty remnants of the old swing set now, fallen over in the back yard.

"You know what I'm going to say," Calvin said, after giving me a few moments to reflect.

"That if I hadn't risked Michael's life, he would have died anyway," I said.

"So you made the right choice. The fact that Michael is still alive now is an added blessing."

"I don't know. It still pretty much feels like something I did to him. All of this is my fault. He was possessed by Anton Clay. How did that happen? How..."

I fell silent as Calvin brought the truck to a stop. I stared out the window.

The cheap wooden fence, which had surrounded the weedy lot to discourage juvenile delinquents and other trespassers from hanging out there, was completely gone. Heavy machinery had churned up the space where my family home had once been, exposing a deep trench of sandy red earth. It was a light red, not an unusual shade for Georgia dirt. A little bit of orange plastic netting had been set up for erosion control, but other than that, the site was ripped wide open.

"Oh, no." I opened the truck door and stumbled out toward the construction site. "How can they do this? People died here."

"Careful, Ellie," Calvin said. "Watch your step."

I stopped at the broken chunks of the curb. The entire lot, including the old trees that had stood at the back, had been completely leveled and then ripped open. Some construction company had really ravaged the place.

"How can they build a new house here?" I asked. "Why? The whole neighborhood's gone to..." I glanced around to make sure none of the neighbors were outside. "...gone to seed," I finished, in a lower, quieter voice.

"At least we have some idea of why Anton Clay is running around," Calvin said. He remained behind the wheel of his truck. "There's been interference with the site."

"It's a start," I said. "But he's always been rooted to this site, as far as we know. And he doesn't have any known history of possessing the living, either. He's growing more powerful and more dangerous."

"I did not foresee this," Calvin said.

"Well, you're not psychic." I gave him the most obviously fake half-smile I could muster. "Anyway, it's not your problem. You'll be escaping down to Florida and leaving this with me. I bet you're pretty happy you sold the firm before this happened."

"I'll stay in town until this is resolved," he said. "Anton Clay is too dangerous for you to face on your own."

"But you have no problem leaving me alone to face all the other dangerous ghosts in the world."

"You won't be alone. You'll have the resources of a much larger organization behind you. It wasn't an easy choice, but believe me when I say I have put your safety first," Calvin said. "You will be less alone than ever, and you'll have more backup than just an old man in a wheelchair."

"You're not as old as you act."

"I'm not as old as I feel, either," he said.

I stared at the ripped red earth in silence for a moment. It seemed insane that someone was building a house here yet again. Maybe they didn't know that six houses had burned down on the same spot, or that the ashes of generations were mingled into the soil. Maybe they just didn't care.

"I wish you weren't going," I said. "I wish you hadn't sold out. Especially now. It feels like everything's turning upside down."

"There will be a number of moments when your life turns upside down," Calvin said. "Each difficult challenge makes you stronger for the next."

"You should put that on a poster. Maybe with a fuzzy little kitten stalking a big eagle or something."

"I'm not joking."

"But I am," I said. "Okay, I get it. You have to move on. I have to get shoved out of the nest like a baby bird or something. Tough love. It's what's best for me. I guess I'm lucky there's just so much of it available."

I looked into the deep trench carved about where the kitchen had once been. A light, drizzling rain had begun to fall, slowly converting the sandy earth to soft mud, bit by bit. Droplets vanished into the shadows of the trench. Maybe they'd dug so deeply that they'd unwittingly released Anton Clay. Some part of him might have been cracked open, some old bone fragments turned to powder and set adrift on the wind.

The rain grew heavier. The drops were icy cold, hinting of the winter to come. I turned and climbed back into the truck.

"We have to find him," I said. "Sometime before he burns down half the city."

Calvin nodded. He'd taken some images of the site with his clunky, whirring old film camera. He set the camera aside as I buckled my seatbelt, and then we drove away.

I kept my eyes on the side mirror, watching the site of my old house retreat behind us. I didn't visit it often, but whenever I had, I'd always felt something. Usually it was Anton himself. I could feel his heat, his anger and desire, his craving to burn and destroy. I might even catch a glimpse of him, sometimes looking youthful in antique finery, a silk cravat, and long golden hair. Other times, he would look like a smoldering corpse, tongues of fire licking out from his eye sockets as he stared back at me.

This time, I felt nothing. The churned-up, muddy lot was just an empty place where my childhood and my family used to be.

The monstrous old ghost hadn't returned to his usual haunt after the corn maze. He was out there somewhere, charged up and powerful, eager to kill me and anyone who happened to be close to me.

Later, I returned to the small hospital in Sylvania where Michael was still unconscious. I sat with his sister Melissa, who was his only immediate family. Their mother had died, and their father had taken off with no forwarding address many years earlier.

Michael didn't stir. He lay somewhere in the gloom between life and death. I tried to call out to him mentally, to steer him back into the direction of life.

Through the hospital window, I watched the sun gradually set, painting the lawn outside with reds and oranges. Then darkness settled in for the night.

THE END

From the author

Thanks so much for continuing to read this series. I love researching and writing these books and I'm glad so many of you keep asking for more!

I'm already hard at work on book seven. Things are about to get very complicated for Ellie with Nicholas and Kara moving in!

If you're enjoying the series, I hope you'll consider taking time to recommend the books to someone who might like them or to rate or review it at your favorite ebook retailer.

Sign up for my newsletter to hear about new Ellie Jordan titles as soon as they come out. (You'll immediately get a free ebook of short stories just for signing up.)

If you'd like to get in touch with me, here are my links:

Website (www.jlbryanbooks.com)
Facebook (J. L. Bryan's Books)
Twitter (@jlbryanbooks)
Email (info@jlbryanbooks.com)

Thanks for reading!

Made in the USA
Lexington, KY
23 October 2016